P. M. Hubbard and The Murder Room

〉〉 This title is part of The Murder Room, our series dedicated to making available out-of-print or hard-to-find titles by classic crime writers.

Crime fiction has always held up a mirror to society. The Victorians were fascinated by sensational murder and the emerging science of detection; now we are obsessed with the forensic detail of violent death. And no other genre has so captivated and enthralled readers.

Vast troves of classic crime writing have for a long time been unavailable to all but the most dedicated frequenters of second-hand bookshops. The advent of digital publishing means that we are now able to bring you the backlists of a huge range of titles by classic and contemporary crime writers, some of which have been out of print for decades.

From the genteel amateur private eyes of the Golden Age and the femmes fatales of pulp fiction, to the morally ambiguous hard-boiled detectives of mid twentieth-century America and their descendants who walk our twenty-first century streets, The Murder Room has it all. 〉〉

The Murder Room
Where Criminal Minds Meet

themurderroom.com

P. M. Hubbard (1910–1980)

Praised by critics for his clean prose style, characterization, and the strong sense of place in his novels, Philip Maitland Hubbard was born in Reading, in Berkshire and brought up in Guernsey, in the Channel Islands. He was educated at Oxford, where he won the Newdigate Prize for English verse in 1933. From 1934 until its disbandment in 1947 he served with the Indian Civil service. On his return to England he worked for the British Council, eventually retiring to work as a freelance writer. He contributed to a number of publications, including *Punch*, and wrote 16 novels for adults as well as two children's books. He lived in Dorset and Scotland, and many of his novels draw on his interest in and knowledge of rural pursuits and folk religion.

Flush as May
Picture of Millie
A Hive of Glass
The Holm Oaks
The Tower
The Custom of the Country
Cold Waters
High Tide
The Dancing Man
A Whisper in the Glen
A Rooted Sorrow
A Thirsty Evil
The Graveyard
The Causeway
The Quiet River
Kill Claudio

Flush as May

P. M. Hubbard

An Orion book

Copyright © Caroline Dumonteil, Owain Rhys Phillips and Maria
Marcela Appleby Gomez 1963, 2012

The right of P. M. Hubbard to be identified as the author of this work
has been asserted in accordance with the Copyright, Designs and
Patents Act 1988.

This edition published by
The Orion Publishing Group Ltd
Orion House
5 Upper St Martin's Lane
London WC2H 9EA

An Hachette UK company
A CIP catalogue record for this book is available from the British Library

ISBN 978 1 4719 0067 9

www.orionbooks.co.uk

CHAPTER ONE

The body sat comfortably against a bank, facing the
early summer sunshine. The face was middle-aged and undis-
tinguished, and wore a slight smile, almost a smirk. If the man
had been alive when she found him, Margaret would have
been instantly irritated by his affectation of mystery. Even
when she saw that the mystery was not of his making, some of
this irritation remained at the expense, she felt, of more suitable emotions.

She was aware of a total absence of pity or terror. Surprise,
naturally, but even here she was more surprised at finding him
there at all than at subsequently finding that he was dead.
The annoyance that quickly supervened on her first surprise
survived the second. It was a bit silly, at her age, to go walking
in the fields at sunrise on May Morning at all, when most of
her friends were hitch-hiking home across the Continent or
waking up on pavements ready to ban the bomb or demon-
strate the solidarity of the Left.

That she should be caught at it by this smirking little nondescript was bad enough. That she should have to admit it, as
now no doubt she would, in every circumstance of publicity
was almost unbearable. And it was his doing, with his neatly
composed mortality and his knowing look. She considered the
possibility of ignoring him and saying nothing to anyone, but
there were obvious difficulties in that too.

It was the flies that decided her. A big blue fly first, which
came droning from behind her in a powerful curve and landed
slap on the smiling mouth. She moved instinctively to brush it
off, but was anticipated by several smaller black flies, which
came gyrating eagerly out of the bank, ánd after a few ex-
ploratory flights landed on his chest and crawled busily one
after the other into the top of his waistcoat. Margaret turned
and made for the village.

The sun was well up now and behind her as she climbed the

steady slope, throwing up the small conical hill in a pyramid of pale green and gold. The tiled roofs emerged from, and cut horizontally across, the bunched trees, and the church tower, golden and vertical, stood up cunningly off-centre. Even in her distress, which was now growing on her, she was amazed, as so often before, at the village's perfection of general design, which seemed perpetually able to absorb the individual outrages inflicted on it from within.

The morning was mild and silent. An early tractor snorted several fields away to her left, but the village itself seemed lifeless. Margaret came to the gate on to the road and turned to look back. He was invisible from here, but she knew pretty well where he was, and nothing stirred. The valley dropped away in close-cultivated perfection until the hedgerows merged in a general drift of trees hiding other villages. Beyond, the Beacon threw up a grey-green curve of that startling significance peculiar to weathered chalk. May Morning was all hers.

For the first time Margaret was suddenly embarrassed by what she had to do. She was not herself a villager, though she had visited the place before. She was on the friendliest terms with many of the people, but remained not one of them. They were fond of her, she knew, as one is fond of a beautiful but exotic bird, and they talked to her freely about themselves and each other; but the very freedom was a measure of her detachment. She might, she thought, have got away with bringing in a may-bough, but she was bringing in a body, and did not quite know where to start.

Close to the first house there actually was a may-bough, broken and bedraggled on the grass verge. Three gardens along two girls, whose need for even desperate measures was all too obvious, tried with muffled hysteria to wash their faces in the dew that stood on a pocket-handkerchief of ruthlessly cut grass. Margaret nodded vaguely in their direction, conscious of her own lack of need.

The police cottage was on the far side of the village. She could not remember having seen the constable, but there must be one. She pushed the gate open and walked up the brick-paved path. Here too nothing stirred. She knocked on the door and stood back, rebuked by the silence. Then the absurdity of her hesitation struck her. She had every right to be at least

2

half hysterical. She knocked again, picturing a man waking grudgingly after a night on duty.

The door opened very suddenly and silently, and a man stood looking down at her. He wore police trousers, but his face was uncompromisingly hostile. In spite of herself Margaret apologised. 'I'm sorry to trouble you so early,' she said, 'but there is something I must report, and I thought I'd better come at once.'

The man said nothing, but looked at her. He had little pig's eyes with no sleep in them. 'There's a man down in the fields,' she said. 'He's dead. It's a dead body.'

'How do you know?'

'I saw it. I found him there.'

'How do you know he was dead?'

His pointless hostility galled her. 'He's dead all right,' she said. 'If you don't believe it, you had better come and see for yourself. In fact, I think you had better come anyhow.'

He said, 'When was this?'

'Just now. I came straight here.'

'What were you doing, then, out there as early as this?'

'I went for a walk. I'm staying at Mrs Besson's.'

'I know where you're staying. What time did you go out?'

She thought. 'Soon after five. About ten past.'

His mouth turned up slightly on one side and she knew, with a sense of helpless resentment, that she was going to blush. He watched her unhappiness appreciatively but offered no comment. Finally he said, 'Wait a minute, then. I'd best come along and see.'

She swallowed a childish retort, turned her back on him and sauntered down the path. She came to the gate, looked up and down the street and had nerved herself to turn round when she heard the door shut. When she did turn, the garden was empty except for a bullet-headed tabby which watched her from a window-sill. She walked towards him, but hesitated. He was not that sort of cat.

Golden hazed and exquisitely scented, the village slept around her. Minutes passed. She looked at her wrist and saw that she had forgotten to put her watch on. Her stomach produced a ridiculous and unladylike bubbling, and she found she was almost desperately hungry. Black resentment struggled in her with a wholly unreasonable feeling of panic

3

and guilt; and still the policeman did not re-emerge. When he did appear, he came from behind the cottage and she saw that he was fully uniformed. He was pushing a bicycle.

She said, 'It's only just down the road,' but he did not appear to accept the implication. He shut the gate firmly behind them, and she had a feeling that he was going to mount his bicycle and leave her to run behind. Instead they processed through the village with the bicycle ticking quietly between them. Now there were heads everywhere. They craned over the sills of dormer windows and peered from behind ground-floor curtains. Doors opened momentarily to afford a glimpse of them and then shut silently. There should have been wood-smoke and the smell of cooking, but the cottages burnt coke in slow-combustion stoves and did not breakfast till later.

The giggling girls had given up and gone indoors. The trampled may-bough was still there, and the constable turned his bicycle slightly and wheeled it firmly over it. When they came to the gate, Margaret pointed and said, 'Over there.' He looked at her for the first time since they had started out. She forced herself, out of her mental disarray, to stare back at him, and found his little eyes full of a sort of truculent good humour. He nodded, put the bicycle against the hedge, took a padlock and chain out of the carrier-bag and locked it elaborately round the back wheel.

'You go on,' he said. 'Go just the way you came.' She started off down the slope, walking into a sea of uncertainty as if she waded into dark water. Half-way across the third field she hesitated and the water closed over her head. She turned left, making for a likely-looking bank, but saw that it could not have been facing the sunrise. The Beacon was golden-green now, and the sloping sun threw up on its summit and sides the scars and dimples of primordial occupation. The tractor had stopped working. The morning was absolutely still. She turned to get a sighting on the village, and found the sun striking back at her dazzlingly from a hidden window. She was too far left.

She doubled back along the side of the next field. The constable walked heavily behind her, his silence goading her to panic. They came to the end of the field without finding a gate, and she turned because she had to. She said, 'It was here somewhere,' and he pounced on the past tense with a sort of ponderous brutality. He said, 'Not here now, though, is it? Or perhaps it's got up and walked off a piece.'

This time he had pushed her too far, and she turned on him in a fury. 'Look,' she said, 'it doesn't matter to me in the slightest whether you believe me or not. So far as I am concerned you can have bodies under every hedge in the parish, and I hope it keeps fine for them. I needn't have reported this one, and I wish now I hadn't, but I thought it was the proper thing to do. Anyway, there you are. I've made my report and it's up to you. I saw a body not far from here less than an hour ago. Now I don't know where it is and I don't care.' She sobbed ridiculously twice, blew her nose and started to walk back in the direction of the road.

'Now wait a bit,' he said from behind her, 'let's hear a bit more about this. You were going for a walk you said?' She refused to stop, and he pulled alongside her, walking two steps to her three. He was an immense man. 'Yes,' she said.

'Always go for a walk this early?'

'No.'

'Special today like, to see the sunrise?'

'I suppose so, yes.'

'Then what?'

'Then I saw him, propped up against a bank, facing the sun. I didn't realise he was dead at first. Then I saw.'

'Saw what?'

'His eyes were open. He was quite still. He wasn't breathing. And then there were flies.'

'Flies?' he said appreciatively. 'What did he look like? Old or young? Fair or dark? Tall or short? How was he dressed?'

She thought. 'Middle-aged, I suppose. I didn't notice his colouring. All very ordinary. Ordinary sort of clothes, a suit. I couldn't see how tall he was, sitting down like that. Not specially tall, I think.'

'Well now,' said the constable, 'practically got him identified, haven't we? Age medium, ordinary appearance and clothes, not too tall. Shouldn't be any trouble finding out who he is.'

Margaret said nothing and they came to the gate. The constable unlocked his bicycle, stowed the chain in the carrier-bag and took out a pair of bicycle clips, which he adjusted round his ankles with close attention to the crease of his

5

uniform trousers. He pushed the bicycle back on to the road, heading away from the village, and put one foot on the pedal.

'Officer,' said Margaret. He turned and faced her. 'I forgot to tell you. He had a beard, rather foreign-looking, and a scar on his face. He had a ruby ring on his hand. And there was a curiously-carved oriental dagger sticking out of his chest.' She remembered the flies crawling one by one under the nondescript waistcoat, and choked slightly.

'Ah,' said the constable, and Margaret saw at once that she had not made him angry at all. 'Irrelevant detail you were right to omit as unlikely to assist identification. Thank you, miss.' His savage joviality caught up her exasperation and seemed to find it unexpectedly enjoyable.

Her defiance collapsed. 'Have it your own way,' she said. 'I don't expect I shall see you again. I'm leaving this evening, and I don't think I shall come back here. But you know, there was a dead man in the field here this morning. It seems only fair to you to say so.'

The constable nodded. 'I'll remember everything you've said, miss,' he said. 'I'd advise you to forget it.' He mounted his bicycle heavily, as he did everything, and started off down the road. She waited until he was out of sight and then sat suddenly on the grass and put her head on her arms. Then, finding this inadequate, she lay full length, wrapped her arms round her head and cried briefly but fiercely into the roadside grasses.

This met her immediate requirements, but did not conceal from her essentially sensible mind her overriding need of food. She sat up, grief-ravaged but still superb, and faced the road that climbed back towards the village. As she did so a long black car, expensive and certainly not local, crept out from among the houses, hesitated and stopped fifty yards from her. A chauffeur, elegant in olive green, got out. For a moment he turned the pages of a book propped on the paintwork and then, seeing her coming slowly up the hill, shut the book and walked down to meet her.

Margaret and the chauffeur studied each other frankly and with growing confidence. She concluded that he had a sense of humour and would not, whatever he wanted of her, call her miss. She wondered how he would manage the chauffeur's cap. A salute seemed over-dramatic and any other gesture impossible. He solved the problem by pulling it off and smiling at her. His eyes were rather tired and not at all piggy.

'Do you think,' he said, 'you could possibly tell me anywhere round here we could get breakfast? I mean – it must be rather a good breakfast, you know, something a bit elegant.' His expression, and perhaps the slightest movement of his head, indicated the silent black car behind him. He himself, he suggested, would gladly share a roadside crust with her this fair May Morning, but he was in duty bound elsewhere.

'There's the Ram at Rushbourne,' said Margaret. 'Very special. It's in all the books. It's a good ten miles on, but you wouldn't get breakfast at this hour in any case. I should go on there, if – if you think that would be all right.' Her eyes went to the car.

'The Ram, of course,' said the chauffeur. 'I should have thought. And ten miles is quite all right. Sir James' – he indicated the car – 'is asleep.'

'You don't come from around here, do you?' Margaret asked. He shook his head. 'Just passing through?'

'That's it.'

'What would you do if you saw a body – a man's body – lying in a field by the road?'

'Sir James being asleep?'

'Yes, I think so. At any rate, you being on your own.'

'What sort of a body? Fairly fresh?'

'Oh yes, absolutely mint-fresh. We don't let them lie hereabouts.'

He considered. 'I should probably go through the pockets for anything of value and drive quickly on.'

'You wouldn't tell the police?'

'The police? Oh no, surely not the police. The *Express*, perhaps.'

'And by God,' said Margaret, 'you'd be right at that.'

He looked at her with a fresh sort of interest. He said, 'Your tone suggests recent, harsh and personal experience. It is no business of mine, but you started this conversation. I suppose there's nothing I can do?'

'I don't think there is really, but thank you for asking. And Sir James will be wanting his breakfast.'

'Not till I wake him, he won't. You do come from around here, I gather?'

7

'Not really, no. I know it pretty well."

The silence blanketed them. The sun, already surprisingly warm, winked on the curved convexities of the black car. 'I'm afraid I need breakfast myself,' said Margaret. 'Nothing elegant in my case, but I can't wait like Sir James. I could cry with hunger.'

'Yes. You have just been crying with something, haven't you?'

'Yes. I told you – hunger. Hunger and frustration.' She walked firmly up the hill and he fell into step beside her. 'Anyhow,' he said, 'thank you for suggesting the Ram. I am sure it will do me credit.' He got into the driving seat. 'I hope we may meet again.'

She nodded. 'I'll think about it. I have taken the number of your car – Sir James's car, I suppose.'

'Not actually. It's hired.'

'And you with it?'

'Me with it.'

She looked past him into the cavernous elegance of the car. Sir James slept peacefully with a tartan rug round him and a slight smile on his lips. He had a long scar on his left cheek and a small pointed beard. There was no ruby ring, and it seemed unlikely that the tartan rug concealed a curiously carved oriental dagger. But it was near enough.

She turned back to the chauffeur. She said, 'Will you do me a favour?"

'Almost certainly. What do you want me to do?'

'You'll pass a policeman down the road, a big red man on a bicycle. Will you engage him in a few moments' desultory conversation without getting out of the car?'

'Conversation about what?'

"Anything. Ask him the way. Ask him if there's much crime in these parts. Anything really.'

'You aren't landing me in anything?'

'Not you, no, I promise.'

He sighed unbelievingly. 'All right. But if I don't see you again, I can't tell you about it, can I?'

She said, 'That's my risk.' He nodded. 'My name's Garrod, by the way,' he said. The great car sighed into movement. For the second time that morning, Margaret set her face to the village.

8

Chapter Two

'What are you thinking of doing next vacation, Margaret? Do you expect to be here?'

'I do not think I expect anything of next vacation, grandmother. I have the intention of being here and of doing a great deal of reading, and that is what most people would say I expected. But I do not really know whether my intention will be fulfilled.'

Her grandmother sighed. 'I do wish you would try to stop talking like a Compton-Burnett character,' she said. 'You don't do it very well, and you don't do it with your friends at all. I don't see why you should try it on with me. Even with me it sounds very affected.'

Margaret laughed. 'I'm awfully sorry,' she said. 'It's the temptation of calling you grandmother. If you had brought me up to call you Grannie or Grandma, I shouldn't have half the trouble. Anyway, I should like to be here, I think, if that's possible. I haven't really got through as much as I wanted this vac., and I shall be pretty busy.'

'I thought you were going to Lodstone *to* work. Of course I like you to be in the country over Easter, but I can't think what else you found to do there. Or did Mrs Besson feed you too well? And you're going back late as it is.'

'I know, but I'm glad I stayed the extra days. I had an experience on May Morning.' She smiled reminiscently.

'Oh. Well, that's very nice. Spiritual, occult or merely carnal?'

'Not carnal. Not very occult, I don't think. Spiritual, perhaps. Is there a very wealthy person called Sir James Something with a scar on his cheek and a beard?'

'Yes, darling, of course, Sir James Utley. I do think you ought to try to watch television more. I think it has a broadening effect on the mind, especially the academic mind, but I suppose that is very old-fashioned of me. But if your May Morning experience had anything to do with Sir James, I'm sure it was spiritual or nothing. He's very respectable, despite his appearance. The beard is, I suppose, a harmless affectation and the scar is strictly honourable. He was an Air Raid Warden or something. I heard him asked about it. Did you meet him? He might be interesting, despite his respectability.'

'No,' said Margaret. 'No, I didn't really what you might call meet him. I saw him, but he was asleep.'

'I refuse to be tempted into mere curiosity, Margaret.'

'I am not trying to tempt you. But what does he do, this Utley man? How did he get his money and what does he do with it?'

'I don't know how he started. He's one of the popular academics, and does a lot of lecturing and broadcasting. But he really is an anthropologist and, well, sociologist, I suppose they'd call it, in a very serious, respectable sort of way. Expeditions and surveys and things. He's a most interesting speaker and rather fascinating, though of course I have only seen him awake. But I didn't think he lived anywhere near Lodstone.'

'Where does he live, do you know?'

'Somewhere in London, I think, when he's not on his travels. But he has a lot to do with Oxford. That's why I was surprised you didn't know who he was.'

'Not my school,' said Margaret. 'But I must try and meet him some time and see how he looks awake.'

But the olive-green chauffeur, she reflected, would not be with Sir James; and this seemed a pity when her heart still bumped pleasantly at the recollection of him. Also, pleasure apart, she badly needed to discuss with someone the incident of the disappearing body and the disbelieving policeman; and although the Garrod man had laid no claim to expertise in such matters, she had sensed his interest and found him sympathetic. More important, she had already gone halfway to telling him. There would be much less explaining to do. Nevertheless, she made little attempt to conceal from herself the fact that she would have been glad to discuss anything from child-care to bi-metallism if she could discuss it with Mr Garrod.

The train to Oxford was still uncomfortably full, even with the term well started. The woman next to her said, 'He doesn't

10

mean it, dear, does he then, ducks?' every time her child laid chocolate-coated hands on the sleeve of Margaret's newly cleaned mackintosh: but this Margaret did not believe. She had an unfeminine dislike of babies, and had found that, like cats, they knew it and lavished their attention where it was least welcome. He meant it all right. After an interval long enough, she hoped, to disguise her feelings, she looked at her hands as if they, and not the baby's, needed washing. Then she muttered an obscurity and went into the corridor. Not for a moment deceived, the mother sniffed and dumped the child in Margaret's corner seat.

'I don't see how you can maintain your view,' said a young-ish, bony man draped diagonally across the corridor, and so long that he clearly could not fit into it at any other angle: 'not, that is, if you accept the possibility of becoming, which I take it you do.'

'Excuse me,' said Margaret, wondering which side of the diagonal she should attempt to negotiate. 'Sorry,' said the young man, arching himself ogivally. 'I mean,' he said, 'on your original hypothesis, of course.'

A solider, squarer man, whom her thrusting head met about half-way up, said, 'That's nonsense, Charles. Of course it is necessary to postulate becoming. Hullo. You were perfectly right about the Ram. They did Sir James proud.'

'Oh, hullo,' said Margaret, straightening herself cautiously in rather breathless proximity to a tweedy shoulder, 'I didn't expect to see you in these parts. Hath no man hired thee or has the car broken down?'

'Neither really. I had to hand in my cards and my uniform the day after I saw you, as a matter of fact. A pity. I liked the life, and I rather fancied myself in green.'

'Yes,' said Margaret, 'an impressive figure. Hungry as I was, I could not but admire.'

'I saw the constable.'

'You did? Look, I must go and wash this filthy witness from my sleeve and you must settle this business of becoming. But I'd like to hear about that some time.'

'This evening?'

'Yes, all right.'

'Seven at the Mitre?'

11

'All right. For the moment shall I pass you face to face or turn my back?'

'I should much prefer face to face. I will make a slight but honourable pretence of trying not to squeeze you.' For a timeless fraction of a second grey eye looked into grey eye at very close range. 'Seven, then,' said Margaret.

'Seven,' said the man Garrod.

'I'm afraid I may seem stupid over this,' he said later, 'but the truth is I don't understand why you wanted me to speak to the policeman.'

'What did he do when you did?'

'Answered. With unexceptionable courtesy, but a curiously sardonic dignity. A rather frightening man, I thought.'

'Yes. Yes, I think he was. Did he see Sir James?'

'Must have. He was standing right by the car.'

'No reaction?'

'Not that I saw. Look. Do you think it would be possible now to tell me a little more what this is about? You put a very odd hypothetical question to me when we met at Lodstone. I was wearing fancy dress and returned a suitably flippant answer. But you had been crying. I have thought of you since with tear-stains throwing up the undoubted splendour of your eyes. That is a pretty conceit, but it does not alter the fact that something had shaken you fairly badly. Even allowing for the effects of hunger, I do not see you crying easily.'

'You confuse me with compliments. Yes, all right. As a matter of fact I want to tell somebody rather badly. I started with you at the time, partly because I was, as you say, shaken, and partly because I felt, wrongly as it turns out, that you were sympathetic but someone completely detached I should never see again.'

He continued to look sympathetic. 'I found a man,' she said, ' – this was just before I met you – in a field not far from the road. He was dead.'

He nodded. 'Yes. Odd though the idea seemed, I imagined that that must be the case. Anything special?'

'No. Nothing visibly shocking at all. The strange thing was that I was surprised and annoyed, but not really upset.'

'Anything to show how he had died?'

'Not really. He was propped against a bank. I suppose he

12

might have sat himself down and died there. But I don't think so.' She told him, with a rather forced brevity, about the flies.

'Rather nasty, but logical. So you went and told the policeman?'

She nodded. 'It seemed the proper thing to do, though for some reason I was very reluctant to do it. Afterwards, of course, I wished I hadn't.'

'Why?'

'Sorry. I'm anticipating. I went to the police cottage and knocked him up. It was still very early, of course – practically no one about. He seemed – I don't know – hostile from the start. It wasn't so much that he reacted violently – he refused to react at all. He was curiously overbearing. Well, you spoke to him, and you know the kind of impression he made.'

'Yes. What did he do? Refuse to take any interest?'

'No. That was the trouble. He said he would come and see, and after a rather long wait he did. We went down the road and he told me to show him the body. And I couldn't. I couldn't find it.'

'You mean it wasn't there?'

'That's what I don't know, don't you see? I couldn't find it, but I'm not really sure I looked in the right place. I was – I'm afraid I rather lost my head. That was his doing – the policeman's. He got me badly rattled.'

'What did he do?'

'Nothing I could complain of. He didn't do or say anything – just followed me in silence until I gave it up and told him I couldn't find it. Then he more or less told me I had been imagining things and went off down the road. That was what really upset me. I was furious and confused and frustrated, but mainly furious. I felt I had tried to do the right thing and had been made a complete fool of. Of course, I was very hungry, and I'm no good when I'm hungry.'

He waited for a bit. Then he said, 'You realise of course that you haven't explained why you wanted me to stop and talk to him?'

'Oh, I'm sorry. No. I'm afraid this sounds a bit silly, but please remember I was upset. He asked me to describe the body, and I couldn't much – there was very little to say – and he made fun of my account of it. He really had a nasty way of speaking. Then just before he went I got childishly angry and told him some ridiculous invented details. I told him, God help me, that the body had a beard and a scar on its cheek and a ruby ring. I even said there was a curious oriental dagger stuck in the chest. You can see what I'm coming to. Of course he didn't believe a word of it. I didn't expect him to. But when you came along and I looked in the car, there was your Sir James with a beard and a scar, and you couldn't have seen a dagger anyway for the rug; and I thought if that horrible policeman saw him like that, it might shake him, and he might insist on investigating Sir James. And of course the real body wasn't like Sir James at all. But now you say there wasn't the slightest reaction. I'm sorry it was so silly. But say what you like, it was an extraordinary coincidence.'

'Extraordinary, yes. And I can see the temptation to try to cash in on it. But of no significance really. I mean, we know you invented a couple of details which by pure chance Sir James was already exhibiting: it's entertaining but it doesn't matter. What is interesting is that the constable didn't react. Like Sherlock Holmes's dog in the night time. Here was this extraordinary coincidence thrust at him, and he never for a moment, apparently, said to himself, "Oy, what's this?" I don't know why he didn't; but everything he did is clearly of interest. You see that, don't you?'

'You mean—'

'I mean this policeman stinks. Everything about him is wrong, admitting that he rather put it across both of us and we both disliked him. I suppose he was the village constable? He didn't feel like one.'

'I'd never seen him before. But he was in the police cottage after all, and he couldn't have known I was going to turn up. Besides, people saw us go through the village. He can't have been an outsider masquerading as the constable, if that's what you mean.'

'All right. Nasty or not, he was the village constable. Then how do we explain his reception of your report? Can you think of any reason why your report should be false on the face of it?'

'No. Extraordinary, of course, but not necessarily false. You'd think he'd come at the run.'

'That's right. Opportunity knocks. Something has happened in Lodstone at last. I shall be a sergeant yet. That's what the local constable thinks in books anyway. Yet you say he challenged you from the start and then came as slowly as he could.'

'Not only that. When we got to the fields, he – well, I thought at first he just didn't believe there was a body there to find. Then I got the feeling, very strongly, that he didn't want me to find it.'

'You mean he wanted to prove himself right and you wrong?'

'I suppose so,' said Margaret. But she seemed doubtful.

'Have you considered another possibility – that he knew for a fact that you wouldn't find it?'

'But how could he? It was there, you know. Or don't you believe in my dead man either?'

'My dear girl, I do more than that. I believe you saw him, and I also believe you could have taken the constable or anyone else back to him – a few moments' hesitation, possibly, but of course you could have found him.'

'You mean he was there the first time, but had really gone by the time I came back?'

'That must be the explanation. Nothing else will do. All right. Now let's go back to the constable. You report a body that is there. You then go back with him, and it's not there. Now looking back at his whole behaviour again, don't you think it's compatible with his having known both in advance?'

'You mean he knew there was a body there all the time?'

'He knew there was one. He also knew it would be gone by the time you got back. Think, Margaret. Wouldn't this fit in with his behaviour from the start? And what else does? Supposing for a moment that he merely disbelieved you – could he really have risked ignoring your report as he apparently did? Suppose the body had turned up again (which by the way it hasn't, as far as one can tell) and you had then come forward and said, "Yes, I reported it to Constable Jones, but he took no notice" – no sergeant's stripes for Constable Jones in that, obviously. No, he wasn't just being exasperating. He knew something. Whatever the explanation is, he's in it up to the neck. Don't you think so?'

'I'd very much like to think you're right. It may make the constable look a pretty big knave, but it makes me look much

less of a fool. And on any other explanation I don't come out
of it very well, do you think? I mean, prejudice apart,' said
Margaret, looking at him with wide grey eyes.

'I am already deeply sunk in prejudice, but I don't have
to put it aside. You stuck to your guns until the enemy had
withdrawn. You may have had a weep afterwards – and that
was mostly hunger, as you say – but you were on your feet
again and quite ready to bandy words with me by the time
I came along. No, I don't think you came out of it badly at
all. The constable's another matter.'

'All that delay before he came back with me – do you
think—?'

'Yes, of course. That fits too. He had to make sure the
body had gone before he came on the spot. And of course
he wasn't interested in my sleeping beauty. He probably
knew what the body looked like – not like Sir James. And
even if he didn't, he knew perfectly well that the body wasn't
driving round the country in a black limousine with a hired
nobody at the wheel. Whatever had happened to it, he
knew I hadn't got it.'

Mr Garrod sat back and looked at her. 'You're in something
pretty queer, Margaret, aren't you? What are you going to
do about it, do you think?'

'I could always do nothing. I suppose that would please
everybody, especially the constable. And it would be convenient, and easy, and I suppose safe. Only—'

'Only it wouldn't be right?'

'No. Yes. Well, in a sense. It wouldn't be satisfactory. I
am far from clear on the rights of it. But I badly want to
know the facts.'

'Attagirl,' said Mr Garrod.

CHAPTER THREE

'You know everyone round about Lodstone, grandmother. What's my best source of information?'

'It rather depends what sort of information you want.'

'About the present people mainly – but I suppose local history too to some extent. Local gossip generally.'

'I should suggest myself,' said Mrs Canting, 'but for two reasons. First, my knowledge, though extensive, is not recent. And second, you obviously do not wish to consult me. You no doubt have your reasons, and I hope they are adequate ones. This is still the thing to do with Sir James Utley, is it? I have heard nothing more of it since you went back to Oxford, but when you suddenly come home halfway through the summer term with the apparent intention of asking me one particular question, I must assume it is something already well on your mind.'

'In point of fact, I don't think Sir James has got anything to do with it, except very incidentally. I'm sorry about that, because I remember you thought that his mere presence would keep the whole thing respectable. Still – yes, it is the same business. And yes, grandmother, my reasons for not bringing you in are entirely adequate and strictly worthy. And you do know, don't you, that despite my almost unnaturally glamorous appearance I am really a very good judge of that sort of thing.'

'Yes. When I was a girl we were all supposed to pretend that we were not beautiful. This involved us in a great many difficulties and subterfuges. In particular we had to find adequate explanations for the presence and behaviour of a great many young men, even when, as on one occasion, they fought each other and fell into the duck-pond. But I still find something slightly cold-blooded in your frank assumption of beauty. Of course, it is soundly based. Your father as a very young man was one of the most beautiful people I have ever seen; and bone and eyes generally keep their value in either

17

sex. However, that is not what you were asking me about. I should go and see Charlie Mayne. I am sure he will do all he can to help you, and he must know a great deal about local affairs. He lives at Ebury.'

'Ebury? Ebury Manor? That's a show place, isn't it? Gardens open on Sunday, and that sort of thing. Is this Charlie Mayne very special?'

'Charlie was not particularly well off when I first knew him, and the Maynes weren't local people. He was in India for a good many years, in the police, and then when he retired and came home he continued to take an interest in that sort of work. I think they made him Chief Constable of the County at one time, but whether he still is I can't say.'

'Chief Constable, is he?'

'Was, anyhow.'

'Is he like the Chief Constables in books – you know, innocent and enthusiastic country gentlemen, the despair of the local professionals? Will he call me 'm'dear' and talk about me as young George Canting's gel?'

'Not unless he's altered a great deal. Full of charm, of course, but as tough as an old boot and very shrewd. Not very popular locally, I fancy. Certainly not regarded with kindly indulgence. For the same reason I don't know that I'd accept Charlie's views about people as necessarily sound. He'd know what everybody did, but I don't know that he'd be very good at their reasons for doing it.'

'That all sounds most reassuring. I must go and see this Charlie when I can find the time. But by the present looks of things, that won't be yet awhile.'

This indeed was true. The summer term at Oxford, even for those who do not face their finals, is a time of infinite preoccupation. The desultory discussion of plans was a pleasure for the season, and Margaret and the man Garrod discussed them in punts and over coffee and in the damp shimmer of the university streets on summer nights. But to implement them was a thing hardly to be borne; and it was not until the curious half-season of Commemoration that Margaret eventually found her way to Ebury.

But plans of a sort had been laid. They had agreed that, given world and time enough, certain things must be done, and in certain ways. They had rejected from the start any attempt to report the matter, at least without a good deal of preliminary exploration, to the higher authorities. 'I don't see what good it would do,' Garrod had said. 'The constable must have faced the possibility as an immediate threat at the time and have made his own preparations. And until we know a good deal more, it is only your word against his. He hoped to bluff you, of course, into keeping quiet, and it won't do any harm to let him think he succeeded. But you mustn't go hanging round Lodstone asking questions. I doubt if it would be profitable, and it might well not be very safe. I don't think I'd trust that man very far if his interests were seriously threatened. If there's any snooping to be done in Lodstone, it's me that has to do it, not you. Apart from driving straight through in an elegant green uniform, I haven't been near the place. You get all the facts you can on the side, and maybe pay an ordinary visit later and watch your step all the way. But no sleuthing on the spot.'

Ebury was in fact four miles from Lodstone. It was a valley village, sunk in the drift of trees that washed the foot of the downs, and Margaret came to it before she expected it. But no one had seen her, and she was still unobserved as she backed the car into a side lane, jacked up and removed a back wheel, fitted a carefully punctured spare in its place and put the sound wheel in the boot. She worked in gloves, and with a strength and competence out of keeping with her appearance. Then she ran the limping car gently back on to the road, beat the dust out of her gloves and stowed them under the seat.

Three minutes later she walked, hesitant but resolved, up the drive of Ebury Manor. Charlie Mayne, who had been in the police in India and was still interested in that sort of thing, had turned out on enquiry to be Sir Charles Mayne, K.C.I.E., and until very recently Chief Constable of the County. Margaret had learnt her lines. She said, 'Oh – I'm so sorry – but can you tell me if this is Sir Charles Mayne's house and if he is in?'

The two curiously similar heads that had risen to greet her from behind a shoulder-high yew hedge turned to consult one another. Both had copper-brown skins and grizzled hair clipped close to the scalp. Only the eyes were different, one pair being brown and liquid and the other grey and fierce. Then brown eyes said something in an unknown tongue to grey eyes, and both heads wagged with incomprehensible but rather formidable laughter. 'Yes, Miss-sahib,' said brown eyes in an oriental sing-song, 'you please come with me, I take you to Sir Charles.' Margaret hesitated. She felt uncomfortably that the act was somehow going wrong, but decided that there was no going back. Brown eyes emerged as a medium-sized but spare man, dressed in a startlingly white shirt, khaki drill trousers and open-toed sandals. He walked very fast. As they came near the house Margaret said, 'I don't know Sir Charles, but I think he knows my grandmother. Only my car has got a puncture, and I wondered whether someone could give me a hand. The name is Canting.'

Brown eyes said, 'Good God, yes,' spun round and offered her a hand. 'Of course that's who it was – George Canting. You must be the daughter. Very like him – both look like recording angels. Sorry about this foolery – didn't know you were friends of the family. Come along in.' He turned on the doorstep, communicated his change of plans to grey eyes in an incomprehensible torrent of sound and led the way indoors. 'Tea will be along in a minute,' he said. 'How's your grandmother? Sprightly as ever? Should have been dead years ago.'

'Oh, I don't think so at all,' said Margaret. 'Of course to outlive one's usefulness is the constant hazard of old age, but you don't all succumb to it, surely?'

'Ah,' said Charlie Mayne, 'educated girl, are you? Good talker. Well, so's your grandmother – splendid talker. Brought you up to it, I suppose.' He thought for a moment. 'What did you say – something wrong with the car? Want some help with it?'

'Oh, yes please. It's just outside the village on the road from Lodstone. It's only a puncture and I think the spare's all right, but I'm not much good at changing wheels.'

'That's all right. I'll tell Karim. Have you come from Lodstone today?'

'Not today. But I know it. I've stayed there once or twice.'

'Have you? Who with?'

'Mrs Besson.'

'Emma Besson? You'll be all right with her. Queer place, Lodstone, though. Always something going on.'

'Oh? It seemed quiet enough to me.'

'Yes. I don't mean that. I mean under the surface. Nothing ever seemed to turn quite as one expected, but I always found it very difficult to say why. Some one would steal a dozen eggs, and half the village would have seen him and be ready to swear to it. Then a house on the green would go up, burnt out in a matter of minutes, everything stinking of arson, but no evidence at all. No one knew anything – almost like a village in India. One had the same feeling that matters were being settled out of court, and that official intervention was not really wanted. Of course, if something serious had turned up, we should have had to go in and pull things apart. But it never did. It was all very quiet, on the surface anyhow. And of course Robin had his finger very much on things.'

'Robin?'

'The constable there. You must have seen him.'

'Oh yes. What a very unsuitable name. Robin's the surname, is it?'

'That's right. Local man. There have been Robins at Lodstone for donkey's years. You didn't like him, though?'

'I didn't say so.'

'All but. But he's an odd man, I agree. Very able and I suspect well educated, but not forthcoming, and no wish to get on. He could have had promotion and a posting somewhere else for the asking, but he wouldn't do it. All he wanted was to stay at Lodstone. And of course he was very useful there, and he just got left. I don't suppose they'll ever shift him now. What didn't you like about him?'

Grey eyes, now identified as Karim, brought in an elaborate tea-tray. He managed to combine deft service with an almost swashbuckling panache in a way hopelessly beyond the mere Englishman. Charlie Mayne gave him some instructions in which the word motor, given a broad Scottish pronunciation, was identifiable; and when he had gone, busied himself with the tea-tray. Here too was a perfectly serious concentration on doing things gracefully with no loss of masculine dignity. An endearing acquirement, Margaret supposed, from the East. Most of the men she knew would have to choose between clumsiness and effeminacy. She must try Mr Garrod with a tea-tray.

Charlie Mayne asked no questions over the tea. He poured out her cup, put the other ingredients ready to her hand and left her to use them or not. It was only when she had done so that she realised that his last question was still between them and must be answered. She had gained time, and was glad of it. She had not been let off. And Charlie Mayne, for all his elliptical conversation and expertise with the tea-tray, would not be an easy man to answer.

'Constable Robin?' she said at last. 'I don't know. I haven't had much to do with him, of course; but he seemed a rather over-bearing character, I thought. A huge, red man, but not at all gentle. I think perhaps he gave me a feeling of subdued violence. And there was this touch of thinly masked superiority – I forget exactly what you said just now, but it seemed to convey the right impression. He doesn't' – she quoted Mr Garrod's words – 'feel like a village constable. But I think if he told me to move along, I'd do it pretty quickly, and then perhaps feel galled about it afterwards. I'm not surprised he keeps the village in order.'

'For a girl who hasn't had much to do with him, you diagnose your impressions very precisely. It's your way with words, I suppose.'

'Do you associate Robin directly with this feeling you had about Lodstone – I mean the feeling that things were going on under the surface? I mean, did you ever feel that he was keeping to himself things he ought to report – more or less suppressing evidence?'

Charlie Mayne glared at her as though he found the question a hard one. 'Not suppressing evidence, no. We couldn't have had that, obviously, once a report had been made or an offence come to our notice. But in my time I've certainly accepted from him what I felt wasn't the whole story. And I shouldn't put it past him to settle things his own way sometimes. Mind you, the better type of village constable has always done that – used his personal authority and prestige to deal with troubles better kept out of court. But it ought to be his legal position as constable that lets him do it. With Robin I don't know. I've had a feeling at times that his influence doesn't hang wholly on his uniform. I think people might be afraid of him.'

'I was,' said Margaret. 'I mean, I felt I could be if there had been anything to be frightened about. He could certainly be frightening.'

'Yes. Yes, I know what you mean. The truth is, I'm not

much good at going too deeply into things. My instinct is not to get under people's skins: I don't think it's a policeman's job. An old-fashioned view, of course, in these psychological days. India too, partly. You'll have heard it said that it was the Englishman's weakness that he never really got on terms with the people he was governing. But it was also his strength, you know – not to be involved, to stick to the solid physical facts and the law – very simple law it was – that applied to them. They found his lack of comprehension exasperating, but in a way it simplified things. They knew much more where they were with him than they did with their own people. But that view would seem very shocking now, of course.'

He showed her, in an off-hand, unexplanatory way, gardens of breathless splendour. When they returned to the house, Karim made a report. There was a certain amount of quick question and answer, and she felt, as she had felt from behind the yew-hedge, that she was caught in a current of thought between two mutually familiar minds. Then Charlie Mayne said, 'Right. Your car is ready. You'll have to get the puncture done, of course, but it will be bad luck if the spare doesn't get you home. By the gates. I'll walk with you.'

Down the exquisitely laundered drive the fierce pace of his walk slackened. 'You know,' he said, 'that I have no longer any official position. I was Chief Constable, of course – I expect your grandmother told you.'

'Yes, I think she did.'

'Less authority, of course. None at all, really. But it leaves my hands much freer, which in some cases can be a great advantage.'

'Yes. I can imagine that particular job of all jobs being pretty restricting. Worse than being a bishop, almost.'

'Ah, but you see, bishop or no bishop, once a priest always a priest. I'm no longer a policeman of any sort.'

'Yes.'

'Therefore,' he went on, as though he had paused to consider his words rather than to have her reply, 'therefore I am what you might call a safe man to consult. I am still in touch, you know, but I don't have to report everything. Like Police Constable Robin of Lodstone.'

'Yes,' said Margaret. 'Yes, I can see that.'

'On the other hand, it is very difficult to help, or even advise, if I don't know the facts.'

They came to the car and Margaret turned to make her farewell. 'My man Karim, you know,' said Charlie Mayne, 'was also a policeman in India. He wasn't an expert tracker, like some of the aboriginals we employed, but he can read the elementary signs, and is accustomed to it. He thought it curious that your car had acquired a puncture suddenly when it was standing in a side lane, and that the spare had been in use only a very little time before. I know you're Margaret Canting,' he went on quickly, 'and I assume your absolute good faith as I assume my own. But now that we've met it may not be necessary, on another occasion, to adopt quite such an indirect approach.'

He opened the door of the car and handed Margaret in. 'I hope, nevertheless, I have been of some use. I'm full of curiosity, of course, but that's undignified at my age. I have certainly enjoyed your visit, however engendered. But look here. I know nothing of your affairs, my girl, but I don't consider Lodstone and some of its inhabitants a very suitable subject for amateur investigation. That's all. Now you thank me and drive off.'

'Thank you,' said Margaret. She headed the car for Oxford.

CHAPTER FOUR

It was still, Jacob Garrod reflected, a standard convention in detective stories that the outsider gained valuable information by dropping in at the local pub. In earlier days, certainly, and even fairly recently, this reconnaissance had had to be made either by the detective himself disguised as an ordinary man or by his assistant who, though he lacked his master's flair, specialised in being ordinary. But recent extensions of the ordinary had made the convention easier to apply. Sherlock Holmes would now attract little attention in the public bar, especially if he brought his fiddle, and Bunter would almost certainly attract more than Lord Peter. So far as he was concerned, he certainly lacked flair, and did not altogether reject the possibility that he might be Margaret Canting's ordinary assistant. In any case, the pub was still the one place in the village where an outsider could linger without excuse and at least start a conversation without presumption. Whether it was still the sounding-board of local opinion and a hotbed of local gossip he doubted; but it seemed as good a place as any to start.

The Goat at Lodstone had long been the property of the local brewery, which had itself lost its identity in a group of companies which was even now on the point of absorption in a national merger. The building was of no particular distinction. Its beams, though they must have been there, were decently clothed in plaster, and even the saloon bar lacked an inglenook. Nevertheless there had been an inn on the site nearly as long as there had been a village, and there was not the slightest evidence that it had ever been called anything but the Goat. The present sign was a purely pastoral conception of the company's painter. Earlier versions had perhaps been less innocent.

To a man stepping out of a car the heat was uncompromisingly fierce and the sunlight smelt of hay. The village itself was deserted, but the cutters chattered urgently from below

25

the hill, and the heavy air threatened trouble before the hay was in. The door opened silently into hops and darkness. Garrod heard a murmur of voices from the varnished settles of the public bar and turned to his right into the saloon. There was one other customer and a small neat man, who should be the licensee, George Crayle, behind the bar.

Conversation stopped audibly as he came in, and the landlord's greeting was tempered with doubt. He ordered his beer, exchanged comment on the heat and settled in a dark corner. George Crayle polished his bar and looked from one to the other of his customers in the silence. 'Well, there you are,' he said at last to the other man, and Garrod felt he was ligaturing the severed ends of a conversation; 'as I said to Jack, it doesn't pay, I said, and if you've any sense that's the last we'll hear of it.'

The other man, small, bright-eyed and worried, grunted. 'Proper furious he was, though, Jack. We tell him the same before he came in here. "Don't you go starting nothing with Nick Valance," we said, "he's not a man to quarrel with." But he wouldn't listen. "I'm not afraid of that bugger," he kept on saying. "He can't do this to me." Real furious he was.' He got up, an older man than Garrod had expected, and made for the door. The door shut on his farewells, the landlord went through into the public bar and Garrod sat back in the silence.

Next door a new-comer was greeted and more drinks were drawn. Conversation remained desultory and inaudible. When the landlord came back, he drew Garrod another pint and said, 'Your first visit to Lodstone?'

'Yes. Just passing through, as a matter of fact.'

'Ah. Thought I hadn't seen you around. Quiet little place, though. Don't see many visitors.'

'You're not a Lodstone man, are you?'

'Not me, no. Come from further north myself. But I been here five years and you get used to the place.'

Garrod nodded, drank his beer and waited. George Crayle was a talker and by Lodstone standards a foreigner. If only the bar stayed empty long enough, something could be had from him. But he must not be hurried.

The landlord mopped his bar again, watching his guest.

Then he smiled confidentially. He said, 'Proper old barney we had last night. You heard that chap telling me.'

'I heard something. Jack Somebody and a man with a funny name – Nick something."

'Valance. Nick Valance, one of the farmers. And Jack Simmons, he's got a wireless shop, wireless and T.V. Hasn't been here long, but he does quite a business. Saves people going into Messleton, and he's clever at it. But it seems he had Nick Valance's set in and didn't do it right, or Nick said he didn't, and refused to pay. Then yesterday Jack stopped him and asked for the money. And Nick, he's a foul-mouthed chap, see, and he fair tore strips off Jack from what they tell me. Then they bring Jack in here afterwards, like I said, and we tried to calm him down. But he wouldn't listen. Said he'd see a solicitor in Messleton today. And he's gone by all accounts.'

Garrod nodded appreciatively. 'But Mr Valance will have to pay, won't he? Or was there something really wrong with the set?'

George Crayle sucked his teeth. 'As to that I wouldn't know. Of course, Jack hasn't been here long. I've been here five years myself, but in his place I'd go a bit slow. Nick Valance farms his own land and was born and brought up here, and Jack's got his business to think of. I'm an outsider and apart from business I like to keep myself to myself. But it's a funny old place, and I know there's those here I wouldn't quarrel with, not if I could avoid it.'

'Often the way in these little places,' said Garrod. 'Some quite small thing starts it and the row goes on for ever. I've known sisters living next door to each other that hadn't spoken for twenty years. But people don't fight like they used to, do they? I mean actually coming to blows. There's a lot of cursing and back-biting, but not much violence. Not in the country, that is. It's coming back in the towns. In the country I think people are too well known to each other. And to the police. Is there a constable in the village?' He buried his face in his beer, but one speculative eye watched the landlord over the tankard's rim.

George Crayle lifted his own and stared straight into the watching eye. 'I felt as if I had been caught with my eye at a key-hole,' Garrod said later to Margaret. 'I'm afraid I'm not much good at this sort of thing, but I'll swear my question

27

was casual enough. Then when he looked up suddenly like that and found me watching him, I nearly choked on my mild-and-bitter. But his face showed nothing – nothing at all. It was impossibly blank for a naturally confidential, gossipy sort of chap like that. Either he suspected my interest or the subject was one he wasn't talking about. But his face wasn't just a blank. It was a howling void.'

George Crayle dropped his eyes and nodded. He said, 'There's a police cottage on the other side of the village.' Then he said, 'Coming, sir,' and vanished into the public bar. Garrod finished his beer and felt oddly discomforted. He was an ordinary assistant all right; but it wasn't only his own ineptitude for duplicity that worried him. There was something here that even an innocent like George Crayle turned his back on instinctively. Garrod had a queer feeling that in a more religious age the little man might have crossed himself.

The voices rose and fell cheerfully in the public bar, and when the landlord came back he was smiling. He moved some bottles about, whistling breathily through his teeth. The yellow sunlight that had indirectly flooded the bar faded suddenly. The world turned grey, and an enormous man came into the room. He moved very silently and with a deliberate slowness. His voice was very deep, with a husky quality that Garrod associated with some negro voices. He remembered it at once. The constable said, 'I'd like a word with you, Mr Crayle.' The landlord, motionless with both hands on the bar, nodded.

'Simmons came in here yesterday evening after an argument with Mr Valance. What did he say about it?'

'He wasn't talking much, Mr Robin. It was the others talking mostly. I didn't hear the row with Nick Valance myself. Only what was said when they bring him in here afterwards.'

'That's what I'm asking you. What was said?'

'Well, mostly they were telling him to keep calm and not to make trouble, and he was saying Nick Valance would have to pay up, and if he didn't he'd bring a case for the money. He was talking a bit wild, of course, Jack Simmons. They were all excited.'

'Did he threaten Mr Valance?'

'Only with a court case. He said he was going to see a solicitor this morning.'

'He's gone. What did you say?'

'I told him not to make trouble with Mr Valance.'

'Why?'

'Why? I thought he wouldn't do himself any good in the village. He's new here, as you know. I didn't think he understood.'

'What did he say?'

'He said he wasn't afraid of Mr Valance and Mr Valance couldn't get away with it. We all told him not to talk so wild.'

'What then?'

'Well, that was all really. I had my bar to attend to. Jack went off with some of the others and that was the last I heard of it. But we all told him not to make trouble.'

'He didn't take much notice of what you said, did he? Went straight into Messleton first thing this morning.'

George Crayle said nothing. Nothing but his face had moved since the policeman came into the bar. Suddenly, but quite unmistakably, the big man became aware of Garrod's presence behind him. He grunted, a deep animal sound, and the great shoulders stiffened and swung slowly round. Garrod, like the landlord behind the bar, was motionless under the compulsion of a jungle instinct not to provoke the larger animal. The room was very dark now, and he faced the little hot eyes from a comforting depth of shadow.

'How long have you been here?'

'Me? Half an hour, I suppose. I'm on my way through.'

'Been here before?'

'No.'

For a second, for another second, almost for a third Garrod felt himself examined. Then the head and shoulders turned away again and came back to George Crayle. He said, 'I don't want rows in here.'

'Nor do I. You know that, Mr Robin.'

'All right. Better not let Simmons in till he's recovered his senses. Then there's no risk, is there?' Without another glance at Garrod he moved heavily to the door. No one spoke in the public bar next door. In the silence a sudden gusty breeze came over the fields and shook the heavy leaves outside. For the first time George Crayle moved. He moved down the bar, shifted a bottle and dusted mechanically the wood underneath. 'I'll see to it, Mr Robin,' he said. He looked out of the open window and seemed to Garrod almost ready to jump through it. He said, 'Going to be a storm by the looks of things.'

The policeman stopped by the door and turned unexpectedly a face of sardonic amusement. 'There'll be no storm today,' he said.

Conversation started fitfully again in the public bar. The landlord resumed his whistling, but seemed unwilling to talk. Garrod found his throat and mouth dry, but wanted no more beer. He got to his feet, aware of the embarrassment that supervenes on a sudden community of emotion. 'I must be getting on,' he said. He nodded and was nodded to.

The sunlight struck him like a flail as he came out of the door. He looked round, saw no one and made for his car. Then he turned and went to the telephone box outside the post office. The door discharged a wave of congested air as he opened it. He leant in, took out the local directory and turned the pages in the relatively free air of the village street. There was only one Valance. The address was Straightways Farm, Lodstone.

He put his head into the post office and said, 'Straightways Farm?' A head came round the glass screen. It had a halo of white hair and the face of a dissipated cavalry colonel, but the voice was local and feminine. 'Straightways? Go on down the hill for Ebury and bear right. There's a sign. Mr Valance will be in the fields, though.'

Garrod thanked her but offered no comment. She watched him through the shop window as he went back to his car, resentful of his inexplicability. With no plan in his head and his mind a turmoil of frustrated emotion, he got into the stifling car and rolled it slowly down the hill.

Half-way down, on a fair May Morning that now seemed very long ago, he had seen a slender figure haloed in yellow sunlight coming up to meet him out of a still sleeping landscape. Now the hand of summer was heavy on the fields and nothing stirred. The Beacon was a blue-green outline hazed with heat. Only down between the hedgerows the tractors purred and the hay-cutters chattered, one of them, he supposed, under the direction of Mr Valance, whom curiosity urged him to see and ingenuity suggested no valid pretext for seeing. Whatever else he had gained from the day, he had achieved once for all a settled conviction of his own inability to deceive.

As the road began to flatten out a signpost said, 'Straightways Farm,' and a lane led off to the right. Brick chimneys showed among the trees two or three furlongs away. He pulled his car into the shade at the side of the road. He wondered what business a farmer might conceivably have to discuss with a total stranger. There might be something he could make a show of trying to sell without too far betraying his ignorance of it. Insurance? Discount sales? He had a nasty feeling that the foul-mouthed Mr Valance would make short work of either.

The Land Rover slid alongside and turned across him so sharply that one of its massive projections scored his wing. A man leaned out and all but put his head in at the nearside window. He said, 'Were you wanting me?' His mental picture of a blustering, red-faced John Bull of a man was wildly wrong. The face was pale and deeply lined and the slanting green eyes sunk back into their sockets. This was a man of almost urban vices, not one who swore down opposition in a village street.

He said, 'No, just pulled off the road for a minute to get something straightened out.'

Mr Valance got out of his driving seat and walked round to the offside of Garrod's car. Then he seized the door handle, pulled the door open and stood looking down at him. The pursed mouth turned sharply down at the corners and stiff white bristles stood out on either side of the flattened nose. It was the most purely feline face he had ever seen on a man. The voice was soft, high-pitched and throaty. He said, 'You asked for my farm.'

Garrod swung one foot out on to the grass and climbed slowly after it. Mr Valance still held the handle of the door and Garrod, straightening himself in the confined space, found himself, a head taller, looking down into the slanting lashless eyes. He was repelled but not frightened. He said, 'Yes, as a matter of fact I did. Any reason why I shouldn't?'

Mr Valance drew the corners of his lips back slightly. 'Any reason why you did?'

'None. All right then – pure curiosity. I heard them talking

31

about a row you had yesterday and I wanted to see you.'

'You a friend of Simmons's?'

'Never set eyes on him.'

'Then why the curiosity?'

'People interest me. I wanted to see what sort of person would behave in that sort of way.'

'Who was talking, then?'

'Man in the pub first – I don't know any names. Then the constable came in and spoke to the landlord.'

'He spoke to Crayle in front of you? Don't make me laugh.'

'You're wrong, but I know what you mean. He didn't see me. I was in the saloon bar, sitting back. It was dark in there, and he came in and spoke to the landlord before he saw me.'

Mr Valance laid his ears back and told Garrod in detail what sort of an eavesdropper he thought he was. To call him foul-mouthed was to miss the heart of the matter. The thing went deeper. Instead of standard formulae he chose deliberately from some obscene treasury the words which conveyed the appalling pictures his mind conceived. A trace of foam stood on the bristles and he spat slightly as he talked.

There were two distinct reasons why Garrod did not hit him. The first was an overwhelming repugnance, an immediate and intense desire to get away without touching him. The second was a vivid memory of George Crayle and the little sad-eyed man talking in the saloon bar, not half an hour before. 'There's those here I wouldn't quarrel with, not if I could avoid it.' And the other had said, 'Don't you go starting anything with Nick Valance.'

He lowered his face to the level of the white cat-mask, ducked under the stream of abuse and got back into his seat. He started the engine, put the car in reverse and began slowly to back clear of the Land Rover. Mr Valance held the door for a moment and then changed his mind and swung it viciously shut.

Garrod put his head out of the window. 'Thank you, Mr Valance,' he said. 'I'm glad we met. My curiosity was fully justified. Good-day to you.' He pulled off the grass on to the tarmac and accelerated quickly on the slight slope. It was only then that he found his hands unsteady on the wheel and his knees vibrating uncontrollably over the pedals. There was something about Mr Valance he did not like at all.

CHAPTER FIVE

The Bank Holiday fell on the second of the month, and on the Friday evening Margaret drove, alone and unannounced, into Lodstone and pulled up outside Mrs Besson's cottage. 'Go and do exactly what you usually do,' Garrod had said. 'Talk to the people you usually talk to and keep your ears open for anything out of the ordinary. But don't for God's sake convey the impression that you are probing or asking questions. If Robin sees you staying in the village as usual and doing nothing, it will satisfy him more than if you don't go. But he must be sure you're doing nothing. Anyway, don't stick your neck out; and if anything seems wrong, get in your car and drive like hell to Ebury. Odd as it all is, you must remember that this is a business of life and death to somebody. For a number of reasons I'd rather you didn't add another death to it.'

She had left the out-of-town traffic behind when she turned off the main road. The valley lanes were empty, and the evening, sultry with the threat of Bank Holiday storms to come, closed in round her breathlessly as she made for the village. She drove steadily but without relish. Then the trees parted as the lane turned, and for a moment she saw all Lodstone afire, glowing like a red cone of coals in the sudden sunset, with tremendous streamers of fiery cloud fuming up from behind it into the sultry sky. Then she was among the houses, there before she had really made up her mind to go there, caught off her guard by a cold wave of panic-stricken distaste she had not bargained for.

Mrs Besson's cottage was shut and looked deserted. She pushed the gate open and walked firmly up the path, her town heels clacking on the paving. She put her suitcase down beside her, determined to outface a nagging hope that Mrs Besson was not at home. She knocked loudly on the upper half-door.

'Why, Miss Margaret!' The sullen apprehension on Mrs Besson's face melted into broad relief when she saw her, but the relief was clouded at once by a sort of wary distress. 'Oh dear, oh dear. You never said you was coming this week-end my dear. I could have told you – oh dear, I do wish I had known. I could have told you it was no use.'

'Oh, I'm sorry, Mrs Besson. I know I should have written and asked you, and I meant to, but I've been awfully busy. And you did say I could come at any time.'

'I know, my dear, but I've had to promise the room for a gentleman. I could have told you if you'd written, but when I never heard, I thought you wasn't coming. You'd better go back to London, miss, your grandmother will be glad to have you.' Unbelievably, and as if it moved without her volition, her hand began to shut the swinging half-door.

Margaret put her elbows firmly on the top of the lower door. She said, 'Mrs Besson!' sharply. The door wavered to a halt, and Mrs Besson raised her eyes and met Margaret's in a blank unfathomable stare. 'Mrs Besson, you're not to worry. Do you understand? You're not to worry at all.'

She smiled, conjuring up the ghost of an answering smile from the blank face before her. Then she turned, picked up her case and clacked off down the path. The street was empty, but she found herself unwilling to turn her car and go back the way she had come. Instead she drove on towards the church. The top of the tower still caught the red ruin of the sunset, but everything below was adrift with the thick beginnings of darkness.

The vicar wore grey-green trousers, a white cricket-shirt and canvas shoes. He thrust savagely with a hand-mower over the uneven green of the vicarage lawn. On an impulse Margaret braked, pulled the car in to the side and got out. The racket of the machine and the determined agony of pushing it cut him off from the dusky world round him. His bony hands clutched the handle convulsively, and his threadbare shirt clung to his gaunt rib-cage with the sweat of his effort. He had the desperate look of a man to whom inanimate objects were habitually hostile.

Margaret advanced her towny shoes and the elegant legs above them until, nearly carried away by a particularly desperate thrust of the mower, they came within Mr Claydon's field of vision. He checked his next thrust so suddenly that his upper half, already committed to the blow, bowed deeply over the stationary handle and he coughed convulsively as he straightened up to greet her.

'Miss Canting, how nice to see you. And what a mercy I saw you in time. Those shoes would have been no protection.'

'I was ready to jump. But I couldn't attract your attention except by direct frontal attack.'

'No, I'm sorry. I get angry, you know.' His long horse-face puckered into a mask of confusion and remorse. 'I try not to get angry with people or animals, whom it might hurt, but there is anger in me, and it vents itself on things. The truth is, I can't get on with things, and they make me feel frustrated and shut out. Shall you be with us over the holiday?'

'I was hoping to, but Mrs Besson can't have me. Like a fool, I never let her know and came down on the chance. You couldn't possibly find room for me here, could you? I'll come to all your services.'

'I have six what the agents call principal bedrooms, of which I occupy one and Mrs Grendle another. It is difficult to maintain that I can't find room. But it's very bare, you know. Most of the house hasn't really been lived in since the war. Wouldn't you find it uncomfortable, or damp, or of course boring? I won't pretend for a moment that I shouldn't enjoy your company immensely, but it won't be very amusing for you.'

'Mrs Besson's isn't the Ritz, you know. And Mrs Besson, dearly as I love her, is conversationally limited. If I shouldn't cause too much upset, I should love to stay here. Do you think Mrs Grendle would mind?'

'Mrs Grendle endured four London evacuees. Of course, we were all a bit younger then, but I cannot believe that you will stone my chickens or light a fire on the attic floor or even throw food about. Anyway, let us ask her.'

He threw a glance full of menace at the uncut grass and made off for the back of the house, trailing the jangling mower behind him with one hand. Margaret went back to the car, took out her suitcase and rejoined him as he emerged from the huge stable where the mowing-machine lived alone. Together they went in at the back door to tackle Mrs Grendle.

The room was wholly white and looked across the church-yard. The late afternoon and evening sun had burned steadily through the tall sash-window, and the air was hot and smelt of old-fashioned soap. The floor was bare. Margaret raised with an effort the heavy lower sash and sat herself cautiously on the window-sill, drawing cool air from the greenness below. The menace that hung in the fields and streets of Lodstone seemed remote here. The house knew nothing of compromise, but was all innocence. Its peacefulness was a positive quality that filtered and sterilised the intrusions of the surrounding world. She felt safer now than at any time since she had turned and found Lodstone piled up and burning on the far side of the valley.

Later, after they had had their late supper, the surrounding world intruded (though by arrangement with the vicar) in the shape of a pale, gloomy young man who wheeled a bicycle in from the road and was closeted with Mr Claydon in his study. Margaret, reading next door in an armchair big enough to accommodate her entire length in almost any position, heard the voices but not the words. The vicar's voice, rather high but beautifully modulated, began with questions and went gradually over to the attack. The young man's, monotonous and much less audible, stated its case and relapsed gradually into short and often hesitant replies. Then chairs were pushed back and the door opened.

'Thank you for coming, Jack,' said the vicar as the feet moved through the hall. 'I know this isn't an easy matter, but I'm convinced there is only one answer. If you can't bring yourself to say it, write it; I wouldn't blame you for that. But do it before the thing goes any further. I think it's one of those things you will recognise as right as soon as it's done. But don't put it off. Good night.'

The door shut and the vicar came in, the firmness of his exhortations to the departed Jack belied by a face heavy with doubt. He sat down in silence and fiddled with an empty pipe, gazing out of the window to where the tower stood against the still luminous sky.

'Do all your parish interviews worry you as much as this?'

'Good gracious, I had forgotten you were there. I really do apologise.'

'Don't apologise. But do please answer.'

He frowned, as he had when he had confessed his hatred of the lawn-mower. 'I am not worried about the advice I gave Jack Simmons. I know that was right. I'm worried about my

own motives for giving it. In my experience to do the right
thing for an even doubtful motive is seldom wholly satisfactory.'

'Is it about his row with Mr Valance?'

'How do you know about that?'

'It's the story of the week in the village.'

He checked as if not wholly satisfied with this explanation,
but let it go. 'My difficulty is that prudence, common, rather
inglorious prudence, counsels what should also be Christian
behaviour. In a way that is easy. I tell Jack Simmons to forgive
Mr Valance his debt as he hopes to be forgiven. At the same
time I know that it will pay him, as a businessman and a
villager, to do just that. But isn't there a danger that I am
taking the easy way out?'

'But what would the harder way be? Would it be more
Christian for being less prudent?'

'On Jack's part, no. No good Christian should enforce
payment to himself. Whether a good Christian should ever
go into business I don't know: but that is not at the moment
in issue. But on my part, should I not, while by all means
enjoining forgiveness on Jack, make some approach to
Valance? And you see, I haven't suggested that.'

'Why not?'

'Valance is not a member of my congregation. Jack
Simmons is, though a recent one.'

'But Mr Valance would – well, recognise your right to
speak. You may say he is a lapsed member of your congregation, but even people who don't have any truck with the
Church can recognise sincerity when they see it.'

'I never said he was a lapsed member of my congregation.
He is nothing of the sort. That is where my difficulty lies.
This is a dispute between Christian and non-Christian. It
must have been familiar in the early Church. St Paul told the
Corinthian Christians to have nothing to do with the pagans.
"What concord hath Christ with Belial?" he said, "come out
from among them and be ye separate." But then the Church
was a tiny minority community. Now she is established in
strength. I am afraid I am not at all clear in my mind, and
shall have to seek guidance. But I think that what worries me
is the fear that in counselling Christian patience on Jack I am
running away from evil myself. It is a thing I have often been

37

conscious of doing. My dear girl, I have no right to burden you with all this. But it is, to be honest, such a joy to have an intelligent and scholarly mind to converse with, and I am afraid I have put too much upon you.'

He got up, took his tobacco pouch from the mantelpiece and filled his pipe. 'For the moment I shall put it out of my mind. And you, please, put it out of yours. I did not know you were so well versed in village affairs. Perhaps it was my surprise that led me into this discussion.'

'I don't want you to think that I am up to my ears in village scandal. But you know that members of a rather closed community always tend, if they like you in the first place, to talk more freely to an outsider about communal affairs than to another member of the community, except of course their special friends. It is another case of the spectator seeing most of the game. Would you tell me about Mr Valance? I've never met him. He sounds pretty unpleasant. But I thought you talked of him as something different from the ordinary backslider.'

For a moment Mr Claydon did not answer. He sat staring out through the darkening window at the now invisible tower, his forehead wrinkled with thought, his pipe cold. Then he took his pipe out of his mouth and spoke deliberately, his eyes still on the window, as if he forced the words into his own hearing. 'There is a power of evil in this village, and I associate Valance with it. I – I find it difficult to be more precise. But you see' – he turned and spoke directly to Margaret – 'where there is a clash, as in this wretched business tonight, between one of my people and a – a man like Valance, I find it difficult to be sure I am right in counselling submission. I don't really know. There is a great deal I don't know. Sometimes I suspect that I am afraid of knowing too much.'

He got up, went to the window and drew the curtains sharply as if there was something to be shut out. 'Now my dear girl' he said in an altogether different tone, 'you must not tempt me to unburden myself. I live much alone and I have a great deal on my mind, as anyone must who has a cure of souls. You are young enough to be – almost my grandchild, I suppose – but you have an educated mind and considerable beauty. What is worse, despite your dutiful levity of phrase, I think you are essentially serious. The temptation to treat you as a sympathetic confidant is, as has already become only too clear, almost overwhelming.'

'Do you remember my father?'

'No. Why?'

'Nor do I, much. Only someone the other day said that he and I both looked like recording angels. I don't think I could manage a scroll, but it might be in order for me to buy a tape-recorder.'

Mr Claydon laughed suddenly and startlingly, a wholly unaffected explosion of pent-up gaiety. 'Bless you, my dear girl, you set me right on all counts. If there is one thing I disapprove of in a professional man of God, it is undue solemnity. I have been in danger of taking myself much too solemnly. No more recording for tonight. You must excuse me if I go to my study. I have some parish accounts to go over, and I should not like even my recording angel to know what I think about those.'

The white room was still hot, though cooler than it had been earlier. Margaret switched on the light only long enough to make sure she remembered where everything was. Then she switched it off and went to the window. The clouds, which at sunset had been dramatically scattered, had thickened and dropped, and the night was utterly dark. The churchyard mound and the main bulk of the church itself lay, she knew, between her and the houses on the far side of the village. From where she sat in the window not a light was to be seen. The air was close, earthy and absolutely still.

An owl started to hoot in one of the churchyard trees, but broke off suddenly, as though embarrassed by its own dramatic propriety. When it spoke again, it made a ridiculous whistling chatter, which no one could take for ham. As her eyes adapted themselves she could make out the crenellations of the tower and the silhouette of trees against the blank wall of sky. Below everything was impenetrable.

There was a faint whirring in the darkness and the church clock clanged with startling violence. Margaret let the strokes flow uncounted, wondering how she was going to sleep with this cataclysm occurring next door at intervals throughout the night. At any rate, it was time she tried.

She moved back across the room and put out her hand to the switch. Then she changed her mind, groped her way back and began to undress in the dark. Something moved under the window, stopped and then moved again. She crept to the sill and listened. The sounds were louder than she had supposed, but came from farther away, near the church. A diffused rustling gradually took shape as stealthy movements through the churchyard grass under the south wall. There seemed to be more than one source of movement, spread out as though a number of bodies followed each other at intervals over a fixed course. The movements were heavy, half stealthy and infinitely menacing, but there was nothing to see.

Someone in the churchyard laughed, and her stomach turned over. It was a low, slow-coming laugh, full of enjoyment and conviviality and utterly beastly. The movements went on for some time but there was no more laughter. It was near morning before she slept.

Chapter Six

For all the shortness of the night daylight came with difficulty. A blanket of cloud still lay over the valley, and Lodstone, thrust up from the valley floor, dipped its tower and trees into its lower fringes. Four o'clock was the one hour Margaret could not swear to having heard strike. Five she counted consciously, conscious also of an aching head and a mind full of desperate uneasiness. A grey daylight penetrated the recesses of her room but cast no shadows on the white walls and floor. Ten minutes later she got up and opened wide the window she had, indefensibly but compulsively, shut before she went to bed.

The outside air had lost some of its heat but gained little freshness. The churchyard had an unreal, photographic quality in the unrelieved daylight. It was, she now saw, the highest point of the village, a circular green platform levelled off where the hill came up steeply on the northern side and almost certainly at some time terraced out over the gentler slope to the south. The church itself stood clear of the churchyard to the north, where a shelf had been scooped out for it at the top of the steep slope and just below the level of the central platform. That was why, when the village was seen from the west, the tower looked off-centre. But the trees grew thick everywhere, and contours were uncertain.

Dressed as lightly as seemed decent in her surroundings, Margaret tiptoed down the stairs. Neither door was locked and as far as she could see none of the ground-floor windows had been shut. Guarded only by poverty and its intrinsic integrity, the house stood open to the world while the vicar slept soundlessly upstairs.

There was no dew. The grass and leaves looked stale, as if they too had not slept. The road curved round the southern side of the churchyard, and underneath the trees the embankment rose sharply from the roadside to the stonework of the retaining wall. From there it spiralled up towards the eastern

41

side of the hill till it reached the level of the churchyard, above the floor level of the church itself. Here a gate led straight into the yard and a low flight of stone steps dropped to the flagged path that ran under the church walls.

Margaret turned into the gate and faced the brick gable-end of the vicarage across the perfect circle of the churchyard. There was her open window, and here, late last night, someone had laughed in the pitch-dark shadow of the trees, and she could not get the sound out of her head. The tombstones of centuries crowded the green space. All round, next to the wall, a grass path circled the churchyard, and here there was no graves of the faithful to hinder the persistent feet that had beaten the grass flat.

She walked clockwise round the path, and on the south side found herself, as she had guessed, on the broad top of an earthwork which must, before the trees grew, have commanded a view clear across the valley to the downs beyond. Moving westwards she passed within yards of the vicarage wall and then, through a sudden gap in the trees, saw the Beacon, dark under its hanging canopy of cloud, standing opposite her over the village roofs. Here there was a second gate in the churchyard wall, and a grass path led downhill and ran into the line of the village street at the point where it turned off to take the hill obliquely on its south side. She completed the circle along its northern segment under the church wall and went out again by the east gate. At different points of the path she saw, but left lying, a bone button, a safety-pin, a local bus ticket and what looked like a tuft of animal fur.

She came in by the back door and found Mrs Grendle in the kitchen. She said, 'You're up early. Couldn't you sleep?' a little sharply.

Margaret shook her head gingerly. 'It was a hot night. And I'm not used to the clock.'

Mrs Grendle pushed a large white cup across the scrubbed table top and said, 'Sugar?'

'Oh, yes please. I'll get some aspirin.'

'Aspirin,' said Mrs Grendle with contemptuous sadness. 'Breakfast is what you want. Ready in ten minutes. Mr Claydon is in his study.'

Margaret found her way, cup in hand, to her armchair of yesterday evening. She coiled herself into it, drank the tea as hot as she could bear, put the cup down and sat with her eyes shut. Her head throbbed miserably and she felt, despite the tea, empty and slightly sick.

'You look washed-out,' the vicar said over breakfast. 'The weather is certainly very trying. I'm afraid perhaps you didn't sleep much.'

'Not much, no. The clock is terribly insistent. I suppose you get used to it.'

'The clock? Do you know, I never hear it once I am in bed. I am afraid I am a grossly sound sleeper. I should like to think it was the sleep of the just, but there have been times in my life when I have been anything but a just person, and I never remember sleeping any the worse for it. I should not hear a besieging army.'

'There needn't be any siege. Everything is wide open. I suppose it wouldn't matter if people came in and walked all over the house.'

The vicar looked at her with mild speculation. 'No, I don't think really it would. I don't see what harm they could do. There is nothing valuable in the house, and nobody need steal food and clothes nowadays, thank goodness."

'I went up to the churchyard.'

'Not last night?'

'No, this morning early. It's an interesting site, isn't it?'

'Archaeologically? I'm afraid I am rather ignorant in that direction. The church is a very old foundation certainly, though there is little of architectural value left. It has suffered some unusually ruthless restorations. But you think there are signs of prehistoric occupation?'

'I'm no expert myself. But yes, I should say the church had clearly been superimposed on a much earlier occupation site.'

'It is very possible. The downs, of course, have been continuously occupied since very early times. The Beacon has at least one neolithic site. And I suppose any hill-top would attract occupation.'

'I think so. The valley would have been all marsh and forest, you see, with the downs struggling clear of the trees on their higher slopes. Lodstone and the Beacon would have faced each other across the treetops – well, they still do. This would have been virtually an island.'

'Recorded history, as in so many places, starts with Domesday. Then there were twelve farms in the parish. But that is all long after what you have in mind. The trees would already have been cut very largely.' He got up, folded his napkin and said a short Latin grace. 'I must concern myself with the present. But if I were you I should take it quiet today. The weather must break soon, and then we shall all feel better.'

But the clouds hung low all day and the heat mounted till by early afternoon the oppression was beyond anything Margaret could have believed possible. She wandered listlessly down through the village, but found it so silent under the yellow murk that she could imagine it deserted, with all its people gone away or dead in their kitchens and the houses waiting for the coming storm to start their long process of decay.

After tea she slept long and deeply, and woke to such a presentiment of evil as she had never experienced. Her watch had stopped, but it was already dark and the silence was absolute. She went downstairs but there was no one about. Remembering her fantasy of the afternoon, she went out into the village to see if lights were burning in the houses. For a moment she believed there were none, and half the houses at least were in darkness. Then scattered lights appeared, but the houses seemed blind and the people, despite the stifling heat, shut away inside.

The church clock struck ten as she turned into the vicarage gate, and almost at the same moment a light went on in the hall. The vicar stood under the ceiling light, his thin clothes hanging limp on him and his bony face lined with sweat. 'Margaret? Ah, I am glad to see you. You were in your room when I went out, I think asleep, but I found your door open just now, and I wondered what had happened to you. I have been up to the church. It is a terrible night.'

'I am more than glad to see you. I had made up my mind that I was alone in a doomed world. Do you think that is what it is? I have never felt so abject.'

'Doomed? It is, of course, in God's good time. But I don't think this is necessarily the time chosen. Mrs Grendle is out, but she left us a cold supper. I think we should be well advised to eat it in case we are after all called on to face another day.'

They ate mostly in silence, and Margaret very little. After grace she excused herself and went upstairs, to find a rush of warm air flowing down to meet her. She hesitated, and at the same moment a door banged loudly above her head and she heard the trees threshing in the churchyard. Then the wind was everywhere.

She ran upstairs, forced open the door of her room and reached through the flapping curtains to slam the window shut. She heard Mr Claydon call downstairs and ran down to the accompaniment of a tremendous crash in the kitchen, where the wind had brought down a pile of crockery. The vicar came out of his study over a drift of flying papers and said, 'Shut everything quickly, will you? This is going to be very bad.'

Before the last window was shut the wind was hurling itself at the roofs and gables and the world outside had gone mad. No rain came with it, only dry gusts of hurricane strength that went howling through the village and dashed themselves at the church tower and its surrounding trees.

Margaret said, 'I'm sorry, because I like your thinking me scholarly and serious, but I'm scared stiff. Are we going to be all right?'

'Yes, yes. They cannot blow us off our holy hill. The church has stood on it six hundred years at least and this house is Victorian brickwork. There will be thunder and lightning presently, and then rain. But the morning will be fair, and I think you will live to see it.'

'Is there anything we ought to do? Will there be anyone needing help?'

'Possibly, yes. But I think we should let the worst of the wind go over before we attempt anything. It may blow for some time yet.' He picked up the telephone receiver and listened. 'The line has gone, of course, so we cannot be called on that way. For the moment I'm afraid there is nothing to do but wait.'

They waited while the house shuddered and creaked round them and the wind squealed with demoniac fury in the eaves and chimneys. Later, it seemed to Margaret a long time later, the gusts began to lose their venom. Then the whole world outside went white for a long unnatural second and the sky split over their heads with a crash that came back as a solid thud in the ground beneath their feet.

The vicar got up suddenly, his face white. 'There will be

45

more of this. We are all right here, but there are thatched roofs in the village. I think, if you will excuse me, I will go and pray.' The study door shut behind him, and the lightning struck again twice in such quick succession that the thunder merged in one tumultuous explosion. The shelter of two thousand years of civilisation stretched and parted over her head, and she was abject before a personal malignancy expending itself in the air above her. She cowered in the huge chair, sheltered only by the integrity of Victorian brickwork and the prayers of a gaunt man on his knees in the next room. With her arms round her head, she cried for fear as she had not cried since she was a child, without pause or hope.

She looked up only when he touched her shoulder. 'I am going out,' he said. 'There is no reason why you should come, but if you prefer to, please do. I should put on a jersey and a mackintosh. It will rain soon, and we shall be cold.' She sat up, blew her nose inelegantly but thoroughly and scuttled upstairs. The thunder still rolled incessantly and from her window she saw the tower, still stubbornly vertical, floodlit by an almost continuous flicker of lightning. But the appalling individual blows seemed over, and she took fresh heart.

They turned out of the gate, heads well down into the gusty wind and the long bombardment of the thunder. The village huddled blue-white in the intermittent flashes, but beyond the roofs a steady red glow poured up into the sky. Mr Claydon said, 'Oh, dear God,' and started to run. Margaret ran with him and at once came down full length over a young tree spreadeagled across the road. She got up shaken but unhurt and found herself alone. The red glow was brighter now, and had begun to flicker back with its own slower tempo at the white flickering of the sky. She ran on, and was conscious in the uncertain darkness of other people running with her.

The building burnt like a torch in one continuous column of flame. Now the whole village, which she had earlier imagined dead or withdrawn, was abroad in the streets. An unbroken wall of faces ringed the fire, and she heard, at first with incredulity and then with sick recognition, the mutter of excitement that passed from mouth to mouth as the fire took its final hold. Mouths gaped, eyes reflected the red inferno they stared at, nostrils flared in the harsh waft of smoke. This was the fury's chosen victim, the scapegoat burned in their place. Their exultation was inarticulate but beyond disguise.

The front of the building buckled, swayed and fell slowly inwards. For a second the darkened paint of a signboard was lit by the flames behind. It said, 'J. Simmons, Radio & Television Dealer and Engineer.' Then it dropped backwards in a cloud of sparks, and the village growled deep in its throats and swayed a foot nearer to the fire.

Margaret seized a shoulder in front of her and shook it fiercely. A face turned and she said, 'Where's Jack Simmons? Is he all right?' The face withdrew its eyes unwillingly from the fire and said 'Who?'

'Jack – Jack Simmons – is he all right?'

The shoulder shrugged. "Should be. Don't think he's here.'

She worked back along the fringe of the crowd, looking for Mr Claydon, but could not find him. A drop of rain struck her cheek and a moment later another splashed on the back of her hand. The wind dropped momentarily and then blew up again, bringing a spatter of hissing drops on to the smoking outskirts of the fire. Margaret seized the man in front of her by the arm and pulled him half round. 'Where's Jack Simmons?' she said. 'Was he in the shop? Is he all right?' He turned back immediately to the fire but answered coherently. He said, 'I don't think anyone was in the shop. I can't say where Simmons is, but he wasn't in the shop.'

Margaret let him go. The rain came heavily at last, driving down in huge drops. A faint wail went up from the crowd and the line wavered and broke. Dim figures ran in all directions in the now uncertain light of the fire. The lightning had stopped altogether, and as the rain gathered force the wind fell away, till the swish and drum of the rain ousted all other sounds. Darkness came back as the fire sputtered under it.

Margaret walked a dozen steps, hesitated and turned. She ran back towards the fire, looking for the man she had last spoken to, but could not find him. All at once the streets had emptied themselves under the rain. The village, assured once more of its security, had crept back into its houses and was already half asleep.

Then she saw the vicar. He stood gaunt and bareheaded in the downpour, silhouetted against the sputtering fire. She ran to him, catching as she went a glimpse of another figure, enormously tall and red to all its height in the fireglow, facing

47

him across it. She pulled at his arm and he took her hand without turning his head. A gust of rain brought momentary darkness. Then the fire flared up again, but the red figure had gone. Mr Claydon, still holding her with his left hand, crossed himself deliberately with his right. Then he turned and walked back with her to the vicarage.

Neither of them spoke. They left shoes and mackintoshes in the kitchen and then, in the hall, he raised his hand in a half-conscious blessing and went upstairs. Margaret, grateful in the sudden chill for the weight of her blankets, lay in exhausted warmth but could not sleep. How much could she have imagined, and why of all things should she imagine this particular thing? Had anyone in the village a pointed beard and scarred cheek? And if not, what was Sir James Utley doing in Lodstone watching, in the small hours of a summer Sunday morning, the burning of a village shop?

CHAPTER SEVEN

'But Simmons is still alive?'

'Yes. He wasn't in the shop at night ever. It was a lock-up. But he lost the lot, and apparently wasn't properly covered. It's put him out of business. And in any case he won't stay.'

'I suppose the shop *was* struck?'

'Who's to say? I was there, remember. The difficulty was to see why the whole village wasn't flattened. I never saw or heard anything the least bit like it. On the face of it no other explanation is needed. We all went in fear of our lives. Jack Simmons was just unlucky, that's all.'

Garrod straightened his legs and dabbled his toes in the green water below them. 'You know,' he said at last, 'it's awfully difficult to be sensible over this business.'

Margaret snorted. 'If it's difficult for you, what do you think it is for me? All you've done is to meet a couple of village nasties over a pot of beer. I've seen all hell let loose against a holy hill, not to speak of having a jovial fiend under my window when I was half undressed. I wasn't sensible at all. I was scared out of my wits. If I'd been at Mrs Besson's and not the vicarage, I think I should really have gone out of my mind.'

'How sure are you it was Utley you spoke to?'

'Well – I saw him once in your car asleep. I never saw him move and I never heard him speak. But yes, I think the face must be the same, apart from the well-known trimmings.'

'How did he speak at the time of the fire?'

'Not like a Lodstone man. Much more prissy. Rather donnish, if the expression may be permitted. "I can't say where Simmons is. He wasn't in the shop." Something like that.'

He looked at her, startled. 'You are perpetually revealing new talents, and I get more and more alarmed. Mimicry is a fresh departure. That was Sir James all right, unless the whole thing was a put-up job. But he would be a tough

49

impersonator who could keep it up over his shoulder at a village fire in the small hours. I think we must assume that Sir James was present. And where does that get us? Margaret – shall we get married and drop the whole thing?'

'You have a damned donnish, off-hand way of proposing. No. Not till I get my degree and not till I know who the body was.'

'You will get your degree, unless the system has broken down. Not a First, of course,' he added hastily, 'but a good Second.'

'You're a mean man, Jacob Garrod. I thought I was as brilliant as I was beautiful. I'll get my First yet, you see if I don't.'

'Darling Margaret.' Mr Garrod got up and pounced on her with tremendous speed and skill, but then held her disconcertingly at arm's length. 'Darling Margaret, I think you are perfect. But Firsts are my job, and it's no good blurring the lines. I haven't seen your work, but I'd give you a good Second. And if you don't marry me, I'll go and lecture at a Middle Western college until I die under the sheer weight of co-eds.' He bent his arms suddenly, and there was a minute of desperate silence.

'You're very young, aren't you? What are we going to do about Sir James?'

'Oh, damn Sir James. I am not very young, and you are intolerably superior. You put your first-class brain to work and tell me what to do. Perhaps if you write your instructions in Basic English I shall be able to grasp their general sense.' She turned her back on him and stared morosely at a cow which had edged up to overhear their discussion. 'Where was Sir James coming from the day you brought him through Lodstone?'

'I wondered when you'd ask me that. Of course, it has only now become important. Sir James interests us if he was in Lodstone or thereabouts on the two significant occasions we are now concerned with. On the second occasion he was, on your evidence, there and wide awake at a most unchristian hour. All we know about the first is that I took him there, and that he was asleep at an hour when some at least of us were awake. But as you rightly ask, where was he coming from? So far as I am concerned, only from Messleton. My orders were to pick up a gentleman in front of the George Hotel a bit before six and take him to London. I got there at about a quarter to and he came straight down the steps, asked if I was from Barker's, got in and went fast asleep. The rest you know. Oh, and he told me to stop at a good place for breakfast and wake him when we got there.'

She turned round to face him. 'Do you have to do jobs of that sort in the vacs?'

'You mean am I in a position to support you in the manner to which you have been accustomed?'

'I still want to know why you did it.'

'I don't have to as a matter of financial desperation, as I did when I was a freshman. I do it because I find it immensely stimulating and useful to do short spells of work completely unlike my own. I do it in my own time and – yes, I find the extra money a pleasant acquisition, especially if it has been hard earned. This particular job was a snip. Shall we go on talking about me or go back to Sir James?'

'Sir James every time for me. I'm sorry I digressed.'

'Well, you see what that means. It means he was at Messleton only – what? – five miles from Lodstone about when you were talking to Robin about the body. And we don't know how he got there or where he came from. The suggestion was, of course, that he was making an early getaway from the George, but I've no evidence he was ever in the hotel at all. He came down the steps, alone, with a small bag as I drove up, and I assumed he came from the hotel. But he may have walked from Lodstone with a curiously carved oriental dagger, slightly blood-stained, in his case. It oughtn't to be difficult to find out if he stayed at the George.'

'No. But anyway, suppose he didn't and suppose he did come from Lodstone, how does that help us?'

'Surely because he is a public figure who has no apparent business to be in Lodstone at all. His presence there, unlike that of Robin, or the vicar's, or even yours, must have an explanation which can be investigated. As his presence is also, apparently, associated with odd and violent doings, its explanation is well worth looking for. It may not mean a thing, but it's an interesting line to follow. And we haven't many others.'

'It's a far cry, though, isn't it? The only real link between

51

Sir James and the body is that in a moment of emotional stress I attributed to the body a couple of purely imaginary attributes which in fact belonged to Sir James. And that, as you pointed out at the time, is curious but of no significance. Otherwise all we know is that Sir James was within five miles when I found it.'

'And that he has visited Lodstone at least once since, and to say the least of it in a very unobtrusive way.'

'Do you suppose he was Mrs Besson's gentleman – the one who got in first for my room?'

'I shouldn't think so for a moment. On the little we know I should say it was very unlikely that he spent the night at Lodstone. From what you said I rather imagined Mrs Besson's gentleman was a figment – she didn't want you, or had been told not to have you. But I tell you what. I'll do two things. I'll go to the George at Messleton and see whether he stayed the night there before I picked him up. And I'll go to Barker's – that's my car-hire bosses – and find out if he hired a car on the Sunday morning after the fire. If the answers are no and yes, then it's at least a good bet that on both occasions he was at Lodstone during the night and left in the early morning.'

'What shall I do?'

'Get on with your work, my girl, if you want to get that Second.'

'First.'

'Second. But in any case, don't go to Lodstone.'

'I wouldn't if I was paid. For the moment I think I'll go home.' She rolled out of reach of a clutching hand and got to her feet. 'Don't bother. Buttercup here will see me to my car. You put your shoes and socks on. You'll look even sillier carrying them than you do dabbling your feet in the water.'

'You have a tough mind and a mean turn of speech. I think I must love you for your purely physical qualities, which I am bound to say are splendid.' He sat on the grass and looked up at her till her heart turned over. 'Anyway, I do love you. Are we engaged, do you think?'

'Only in a search for a body – which must by now be in no fit state to be found. Had you thought of that?'

'We are not searching for a body. We are searching for an

explanation and a name. I don't think I want anyone tried for murder, not even Mr Valance.'

'Let me know how things go. Good-bye, Jacob. Come on, Buttercup. Cusha, cusha.' She picked her way across the water-meadow with her hand on the cow's golden neck, while he dragged his socks distractedly over still damp feet.

'I hoped you'd be in earlier,' said Mrs Canting. 'Did you have a good day?'

'Yes. Oh yes, very good. We went to the river.'

'I get the impression that this is rather serious. I hope it won't get in the way of your work.'

'What is?'

'Not the mystery, the man.'

'Yes. Yes, he does tend to get rather serious. But I'm going to get my degree, grandmother, even if it is only a Second.'

'I thought you hoped for a First.'

'I did. I still do. But I don't really think I'll get one. Why did you say you hoped I'd get in earlier?'

'Oh yes – there was a talk by your friend Sir James Utley. I think it's over, but it may not be quite. He is talking about The Savage Inside Us.'

Margaret dived for the controls and suddenly, out of the mysterious background noises, there emerged quite unmistakably the voice that had told her that Simmons wasn't in the shop. The face was bland, wise and assured, the eyes quizzically narrowed, the eyebrows nobly arched. The beard conducted the modulated speech like a baton.

'When I was a boy in Wiltshire, there were still to be found among the country people practices and usages of speech every bit as remote from this scientific civilisation of today as many of those I have been talking about. Some have now disappeared, some survive. But those that have disappeared have in many cases not, in the anthropologist's eyes, completely ceased to exist. They have been replaced by forms and practices drawn from contemporary life but serving, in the minds of the people who use them, the same essential purposes.'

He paused and let his quizzical glance penetrate the camera. 'The mind of man has taken a tremendously long time to develop, and recent discoveries serve only to push the beginnings of human history further and further back. Compared with all that vast stretch of time the period to which we can now attribute exact or approximate dates is almost insignificantly small. From neolithic times to the present is only, as it were, the last minute or two of a process of many years. The people who built the long barrows had a mental and emotional experience in no essential respect different from our own. The forms and symbols in which they expressed it no doubt reflected the differences between the world they lived in and that which surrounds us. But these symbols would, I am convinced, if we could rediscover them, convey to the sympathetic and experienced eye truths as familiar and important now as they were then. Good night.'

'H'm,' said Margaret, turning the switch sharply on Sir James's sympathetic and experienced eye, 'he's got all the tricks, hasn't he? I bet he had the make-up girl put lipstick on that scar of his instead of powder.'

'I like him, I must say. But as a performer, I admit. I don't think I'd really much care for the man himself, but the figure he presents is very pleasant and interesting.'

'And familiar, for some reason. To you naturally, because you have seen many previous performances. Why to me, I wonder? That feeling of benign superiority, the knowing smile.'

'He must look like that when he is asleep. Many people look unbearably irritating asleep. It is one of the perils of matrimony.'

'I suppose that must be it. I don't think we missed much that was worthwhile, even if we did get only the last minute or two. The rest would have been all Polynesians and potlatches. The last bit was what he really wanted to say. Pop stuff, of course, but I thought sincere, didn't you? That sympathetic and experienced eye bent on the neolithic mind. I can't answer for its experience, but I did get a feeling of genuine sympathy for the past.'

'Does this throw any light on the mystery, or is it still not permissible to ask that?'

'To tell the truth, I don't know. It may. I did tell you that Sir James's connection with the mystery was a purely fortuitous one. This doesn't seem as certain now as it did. But it is still very difficult to say. Still, I'm glad I saw him performing.

Did you notice he said he had been a boy in Wiltshire? I thought it was London.'

'I have no idea where he was a boy. All I said was that he lives in London.'

'Isn't there a *Who's Who* in the house?'

'Yes, downstairs on the shelf by the window. A year or two old, but near enough.'

'Here he is,' said Margaret, propping *Who's Who* in front of her as she came back into the room. 'Let's see. Knighted in 1948. Born 1908. Son of John Utley, Devizes. Educated – yes, a Wiltshire school and then Oxford. That's it. Wiltshire boyhood, then Oxford on a scholarship, sociological and so on interests, then the Utley Committee and a Labour knighthood on the strength of it. Don't you think it would be nice if public men composed their *Who's Who* entries like famous actresses, by listing the roles they have played and in whose company? "Played (with Lord Snort) the role of peacemaker, Labour Party dissensions, 1958: acted as go-between in appointment of Sir Charles Faceless as Chairman of Imperial Vehicles, 1960: and as agent-provocateur (with Herr Otto Koltz) in dismissal of Foreign Secretary, 1962." That sort of thing. You could really follow a man's career then. This listing of titles and offices and clubs is useless as information about the man himself, except on certain general qualifications. You have to read all the rest between the lines.

'But Sir James is fairly easy to read, I should say. A genuine interest, and some pretensions to scholarship, in anthropology. Then the public role of sociological reformer, beginning with his chairmanship of the Utley Committee in the early year of the Glorious Revolution. Thence his knighthood and in due course, better still, a T.V. personality. Now, having got there, he can afford to be the wise old humanist whose only proper study is Man. A bit of an old mountebank, but no more than most. Or can you see him as a sinister figure?'

'I'm sorry, I'm afraid I didn't hear your question.'

'You haven't been listening at all?'

'No, darling, of course not. I didn't think you wanted me to. I thought you were perfectly happy talking, so I left you to it. But I am quite prepared to give an opinion if you want one. Only you'll have to go back a bit.'

'Do you think Sir James is a crook?'

'No, I shouldn't say so, not deliberately crooked, anyhow. I should say he would be defensively tough. Most of these people who have got somewhere are unexpectedly ruthless in maintaining their position. I think that if anyone were to suggest, for instance, that he was an old mountebank with no social conscience posing as a wise old humanist, he would react very sharply.'

'Yes. As you know exactly how exasperating you are being, I refuse to be exasperated.'

'That is the wisest course, certainly. I hope this man does not listen to you with uncalculating admiration.'

'He listens to me with, I really do think, affection but considerable intellectual contempt. He says it is only my physical qualities he admires.'

'Well I must say I find that very reassuring. He seems to be a man of character and taste.'

'Oh, do you think so? That is interesting, though of course a bit disconcerting. I must consider him in that light and see how he appears.'

But it was Sir James Utley she mostly considered. He showed such civilised sympathy with the verities of stone-age experience and joined so cheerfully in the village's rejoicing when the wrath of God passed over its houses and destroyed that of the stranger. Crooked or straight, Sir James certainly did not lack interest.

CHAPTER EIGHT

From the bar-parlour window Garrod watched the long black car roll into the yard gate opposite. He sighed, finished his beer and went after it. A stocky, red-faced man, whom not even his bottle-green uniform could make elegant, was climbing stiffly out of the driver's seat. He said, 'Gawd, it's the professor. Want the job back, Prof? I knew you'd never settle down to teaching after tasting the joys of the open road.' He put out a hand. 'Nice to see you. How are you?'

'Fine, thanks. No, I don't want the job at the moment. I'm going to work in a zoo. The reptile house. Very fond of snakes. Look, Jim, who was on over the Bank Holiday?'

'Not me, that's for certain. Reptile house, eh? Nah, you're kidding.'

'I'm not, you know. They pay danger money, and the conditions are good, especially in winter. Always warm. But who was on then, Jim? I want to know about a job.'

Jim thought. 'Charlie,' he said, 'mostly. And Harry did some nights. Anything wrong?'

'No, no. Only about a chap I drove. Said he was doing the same trip over the Bank Holiday, and I wondered. I want to get in touch if I can. Charlie in?'

'Probably having a manicure or a wash-and-set. You know Charlie. But you could try the café.'

He met Charlie half-way. Bunches of golden curls peeped ingenuously from under the rim of his green cap, and he fluttered his sandy eyelashes at Garrod when he saw him. 'Oh Mr Garrod, this is a surprise. I've been hoping you'd come back to us.'

'I haven't, Charlie. Just looking in. I wonder if you can help me.'

'Me, Mr Garrod?' Charlie's blue eyes got suddenly much narrower and seemed to crowd in on his nose. 'What can I do for you?'

57

'Just this. Jim says you were on duty over the Bank Holiday. Did you do an early-morning run out to Messleton on the Sunday, same as the one I did at the beginning of May? To pick up a man at the George, chap with a beard.'

'Oh, you mean Sir James Utley? No. I was going to, you know, but it was cancelled. I was ever so disappointed. I've seen him on T.V. and I came on very early specially to do it. Mr Barker wasn't half upset. Cancelled the order by phone only an hour beforehand. I was already on my way here. I think he made it all right with Mr Barker, but I was disappointed, I must say. Still, one can't help illness, can one?'

'He was taken ill, was he?'

'That's right. That's what Mr Barker told me, anyway. Anything wrong, Mr Garrod? You could always write to him at the B.B.C. I'm sure lots do.'

'No, don't worry. I only wondered. I must get on.'

'Oh, you going already? We've hardly seen you.'

'I must, Charlie. When are you coming to the university? You'd do well there.'

'Me? Oh, Mr Garrod.'

Unable to hold up the heavy fun any longer, Garrod waved rather vaguely and made for his car. So Sir James had changed his plans at the last moment. More important, he had made plans. He had arranged to be picked up in Messleton as he had been on May Morning, only this time they knew he hadn't spent the night at the George. It was reasonably certain that he hadn't the first time, but it might be as well to make certain. Anyhow, he had told Margaret he would get the answer to both questions, and get them he therefore would.

But it was obviously market day. A Land Rover towing a trailer full of young pigs under a net was only a foretaste. Cattle trucks soon filled the narrowing road, and there was even a flock of pedestrian sheep in charge of a lean man in a mackintosh and two grinning dogs. The space in front of the George was filled with the cars of farmers keeping their agricultural depression at arm's length in the bars; and he was struck, not for the first time, by the fact that for the farmer, who now dressed like a business man, the car had become a professional symbol rather than a status symbol. The possession of a Jaguar represented little to a man whose credit already ran to several tractors and a combine-harvester. He drove a utility as his father had worn breeches and gaiters, not because it was necessarily vital to his job, but because it was part of the uniform. But there was nothing shoddy about the cars any more than there had been about the breeches.

The George was crowded, noisy and extremely cheerful. Red-faced men hailed each other in local voices, and large mixed parties sat round tables working their way through rapid rounds of short and expensive drinks. It was a difficult day for disingenuous enquiries at the reception desk; everybody was rushed. On the other hand it was a good day for going unnoticed. Unnoticed in the smoke-laden tumult, Garrod approached the desk.

There, straight away, was what he had counted on – an old-fashioned printed register covering months and even years, not the carboned-in-triplicate reference card now fashionable in the bigger hotels. There was even pen and ink ready for the visitor. Two girls were on show, a blonde of transparent simplicity and a dark girl with a calculating eye, obviously up to no good. The dark one was doing figures at a table. The blonde listened half-heartedly to a telephone call and conducted a whispered conversation with a copper-faced man who leant confidentially across the desk. Garrod simply pulled the register to him and started to turn the pages back. He overshot to the middle of April and was beginning to work forward again when the dark girl said 'Can I help you?' in a tone which clearly meant nothing of the sort. Her face was a foot from his, full of outrage but ready to be persuaded.

He smiled warmly into the snapping black eyes and said 'Oh, I say, I'm awfully sorry' in the voice used by romantic juveniles in radio comedies. 'I was wondering whether this was the place some friends of mine stayed at at the end of April. I thought I'd see if their names were in the book.' He spoke as if this brilliant expedient had only just occurred to him and would need explaining to anyone else.

She plainly thought this too silly to be true but could not see, off-hand, what objection she could raise to his looking at the register. To reassert her authority she said, 'What was the name, please?' and pulled the book towards her.

'Wait a minute, there it is!' He grabbed the book and pointed with great excitement to the name of Mr and Mrs J. A. Kraski, who had booked in on the 15th April. 'Those your friends?' the girl said, relaxing at the prospect of a *fait accompli*.

'Oh no, dash it – I thought it must be—' He flicked over a couple of pages, read calmly through the names entered on the last two days of April and said, 'Never mind, perhaps it was somewhere else. Sorry I've been such a nuisance.' This time his warm smile splintered on naked hostility, but he had got what he wanted. No Sir James at the George.

He turned to go out, but somebody took and held his arm. 'Come and meet my friends,' said Mr Valance. There was no logical reason to break away, only an instinctive urge which logic forbade him to indulge. They moved off through the tobacco smoke between the noisy parties. 'Did you hear about Jack?'

'Jack?'

'Jack Simmons. Chap who threatened to sue me.'

'Oh, I remember. No.'

'Lost his shop in a fire. Struck by lightning. Terrible storm we had. In here. We get this room to ourselves.'

The small room was dark with smoke, through which the faces appeared puckered and distorted. They were in a circle, like all the other parties. He tried to count them, but could never make out which one he had started with. There were a dozen of them, more or less. The door opened on as much noise as there was outside, concurrent conversations, rather loud, with a cross-fire of laughter and shouting. Then the door shut and there was silence.

'Friend of mine,' said Mr Valance. 'Knows Jack Simmons.'

There was laughter, and someone pushed a glass into his hand. He waved it and said, 'Here's luck,' but no one responded. He said, 'As a matter of fact, I don't know Jack Simmons at all. Never set eyes on him.' He drank. It was sweet and extremely strong. A youngish man said, 'That goes for me, among others. We had to take Nick's word for him.' This was clearly some sort of joke. There was an atmosphere of intense but secret amusement, which gave exaggerated significance to whatever was said. It was like a dormitory feast that had somehow lost its innocence.

A woman sitting opposite said, 'Do you live around here, Mr——?'

'I don't know your name,' said Mr Valance.

'Kraski.'

There was an explosion of merriment at Mr Valance's statement and a fresh one at his reply. He emptied his glass and joined in the laughter, but his mind was fixed on the woman opposite. She was like Life-in-Death. Her lips were red, her looks were free, her hair had been recently gilded at one of the new and surprisingly expensive shops in the Market Square. It was piled up in elaborate convolutions. 'It must come down to her waist,' he kept thinking: 'it might come down to her knees.'

He said, 'No, just passing through. Do you live at Lodstone?'

Her lips parted before she smiled. She said, 'Not now. We used to.' He could have pushed the table over and gone across to her. Someone refilled his glass from a cocktail shaker.

'Mr Stallard is from Lodstone,' said Mr Valance; 'so are Belling and Marston there. They all farm, like me.' Stallard was an older man, of an age with Mr Valance. The other two looked younger. They all looked like farmers. The man who had not known Simmons was the youngest of all and evidently not a Lodstone man. 'Of course,' said Mr Valance, 'we're all Lodstone people originally.'

They had baskets and sling-bags and brief-cases put down on empty chairs or on the floor beside them, like all the other parties. The woman opposite had a heavy gold wedding-ring on her left hand and a housewife's basket of food and detergents. Everyone called her Mary. She was full of a placid and absolute familiarity, that left everything unsaid and nothing that needed saying. She did not laugh with the others, but seemed to be the point of rest round which the laughter revolved. When she stood up, Garrod saw that she was of no more than medium height and broad-built. Every movement was perfect and predictable. She said, 'We must go now,' and everyone got up and stood round her in the blue tobacco murk. It was not conventional gallantry. Her female authority was complete, so that whatever she decided was automatically desirable.

She moved towards the door and the place where Garrod stood. She said, 'We shan't meet again,' and touched his hand lightly with a gloved finger held free of her shopping basket. He was conscious of the complete and irredeemable loss of the

61

waking dream, in which the loss is itself part of the realisation. She went out with the others round her.

What he had drunk had been even stronger than he had suspected. His sight and movements seemed perfectly co-ordinated, but his mental imbalance was chaotic. It seemed natural, though still objectionable, that Mr Valance should be with him, piloting him out into the cheerful noise of the hotel. He groped for a more or less rational attitude and course of conduct, but could fix on nothing, and was ready to accept passivity. There was no danger except that of indiscretion, and passivity can be perfectly discreet.

Mr Valance said, 'I wanted my friends to see you. We generally meet here for a drink market days, or as many of us as can manage it. Nothing special in that, is there?' They came out on to the steps, where Sir James Utley on one occasion, but not on a second, had appeared bag in hand to claim his hired car. 'Mary liked you,' said Mr Valance.

'She said we shouldn't meet again.'

'That's right. You have to accept that, of course.'

This was quite clearly so. There could be no discussion of her because there was nothing either of them did not know. The knowledge, and the blind peace that flowed from it, were universal and incommunicable.

At the top of the steps Mr Valance stood, waiting for Garrod to go down. 'You go on,' he said. 'You're just passing through. Always just passing through whenever I see you. And I tell you – you just keep on passing us by like that – much better in the long run.' There was no menace in him, but an unmistakable certainty. He remained, in himself, an unimpressive figure. But he would meet his friends again next market day and Garrod would be passing through.

'The answers were, as we anticipated, no and yes,' he said to Margaret later over the telephone. 'That is, Sir James did not stay at the George the night before I picked him up at Messleton. And he did make a similar arrangement with Barker's for the Sunday morning after the fire, but changed his plans at very short notice on a plea of illness. Charlie was ever so disappointed.'

'Charlie?'

'One of my late colleagues. Golden curls and a water wave.'

62

'You have some odd friends. But never mind. Your inclinations seem reassuringly normal.'

'Oh, indeed yes. Powerful but well-directed. But listen, Margaret. I don't like Sir James's changing his plans like that after the fire.'

'Why?'

'Because whatever his plans were, I can't help feeling that their only real disruption was being spoken to by you. Of course this is all speculation. But if he changed his transport plans because of you, it argues a good many things, none of which I care for much. To begin with, it at least suggests that he knew who you were. After all, he's a public face, and easily recognisable by his trimmings. He risked recognition by someone, even joining the throng at a nocturnal fire-raising. He hadn't seen you. But your appearance, conduct, voice – everything about you showed you weren't one of the village. And if he'd been told you were in the village, he wouldn't have had much doubt who you were. What I'm afraid of is that he may have changed his plans precisely because he knew you had seen him and also knew you might have recognised him – as in fact you did. If he did that, it means he knows you are interested in his Lodstone doings, and had been warned against you – presumably by Robin, because no one in Lodstone knows anything about your finding the body except Robin or anybody Robin may have told. It brings him much more into the picture, do you see? I'm afraid I am making this sound all rather confused. I hate telephones. Can't I come round and talk to you?'

'Not tonight. But I think I follow. He changed his plans after the fire. He knew I might have recognised him at the fire. If he changed his plans because of this (which we don't know, but suspect), it means he already knew who I was and that I might be interested in his movements. If he did know this, he must have had it from Robin. And if Robin and Sir James are in touch, it tends to tie Sir James in with the body. A lot of conditionals, aren't there?'

'You are splendidly concise and rightly sceptical. But I still don't like it, even if it is only a possibility. And, of course, there's another, a good deal more far-fetched but a good deal more frightening if true. He could have changed his plans for transport – I mean, he must have got home somehow –

not merely to cover his tracks generally, but because the last time he'd used Barker's I had done the driving, and for all he knew it might be me again. This would mean not only that my driving Sir James on May Day has been connected up with my going to Lodstone since, but also that my movements have been connected up with yours. There again, the link would have to be Robin. I spoke to him on May Day – you asked me to, damn it – and he saw me in the pub before I had my turn-up with Valance. I didn't think he recognised me the second time, but I can't swear he didn't. As for my connection with you, he might have guessed, if he had worked it out, that I might have met you on the road that morning before I caught him up. But he couldn't know we'd spoken, and I can't see any other connection between us he could have traced. As I say, this is a bit far-fetched. But I don't like the idea that we may be doing our fumbling amateur sleuthing in full view of an amused audience.'

'No: though so long as it merely amuses them, I suppose it's all right.'

'There is a curious sort of amusement about. I saw Valance again today and a party of his friends. I think I must have got drunk with them. I still find the whole thing very difficult to assess. But they laughed like hell. Only I'm not quite sure what at.'

'I – I don't like the sound of this at all. Are you all right?'

'Yes, of course I'm all right. Confused, I admit.'

'You sounded rather shaken. Nothing happened today to shake you?'

'Nothing.'

'Oh well. I've got some extra bits on Sir James to tell you. But no more now. Good night.'

'Good night.' A waking dream, after all, never returned, and one did not communicate, unless unconsciously, the incommunicable. But this, he knew, was all a rationalisation. The knowledge of his loss was in fact the most private of his treasures.

CHAPTER NINE

'So that's our Sir James, is it? A Wiltshire lad, an honest anthropologist and a not-so-honest wooer of fame and fortune. This is all for the eye of the world. For ourselves we also know that he has been twice, almost certainly, at Lodstone on occasions of odd and violent events: and we suspect, but cannot be certain, that he may know of your discovery of the body, and may therefore be in some degree privy to the murder – if there was one.'

'It isn't much, is it, really?' Margaret, balanced on the arm of a chair in her grandmother's drawing-room, looked gloomily at the man Garrod arranged with unusual elegance on the sofa.

'No. The trouble is, it is difficult to see what next to do about him. I should like to know a good deal more about the connection between Sir James the public figure and Sir James the nocturnal visitor to Lodstone. Does anyone know about his business, whatever it is, in Lodstone? There is some evidence of his covering his tracks, at least partially, at this end. I wonder whether he covers them at the other. Did his wife (or hasn't he got a wife?) or his secretary or his agent know where he was when he was in the crowd round the burning shop? There's work to be done there, I think.'

'Yes. Do you think it would be fair to describe us as a pair of incompetent, irresponsible, bungling, amateur busybodies?'

'It would be slightly less than just, I think, but I admit a case could be made out.'

'Then why do we go on with it?'

'I think I would give you the same answer as you gave me when we first discussed the thing at the Mitre. I'm not sure of the rights and wrongs of it, but I badly want to know the facts. I applauded that attitude in you at the time because I thought it showed resolution and a scholarly grasp in what seemed rather harassing circumstances. My own present

65

attitude is slightly different. I still want to know the facts, but I think I want to know them at least partly so that I can decide where the rights and wrongs lie. There is so much I don't understand that I am not sure it would necessarily be right, without knowing more, to set the police looking for a murdered man and his murderer – even if we could do so. And of course you realise that the longer the time elapsed since May Day, the more difficult it would be to persuade them to look at all. I want to go on, therefore, partly because my curiosity has been increasingly inflamed by every fresh thing that has come to light, and partly because I think it may be my duty to do something about what seems to be a murder, but I need more facts before I can decide whether it is my duty or not. I admit I am incompetent and an amateur, but I won't admit I'm irresponsible.'

'Grandmother, this is Jacob Garrod.' He shot to his feet and turned to find Mrs Canting standing just inside the door.

'How do you do, Mr Garrod? Margaret, if I hadn't on occasion accused you of trying to talk like a Compton-Burnett character, I should like to come in on an entrance line showing that I had overheard the last thing said. In fact, now that my entrance is made and we have been introduced, I am going to do just that. I am glad you claim responsibility in this business, Mr Garrod, and still more glad that you should wish to make the claim at all. I do, generally speaking, regard Margaret as a responsible person, and I have accepted her assurance that the thing is all right and that her reasons for not telling me about it are sound ones. In view of your claim to responsibility, I should be glad to have, and should be anxious to accept, the same assurance from you.'

'On the first point you certainly have my assurance. This thing came on Margaret by pure chance, but I am sure she is right to go on with it. We were in fact talking about that when you came in, and it was just in this respect that I was, rightly or wrongly, claiming to be responsible. On the second point, Margaret's reasons for not telling you about it, I can't of course claim complete knowledge of her reasons, and we haven't, as far as I can remember, discussed it. But I have little doubt what her reasons are, and I think, certainly, that they are sound. I also think, myself, that she may do well to consult you sooner or later. But for the moment the position is that we were both by chance in the thing from the start and have so far discussed it with nobody.'

'Not Charlie Mayne?'

'I did go and see him, grandmother. But I'm afraid I didn't take him into my confidence. Here again, it may be necessary to do so later.'

Mrs Canting looked from one to the other. 'All right. I suppose you know what you are doing. You do not, I am sure, Mr Garrod, want me to make a speech about my responsibility for Margaret since her parents died. But I do hold you responsible, you know – I can't help it.'

'I understand that. Will it do any good if I say that nothing, not even your laying this responsibility on me, can make me feel more responsible for Margaret than I already do?'

'It won't help much, to tell the truth. But it is nicely said and I am glad to hear you say it. Oh well, get along, the pair of you. I am going out, so you are free to continue your discussion here if you want to.'

'You're lucky, aren't you, as orphans go,' Garrod said when Mrs Canting had gone. 'And I gather your parents' deaths have ceased to be a conscious loss?'

'I doubt if they ever were. I was very young. No doubt skilled analysis would show a splendid collection of resulting traumata, but whatever they do to me, it is all well down in my sub-conscious. My grandmother has been my parents ever since I can remember. And yes, of course, I am very lucky indeed. I know that.'

He stood above her and, tilting her head back, looked at her face long and gravely. 'I think it does show, you know. But as I would not in any circumstances have you other than you are, I am forced to the conclusion that to have been deprived of your parents' upbringing was a good thing for you. There is an emotional independence in you that I admire inexpressibly, even if it makes you, at times, a little alarming. I don't mean that you are cold and calculating. You're not that, are you?' He dropped his face suddenly to hers and presently lifted it again. 'Not that at all. But I always have the feeling that your emotions are less derivative than anyone's I have ever met. You don't ever seem to feel something because you think you ought to or because it is the standard reaction: and I fancy that's very rare. Of course, you might have been

67

the same even with a more normal upbringing; and God knows you might, having lost your parents, have had something worse, not better. As I said just now, you have been incredibly lucky as orphans go. But that being said, I honestly believe you have gained something from being orphaned. Come to that our parents may be the last people who ought to bring us up.'

'Mm. I trust I continue to give satisfaction. But supposing, for the sake of argument, I do, and supposing, having got my degree, I find you prepared to stand on your rash declaration; and supposing, all that being so, I decide to marry you and we then, in due course, have children – would you like your mother to bring them up?'

'I shouldn't, no, of course, because I am sufficiently prejudiced to think that you would do it perfectly and I should like to take a hand at it myself. But the prejudice is there, and I may be quite wrong.'

'Anyway, she won't.'

'You're telling me she won't.'

Presently she pushed him gently away and said, 'Go and sit on that sofa again. You look very elegant there. I suppose you came to steal my grandmother's heart with your fine clothes and your gentlemanly ways. You haven't a hope. Still, it shows a sense of occasion to put that suit on.'

'I try to please. Was it all right, do you think?'

'Grandmother? Oh yes, I think so. But we very seldom dislike different people. We were talking about Sir James. Don't you think it is about time we considered my body?'

'That, for me, would be a busman's holiday. I seldom do anything else.'

'*The* body, then – the one I found – you know perfectly well what I mean. Don't you think we ought to come at the thing from that end for a change? Can't the body itself, and its movements so far as we know them or can guess them, give us some sort of line on the person responsible for its being there at all?'

'It ought to. You could come at it two ways. The obvious one is to try to find out the body's identity by trying to find what man of that sort disappeared on that date. After all, few people can disappear without raising a bit of a storm somewhere. Or you could try to find out more about its movements before and after you saw it. Any evidence on either would, as you say, tell us a lot about those responsible. The trouble about the obvious line of investigation is that we are so extraordinarily ill equipped to do it. That is the sort of thing the police do as a matter of routine. I don't even know where we should start. It clearly wasn't a local man, or we should have heard – and of course, Robin couldn't possibly have taken the line he did with you if he knew that you'd hear next day that somebody's Uncle Fred had disappeared. The whole thing turned on his being able to say, 'Body? Whose body? There's no one dead that I know of.' I think we can pretty well assume that, although your friend did not depart completely unrecorded and unmourned, the mourning and recording were done somewhere where we aren't likely to get notice of them.'

'Not that fabulous creature – though I believe it has happened – the convenient tramp with no family and no connections? He didn't look like a tramp.'

'No, I don't mean that. But even if the chap had disappeared only in the next county, and was fairly well known there, you and I should still not have heard of his disappearance. We know there was a body found here; plenty of people would know there was one missing there. But as we stand, there is no one to connect the two.'

'All right. Then what about the body as a body? I saw it at about half-past five and less than an hour later it was gone. Who put it there, who took it away, where did they take it and what did they do with it?'

'You didn't see anybody at all, except Robin, during that time?'

'No one. Oh yes, two girls as I went into the village, but they were harmless and obviously hadn't been out in the fields. They were trying to collect dew off a tiny bit of lawn.'

'No one in the fields at all?'

'No.'

'No sign of life anywhere?'

'No. I remember thinking how completely deserted it all was. All space and silence. Oh, wait a minute, though. Yes. There was a tractor working somewhere over to my left as I went back to the village the first time, after finding the body. I had forgotten it completely, but I remember now noticing it as the only artificial sound in all that silence.'

'This was at – what? – half-past five or soon after?'

'Yes.'

'You know, that's extraordinarily early for anyone to be working in the fields these days. I know the farmer and his men used to rise at cockcrow, but if his men worked from dawn to dusk nowadays, he couldn't pay the overtime bill for a start. It's the townsman who's the early riser now. I wonder what your tractor driver was up to at that hour? I can't help thinking that a tractor and trailer would be an extremely handy way of humping a body about the fields; in fact, it's the first way a farmer nowadays thinks of shifting anything. Can you remember anything more about it – where it was, whether the sound moved, how long it went on?'

'It was on my left – I've said that. I had found the body and was walking back towards the village, when I was conscious of it away to my left. It was some way away, but I'm afraid I didn't notice it very carefully. I just remember noticing it as the only thing disturbing the silence. It was a superb morning, quite still and golden, and the sun was getting well up. When I came to the road I looked back towards where the body was, but I couldn't see anything.'

'Or hear anything? Was the tractor still going then, do you think?'

'I can't remember to be certain. My impression, for what it's worth, is that it wasn't. I do remember being impressed by the completeness of the silence and emptiness.'

'You say you looked back towards where the body was lying. You couldn't see it from the road?'

'No, definitely not. It was several fields away, and there were banks and hedges in between. The body was at the foot of a bank.'

'How long do you suppose it took you to walk back to the road?'

'It's terribly difficult to say. A matter of minutes, you know. Five minutes, I suppose.'

'Any idea how far away the tractor was when you first heard it?'

'That's also extremely difficult to say. In that complete silence sound would carry a pretty long way. But I don't think it was all that far. Say – what? – not less than a few hundred yards and not more than half-a-mile. Does that sound reasonable?'

'You see what I'm getting at? You noticed the sound of the tractor as you were walking away from the body towards the road. It was on your left – that is, on your side of the road, but farther from it than you were. From what you heard would it have been possible for the tractor to be approaching the body, from a different, but not quite opposite, angle, as you were moving away from it? And if so, could it have reached the body when you reached the road? And lastly, supposing it had reached the body and stopped and cut its engine some time about then, would you have seen it when you looked back from the road?'

'I doubt it, but I couldn't swear to it either way. You know, there's only one way of getting any of this clear to any extent. I must go to the spot, try to fix the place where the body was and see what things look like from there. I never did go back there. I'd certainly like to think that without Robin there to play havoc with my self-confidence I could, even now, find the place with reasonable certainty. You see, when I tried it with him, I was looking for a body, not a place. If there wasn't a body, it couldn't be the right place, and when I found no body, I panicked and looked elsewhere. If I went back knowing there was no body, but trying to identify the place where it had been, I think I should have much more chance.'

'You're not going back to Lodstone at all for the moment, my girl – let alone prowling about looking for traces of the body.'

'Not by myself, no. Couldn't we both go? And of course I don't mean openly, leaving a car at the roadside and making a noise about it. But you know, those fields are pretty deserted as a rule. In fact, if we're on the right lines at all, someone dumped the body where I found it on the assumption that there would be no one around until it could be picked up. It was only sheer bad luck that I went for a walk when I did. As a rule village people don't walk in the fields, unless there's anything to go for. They work in them when they have to, and they go to pick blackberries, for instance, at the right time of the year or do a bit of rough shooting – but they very seldom just walk out. Out of working hours, with any luck at all, there's no one for miles. I know, I've walked all round Lodstone at all hours and never seen a living soul. One dead one, I admit: but even a second corpse wouldn't get in the way of our having a look at the place.'

71

'Could we get there across country?'

'Easily, especially if we had a map.'

'We must have daylight, mustn't we?'

'Yes, but there's a lot of that even at this time of the year. Very early in the morning or in the last of the daylight, whichever you think better. I rather fancy early morning, because then it will be easier for me to feel my way back into what happened before. Dusk would be easier for a getaway if we are seen. But I still prefer the morning.'

'All right. Early morning it is. I suggest Sunday – fewer people about. I'll get a map and let you know details.'

CHAPTER TEN

It was still dark when they left the main road and took to the lanes. Margaret had long shaken off both the agitations of an early start and the stimulus of hot tea drunk in silence in a silent house, and had slept peacefully and unashamedly against Garrod's shoulder; but now the rougher going shook her awake. She yawned, rubbed her face kittenwise against the smooth cloth of his wind-cheater and sat up.

'I'm sorry I've been asleep. I hope I didn't snore or roll about.'

'No, no. You leant your flawless cheek on my shoulder and slept like an exhausted angel. It made me feel very vigilant and protective. The human head, nevertheless, is surprisingly heavy. You won't think me ungallant if I rub my left arm a little?'

'You get on with your driving. I'll rub it. How much farther to go?'

'Five miles or so in the car, if we don't lose our way. Then quite a longish walk across country, starting on a compass bearing. It has a fascination even if we never get near Lodstone. And think of the satisfaction if daylight shows us Lodstone right ahead. Columbus won't be in it.'

He checked at a cross-roads, read the finger-post and grunted contentedly. 'We really are on course, I think. Shan't be long now.' Presently he slowed down, pulled the car on to the grass verge and stopped. They got out. The air was sweet-smelling and mild, and a slight breeze rumpled the hedges in the dark. They crossed the lane to a gate, and he took a compass bearing and pointed.

'That's our line. Any good with stars?'

'I know the main groups. Let's see. Oh well, look – we'll be heading not so far off north. That's the Pole Star. It's half left of us.'

'That's right. Let's go, then. The stubble's good going at this time of the year, but there'll be a certain amount newly under plough, and that's damned awkward in the dark. Let's hope there's not too much of it.'

They walked steadily with Garrod in the lead. When they spoke it was in little more than a whisper. The guilt of clandestine movement grew steadily on them, and they felt like poachers. Half an hour later the trees on the far side of the field took shape suddenly and there was the evidence of daylight all round them. Two fields later Garrod stopped and pointed. Ahead and very slightly to their right a cone of shadow showed against the faint phosphorescence of the sky.

'Land-ho,' he whispered.

'Oh, Captain Columbus, sir!'

They embraced briefly and went on into the growing daylight. After a bit they stopped and Margaret said, 'Now let's see. The road should be closing in on our right now. The Beacon should be pretty well behind us. The road down from the village heads straight for the Beacon and then turns a bit left just about where the gate is.'

They turned, but the sky behind was a blank wall of impenetrable grey. She said, 'I think the only thing to do is to go almost to the road – not quite, in case anybody is out early. But once I'm near enough to the road to know I'm on the right line we'll turn back and I'll see if I can find the place.'

They moved stealthily towards the village until the long outline of trees ahead showed the course of the road. Then Margaret turned. She said, 'That morning I turned off the road at the gate just over there. I came this way, following the line of the hedges.' She began to walk back. 'Then about here I went straight across. I think there's a sort of track. As a matter of fact, I think what I was really doing was walking with my eye on the Beacon. You know how you tend to walk to a mark across country. We ought really to wait till the Beacon shows up to get it quite right. But this is the way all right, so far.'

She set off again, and presently they came to a gate, which they climbed. Ahead of them the line lay along the edge of a field with a bank and hedge on their right. Fifty yards further on the hedges closed in on both sides, and Margaret hesitated. 'It was somewhere here,' she said. 'If only – oh yes, look!'

Straight ahead of them, grey, withdrawn but palpably solid,

the Beacon threw up its huge curve against the paler grey of the sky. 'That's right, do you see? I must have been walking straight for the Beacon. I went over this track, and then for some reason I turned, and – There! That's where he was. Propped up against that bank, facing the sun. It was coming up almost over the Beacon by then. He was in full sunlight.'

They tiptoed to the spot, as though someone still sat there and would not be awakened. There was, of course, nothing to be seen. If the grass and wild flowers had been crushed, the blades now stood straight again, and the flowers had ceased to bloom these months past. If there had been blood, it had long ago soaked away into the roots of the grass and been taken up, as some new, minute trace-element, by the rich top-soil. If there had been human artefacts, they had been tidied away. Nothing of any sort remained. But Margaret had not the slightest doubt.

'What I find so difficult to understand now,' she said, 'is how I could have had any doubt about the place when I came back. Here I am, months later and in semi-darkness, and I come straight to it. That morning I was in trouble almost as soon as we had left the road. It was like walking in a dream. Anything seemed possible and confusion most probable. It can't have been all hunger, can it?'

'No. No, to be perfectly frank, I'd say it was Robin. He is a – well, a most formidable person. My own belief is that if you had been more suggestible – and I should say that in fact you are a good deal less suggestible than most – he might have persuaded you that you had imagined the whole thing. Not normal persuasion, of course. I should think there isn't much he doesn't know about getting hold of other people's minds. That's probably what he set out to do. He succeeded to the point of throwing you into pretty complete confusion about the whereabouts of the body but, you being you, he couldn't loosen your grip on the fact that you had seen it. But I think he probably made you fight very hard for your grasp on reality. I am not surprised it left you shaken.'

'I think, looking back, that that is true. I never believed I had imagined the body, but I thought I had made some extraordinary muddle over where it was. As you know, the obvious explanation – that I knew where it had been, but that it was no longer there – simply did not occur to me until you pointed it out. It was a great relief when you did. Up to then I really believed I had got myself into the muddle. I suppose he must have – put it across me in some way or other. I think my salvation was that he made me angry. If he'd played it more gently, I might have been in real trouble. It's all a bit – a bit nasty, isn't it? Much worse than physical violence. Let's go back towards the road. And please hold my hand.'

It was daylight now, shadowless, almost colourless, but quite clear. The breeze had died out, and nothing moved in all the world but themselves. The birds were not yet awake. They walked back, following their own green tracks through the luminous grey of the dew. The light-headed, unreliable exaltation of the early morning welled up in them. The whole mystery of the world was at their finger-tips, and their finger-tips touched each other. He stopped suddenly and pulled her round to face him.

'Margaret,' he said, 'are you sure? I've asked you this before, but I must ask you again. Are you sure you wouldn't rather leave the whole thing? Whoever he was over there' – he jerked his head back the way they had come – 'it was his doing that we met half-way up that hill, and so far as I am concerned that alone must earn him his place in paradise. Do we need to know more about how he died?'

'I'm afraid so, yes. If we left it now, I should feel guilty and frustrated – as if I had gone down without taking a degree. The thing would nag at me for the rest of my life. I told you I'd marry you when we had the answer to this and I had my degree. I still feel like that, and the more the opposition shows its hand, the more strongly I feel it.'

She looked up at him, very pale and intent in the grey light. She said, 'Supposing I had said, "All right, never mind about this. Never mind about my degree. We'll get married next week and live happily ever after." What, in the most scrupulous honesty, would you have felt?'

He turned and walked on, still holding her by the hand. His eye was fixed on the grass in front of him, where their own tracks came back to meet them through the dew. He said, 'The first thing I should feel would be a jolt of surprise. It would be quite out of character, against all expectations. Then I should start to see the exciting implications, and my heart would skip like a young ram, and I should think nothing else mattered at all. Then I should have doubts. I should wonder why you had done something so unlike the person I thought you were, and whether in fact you really were the person I thought you: and I should feel, and try to conceal, a jab of regret that you apparently were not. Then I should try to bury this new regret in my new excitement; but I don't think it would work. You're quite right. It wouldn't do for either of us. Now what about that tractor?'

'I think it was further on. This is much more difficult, of course, because I never really focused my mind on it at the time. Let's go back towards the road a bit.'

They walked back; and now she took her hand from his and walked a little in front, silent, with her head tilted slightly back, as if she awaited a signal. Finally she said, 'I think somewhere about here I heard it coming from over there.' She pointed not quite square to her left. 'I don't honestly remember its getting louder or seeming to change its position. But that's not to say it didn't. I simply remember that I did hear it when there was nothing else to hear.'

From behind her Garrod said, 'Keep on walking towards the road. Try and do exactly what you did that morning. Think yourself back into it and leave your mind empty. You may remember something else.'

Silently, one behind the other, they crossed the open field and followed the track along the line of the hedges. The road was closing in now on their right, and already he could see the white gate at which it met the path. Beyond the gate the tarmac turned slightly right, so that the road ran up-hill into the village in a direct extension of their present line. They were coming up to the gate now, and he knew the scene was a familiar one, though seen before in reverse. The trees on the far side of the road formed a known group which nevertheless he could not identify. Margaret came to the gate, hesitated, climbed it slowly, and then turned and looked back. He came to the side of the gate and stood watching her. It was from there that he saw, over her shoulder, the finger-post that pointed from the roadside and said 'Straightways Farm.' Then he remembered.

Margaret said, 'It's no good. I can't remember whether the tractor was still running when I got here and looked back.'

'Never mind for the moment. Look, this is important. Show me from here about where the sound was coming from when you did hear it.'

She pointed. 'There.'

'So that's it. Do you know what is over there? You can't see it from here because of the hedges, but you can see it from the road. I have seen it from the road. Straightways Farm – our friend Mr Valance.'

She scrambled back over the gate and came to him. 'Valance? So he joins on somewhere, does he?'

'Joins on? It looks to me as if he was in it up to his neck. You find the body dumped there – probably on his land, though that may not matter much. Then as you walk away you hear a tractor start up at his farm. You hear it for some time. Then by the time you get here it seems to have stopped. And when, half an hour or so later, you get back to the spot, the body's gone. Of course, there are gaps to be jumped, but I know where I think it went. I think it went to Straightways Farm on a trailer.'

She touched his arm. She said, 'I don't like this awfully. It's getting much too light, and we're right on the road. Let's get back into the fields. This needs some thinking about, but I don't think this is the place to do it.'

'You're quite right. Come on. Back the way we came, because that's the way we want to go, but let's cover it as fast as possible.'

They jog-trotted along the line of hedges, stopped and looked round them. The sun would not be up for some time yet, but it was broad daylight. Distance was no longer any protection. They needed solid cover, and there was the open field to cross.

They stood for a moment listening. A bird sang suddenly in the hedge behind them and then as suddenly stopped. He said, 'Come on, close together,' and stepped out. 'After all, we are committing no offence and doing no harm. You haven't seen Valance. He's a bit nasty, but I don't feel frightened of him.'

'Being brave won't help us, still less being innocent. You say Valance made away with the body of what we assume was a murdered man. If he finds us going over the ground at this hour, he's not going to be swayed by niceties of moral

78

ascendancy; and all farmers have guns. I don't want to be taken off to Straightways on a trailer.'

They walked on steadily, and the empty world hung round them full of menace. He said, 'You're not easy to reassure, are you? Too clear-headed by half. But I'm glad you realise what we're up against. Here's the gate.'

They scrambled breathlessly over and shrank into the over-arching hedge beyond. She said, 'Valance may be nothing much, but I don't like some of his friends.'

They walked on again, keeping close under the hedge. He remembered Valance saying, 'Come and meet my friends' across the rowdy bustle of the hotel, and in the clear air of morning the smell of stale smoke and the sweet, treacherous taste of the drink came back on his palate. He walked on alone, with this girl beside him, and such a pang of desolate longing struck through him that he clenched his hands and gasped as involuntarily as if he had been hit. He thought she looked at him, but neither spoke. He walked on in two worlds until the hedges closed in upon them again and they came back to the centre of their search.

He said, 'You realise what this is. This is where the farm road from the house crosses our line. You can see, it goes round the far side of this field and then turns back to the gate where the signpost is. It fits in with our idea that the body was dumped here for Valance to pick up. Wherever it came from it was put down where he could get his trailer right up to it. And remember there was young corn here on May Morning; it had to be on the road.'

Margaret nodded, crossed the farm-track and climbed the gate on the far side. 'You never told me much about Valance's friends when you met them in Messleton,' she said. 'I've only seen Robin.'

'He wasn't there, of course. They were farming types mostly, some actually farming in Lodstone. A man called Stallard, I remember. They said they were all Lodstone people originally, but I'm not quite sure what they meant by that. They were all pretty ordinary, except for whatever it was they had between them. Like Freemasons.'

She nodded again. 'How do we find our way back to the car? It's no good following the line we're on, and nothing much will be recognisable by daylight.'

'I'll take a bearing. It won't be dead accurate from where we are now, but it should bring us out on the road where I left the car, even if we don't hit the car itself first time. Is there anything else we should look at while we're here? You've no doubt at all that the tractor must have been over at Straightways?'

'No. It was over there all right.' She pointed, and with a coughing roar a tractor engine came to life at the end of her pointing finger. It settled down into a working rhythm and came steadily down the track towards them.

'Run,' said Garrod.

Chapter Eleven

Along the rutted stubble, under the lee of the bank and hedge on their right hand, Margaret ran like a startled hare and Garrod pounded after her. The immediate need was some sort of cover before the tractor, moving steadily up the farm road to cross their line behind them, reached the gate they had just left. The driver might, of course, cross the gap without turning his head, but the risk was one they could not take. Garrod measured the distance still ahead of them to the shelter of the next gate, but saw little hope of reaching it. It was difficult, as they ran, to judge the tractor's position, but it could not be far off the gap now.

He said, 'Margaret! Stop!' She hesitated and half turned. 'Down under the hedge. Quick!' He gathered her in a sweeping left-arm tackle and flung her down at the foot of the bank, plunging after her. 'Crawl a yard or two forward.' He gasped, recovered his breath and went on in a fierce whisper. 'The bank goes in a bit, do you see? Crawl in there and get as far under the hedge as you can.' She nodded and wriggled forward. He looked back. The tractor was very close to the gap now, but had still not appeared. He crawled round the protecting shoulder of turf and rolled in sideways under the hedge.

They clung together, breathing desperately through open mouths, while the tractor reached the gap, roared for a moment unmuffled by the hedge and went on. Margaret said, 'He's gone,' but even as she spoke the engine cut suddenly and the tractor stopped. Then it picked up again. It was in reverse, and moving back.

'Has he seen us?' Her wide grey eyes, staring close into his, held a disconcerting hint of panic.

'Not us. I don't think he can have. I'm afraid he must have seen our tracks on the other side of the gap. In the dew – you remember how clear they were on the grass. This last bit was stubble. It won't show much.'

The tractor came back into the gap again and stopped. The engine beat steadily in neutral. There was no other sound anywhere.

Garrod whispered, 'I've got to see what he's doing. Don't move at all.' She clutched his sleeve. Her hand was muddy and bled steadily from the thorns off the hedge. She said, 'Don't leave me, will you?' He shook his head, smiled into her startled eyes and began to wriggle backwards along the foot of the hedge.

Clear of the hedge, he snaked round till his head pointed back the way they had come. Then very cautiously he raised it sideways, till one eye cleared the tufts of stubble and could get a clear view of the gate. The tractor stood beyond the gate. He could see the bright red and blue of farm machinery between the bars, and the exhaust puffed steadily upwards over the top. The air was still, but the smell that is now the characteristic breath of rural England drifted slowly to them over the stubble. He could not see the driver.

Then a head and shoulders appeared and vanished unrecognisably. He dropped his head into the stubble. The engine stopped altogether and there was complete silence. He waited and then, with infinite caution, raised his head again. This time he had a much clearer view of head and shoulders as they heaved momentarily into sight, but the back was towards him. Whoever he was, the driver had climbed the far gate.

He lifted his head, then his shoulders. He got to his knees. Nothing was to be seen but the silent tractor half hidden behind the bars of the gate. On his feet, but crouching, he turned back to Margaret. He said, 'Come on. He's gone into the far field. It's our only chance. Let's get out of this one.' He held out a hand and hauled her to her feet. Side by side and bent ridiculously double, they raced for the far gate.

Nothing moved behind them. No sudden shout stopped them in their tracks. They made the gate, looked back, saw nothing, scrambled over and flung themselves into the solid shelter of the bank beyond. For a moment they knelt, looking at each other. Then Margaret giggled, looked at a bleeding finger, put it to her mouth and gave an unmistakable sob. He gathered her to himself in a comprehensive enfolding movement, and for a few seconds she buried her face in his jacket.

Then she pulled away and said, 'I'm sorry. This sort of thing scares me. I'm too civilised, that's my trouble. I like the contemplation of nature, but I'll never be any good at cross-country work.'

Lacking both a suitable answer and time to consider the matter, he kissed her quickly but firmly. 'Listen,' he said then, 'I don't know who it is, but I think he's gone to look at our tracks beyond the gap. If he follows them right back to the road, it will take him quite a time. He may even think we went off along the road – I'm not sure what will show round the gate. In any case, we must get as far as we can on our way now. It might occur to him to cast for us in this direction, and he may go and get a dog, if he hasn't already got one.'

He saw the fright come back into her eyes. 'Farmers generally have one of two kinds of dog – sheep dogs or gun dogs. They don't keep bloodhounds and they don't keep killers. A farm dog lives loose, and they couldn't risk it. I doubt very much myself whether any dog they've got at Straightways would be of much use following a human trail, but with our tracks invisible on the stubble they might be inclined to try. If they do, I think they'll only waste time getting the dog and setting it on. Now let's go.'

He took out his compass, read it and pointed. 'Do you see that white slash on the side of the down, away over to the right of the Beacon? There's a bunch of trees on the sky-line just left of it. That's our direction, as near as I can judge. Anyway, if we keep making for that, we shouldn't be too far from the car when we reach the lane.' He held out a hand and they set out again, hurrying now in broad daylight through the silent fields, keeping their line as best they could when hedges and ditches made a straight course impossible. It was as they were looking for a way through their second hedge that they heard the tractor start up again and make off at speed back to the farmhouse. They stood and listened.

'Gone back,' said Garrod. 'I wonder what for? He may have lost interest, but I rather doubt it.'

They found a gap, reset their course and went on, struggling now across newly ploughed land. The going was heavy but not, in daylight, dangerous. Through a convenient gate and back on stubble again, they made better speed, but almost at once heard the tractor restart and cover the track fast to a point directly behind them. Then it stopped, and a second later they heard, away behind but clear and faintly menacing, the excited barking of a dog.

'The hunt is up, is it? Good luck to them. Now look, Margaret. We haven't got a pack of wolves running free on our tail, nor even a pack of hounds. We've got one man, as far as we know, probably no faster across country than we are, and an excited dog running rings out in front of him. The dog is there to give him a line, if possible, but in particular to flush us out if we try to lie up and let him go past. All we've got to do is to keep going as fast as we can make it without killing ourselves, and with any luck at all he'll never get a sight of us. But in any case, it's the man we've got to watch out for, not the dog.'

She nodded, saving her breath. They scrambled through a hedge, found themselves on plough again and set off across it at a dogged, shambling jog-trot. The dog had stopped barking now, and nothing broke the silence; but they felt, when they stopped to negotiate a gate or hedge, that a slight breeze had sprung up, blowing almost directly behind them. Dressed warm for their night operations, they were by now much too hot, but had neither time to shed clothes nor the wish to carry them. At the next plough Garrod said, 'We'll walk this. We should have plenty of time in hand, and we've still got some way to go. And a twisted ankle won't help.'

Margaret nodded again, and they negotiated the crumbling furrows at a quick, high-stepping walk. The hedge beyond seemed impenetrable, and they had to mark the spot, go wide round to find a gate and strike back along the far side of the hedge to pick up their line. This was old pasture, and by common consent they broke into a run; but Margaret was now very tired. A stile near enough their line gave them easy access to the next field, but they saw that the far side of the field was plough again with a thick belt of trees beyond. The field was the widest they had yet crossed.

At the beginning of the plough Margaret stumbled. 'Oh damn. I've given my ankle rather a twist. How much further, do you think? I doubt if I can keep this up much longer.'

'It's no good, I can't do more than guess. We aren't even on the same course as when we came, and conditions are completely different. For what it's worth, I can't believe we've got much more than half a mile to go, if that. But don't count on that. Let's get into the trees and have a look at the ankle. It might help to strap it.'

Here there was only a low bank with two strands of rusty barbed wire on posts to make it cattle-proof. A line of elms grew just behind it, and beyond they found themselves between the banks of an old road, thickly grown now with elder and bramble, but holding its course straight between the fields for a stretch of several hundred yards. They dragged themselves into it, putting up a pair of wood-pigeons over their heads, and sat down on the bare earth and leaf mould under the bushes. For a moment neither spoke. The breeze, fresher now, rustled the tops of the elms, and Garrod loosened his jacket at the neck. Then he walked cautiously back to the bank and peered over.

'We've got a long view behind us,' he said, 'and I can't hear anything. Let's have a look at that ankle.'

'I don't think it's anything much. If you say it's not much further to go—'

'I can't say for certain.'

He knelt and felt the ankle gently. 'It's a bit puffy. If I can find some water, I'll at least tie a wet handkerchief round it. If you'll cast your stocking off its moorings at the top, I'll look for water. There should be some standing after the rain.'

He moved off quietly between the bushes. She rolled her stocking down and waited in the green silence for his return, thankful but apprehensive. Then beyond the far side of the field behind her the dog barked suddenly, and she thought she heard a man shout to it. She opened her mouth to call, shut it convulsively and knelt up, peering into the bushes about her. Wherever he was, he must have heard it too. She refastened the stocking, ready to move on the moment he returned.

Suddenly he was behind her, gripping her arm. His hand came over her mouth and her words were cut off in a little throaty gasp. She saw his finger across his lips and he took his hand off her mouth. His head came close to her ear.

'Two men in the field ahead of us,' he breathed. 'They've got guns but no dog, thank God. They may be just shooting, but I don't like the look of it. I suppose Valance could have phoned them when he went back. Anyhow, I'm taking no chances. If I can recognise either, I'll know for sure. In the meantime, we have got to try and get through somehow.'

She whispered, 'The dog behind – did you hear him?'

He nodded. 'If they're working towards each other, it's the pair in front we must dodge. There are two of them, but at least they haven't got a dog. Come after me, and for God's sake don't make a sound if you can help it.'

He went crouching and very slowly, leading towards the bank on the far side. There he stopped and knelt. Margaret, kneeling beside him, peered under the bushes across the stubble field ahead. The sun was suddenly up, and the whole stretch was golden-yellow and diamond-tagged with dew. They were half-way across, breeched and gaitered figures, advancing steadily thirty yards apart with guns at the ready. They might have been walking up birds or hoping for a hare in the stubble. For all she knew they were. But she did not think so.

She felt a touch on her arm. Garrod moved off again, making for a point midway between the advancing guns. Then she saw the pool. He must have found it just before the two appeared on the far side of the field. The bank had fallen away, or been cut into, at one point, and in the gap a small sheet of water, dark with rotted leaves, lay under the over-hanging bushes. He crawled towards it, laid himself not quite in the water but on the clay at its edge and motioned her to do the same.

With the little strip of rotten-smelling water between them they lay face down on the dank leaves and clay, their faces on their arms, and waited. Presently the bushes were beaten back over to their right, and they heard a man moving between the banks.

'Hey, Jack!' The voice was startlingly loud in the silence under the trees.

'Hullo?'

'All clear?'

'Think so. All quiet, anyhow. Haven't heard a thing. You heard anything?'

'No. I'm going through meself.'

'I'm with you, then.'

On either side of them the bushes threshed and fell silent. The elms stirred again and, faint but unbelievably clear on the

86

breeze, they heard the bell of Lodstone church begin to ring for Communion.

A voice in the field behind them said, 'Rot and fall,' and then in a shout 'There's Nick!'

'Nick!' the other voice bellowed, 'Hey, Nick!'

'Come on,' said Garrod. They reared themselves carefully from their mudpatch and crawled forward under the bushes and out into the sunlight on the stubble. 'Can you run?' She put her foot down, felt a jab of pain but decided with relief that it was endurable. She nodded. 'Come on, then.'

They ran straight for the gate opposite. The dog barked again beyond the trees, but not for them; and the men's voices, harsh against the surrounding silence and the distant bell, spoke only to each other.

Through the gate and behind the bank, Margaret sat suddenly and put her head down. He put an arm round her. 'All right?'

'I think so. Give me a minute.' Presently she lifted a face ashen but no longer green. 'All right. I can make it now. But this damned ankle hurts.'

'I'll carry you. It can't be far to the lane.'

'Not yet. It might be further than you think, and you would die rather than surrender. Give me an arm as far as the lane. If the car's in sight, you can carry me to it.'

'All right. But we must go. They may come back this way. We don't know where those two came from.'

His arm came round her. She let it take much of her weight and found it competent. 'I told you,' she said, 'I'm no good across country. But if you're up to it, I am.' They made their way with nightmare slowness across more pasture, hobbled with relief through a gap and stopped in dismay. For fifty yards ahead, and for much further on either hand, the ribbed richness of new plough steamed gently in the sun. Then he said, 'Look.'

Across the field a white gate stood half-open and beyond it, against a background of ranged trees, the tarmac gleamed unmistakably grey. 'The lane,' he said. 'Up you come. Hang on my neck as much as you can, if not for affection at least to take the weight off my arms. This plough is like frozen treacle.'

They came at last to the white gate, and he lowered her gently, sound leg first. 'The car?'

He was fighting for breath. 'Over there. I know. Not far. Five minutes.' After a minute he said, 'I'm sorry. It was that damned plough. This is easy. Up you come.'

He set out briskly along the tarmac. 'You realise of course,' he said, 'that we are both desperately hungry?'

'I am now, but only just this minute. I've only just stopped feeling sick. I'm sorry I'm not better at this sort of thing.'

'I don't want you any better at anything. It wouldn't be the same. Do you, by the way, know of any place we could get a really good breakfast?'

'Well, of course, there's the Ram at Rushbourne. I have heard it highly spoken of. But you realise we're both practically solid mud?'

'Damn the mud. It will brush off. The Ram it is.'

CHAPTER TWELVE

'You didn't recognise them?'

'I didn't really get the chance. But I saw or heard nothing that wouldn't fit in with two of Valance's bunch. I told you – ordinary farming types. And if the man behind wasn't Valance, there are two Nicks at Straightways, which takes a bit of believing. No, I think we must assume that they were two of Valance's friends going to meet him. It wasn't a chance meeting – you heard that. There's quite an organisation here, Margaret.'

She was silent for a minute. Then she said, 'What would they have done if they had found us?'

'I don't know. In a way, that's the most extraordinary part of the whole business. We started playing a game against unknown people for unknown stakes. We didn't even know the rules or what we had to do to win. Now we have at least a slightly clearer picture of the other side, but we still don't really know what's to be done or what's at stake. If Valance and his friends have committed a murder, or are covering one up, and think, or know, that we are trying to uncover it, the stakes must be high. That's not to say they would necessarily have shot us down and buried us where we fell, or even carted us back to Straightways behind the tractor. But we should at least have had to give an account of ourselves, which I shouldn't be anxious to do. You see, we don't know how much they know about us – about me, anyhow. They still haven't to my knowledge any evidence that I am in this with you, or indeed that we are in this at all. They may, as I have said before, know all about us: but there's no real reason why they should.'

'And we still don't know where Sir James joins on. I think it's time we had a go at Sir James. I feel safer with him. He's civilised, even if he has a sympathetic interest in the primitive mind. Men in fields with guns frighten me. Why don't they frighten you? You're civilised to swooning point, but to see you crawling about under hedges and taking compass bearings anyone would think you were king of the wild frontier. Weren't you frightened, or was it all such fun that you didn't notice?'

'I told you I liked doing odd jobs in the vacs. Yes, damn it, Margaret, of course I was frightened, and not only for you, though that certainly counted. But – oh well, I suppose like most men I have a strong streak of anti-civilisation in me. That's why men enjoy wars, at least until the pace gets too hot. It's the women who want them to stay at home and be civilised; and the men go to war to get away from the women. I know this is all commonplaces, but it's fairly generally true. I don't want to be shot at short range with a twelve-bore and taken off on a tractor any more than you do; but I do get a positive satisfaction out of dodging being shot, whereas for you it's all miserable lunacy.'

'All right. In future you do all the gun-play. I'm for a battle of wits myself. I'll have a go at Sir James. I'll play Delilah to this scarred and bearded Samson. He's obviously a professional charmer, and they're easy meat. It's the casual ones you have to fight for.'

'Bah. You leave me cold with your vanity and your predatory generalisations. If you're Delilah, I'm the Queen of Sheba. All right. You go ahead and play Delilah to this carbonadoed piece of easy meat. But don't yell for help if he uses the ass's jaw-bone on you. I shall be busy hiding under hedges and dodging men with guns. Can you conceivably manage another cup of coffee? I don't think I can, much as I should like to. Let's have our bill, then. Waiter!'

They left with much magnificence. 'Thank you, sir,' said the head waiter. 'I hope madam will be none the worse for your accident.'

'Oh no,' said Garrod, 'after all, there is bound to be some risk in every sport.'

'Yes, indeed, sir. Good morning, sir, madam. Thank you, sir.'

'What on earth did you tell him?' Margaret asked as they made for the car.

'I told him we had been bird watching and had been attacked by a rouge marsh-warbler. He was perfectly satisfied.'

'You don't mean he believed you?'

'No, of course he didn't believe me. I said he was satisfied. The explanation met the requirements of the situation, and everyone was happy.'

'It's no good. I don't understand.'

'Well – there we were, don't you see, plastered with mud even after we had got the worst off. If I hadn't said anything, it would have put him and the waiters under the intolerable obligation of pretending not to notice. It would have left a sort of conversational vacuum. As it was, what I said enabled him to go through the proper motions of amusement and concern, and that allowed the others to smile and look shocked –and everyone, as I've said, was happy. It didn't matter what the explanation was, so long as one was offered and the vacuum was filled. You must surely see that.'

'Not really. But men are all mad in their social relations. It won't do for my grandmother.'

'No, but she needn't see me. You can tell her you slipped and came down in the mud. It's perfectly true, in its parts, anyway. You should be thankful you haven't got shot holes in your clothes. That would take some explaining. You're not really going to tackle Sir James direct, are you? Remember he knows you by sight.'

'I don't think it will be necessary, as a matter of fact. I haven't quite decided. Give me time to brood on it, and I'll let you know.'

'All right. Only don't lean too heavily on Sir James's civilisation if he is involved in this. He probably hasn't got a twelve-bore, but remember the curiously carved oriental dagger in his brief-case.'

'I promise I'll keep clear of his brief-case.'

This in fact she contrived to do. It was only Sir James's secretary she saw, and the secretary carried no weapons of any sort, her appearance being evidently her best defence. Whether or not Sir James was a professional charmer, he apparently wanted no glamour in his office. Margaret opened her eyes wide and looked breathless. She said, 'I didn't want to bother Sir James by writing to him, but I thought you could tell me. A friend of mine heard him speak at a meeting in Oxford at the end of April, and said he was marvellous. I wondered whether there was any chance of getting him to come and speak to us. It's only a college society, but we get quite good numbers. Do you think—'

'I'm sorry, Miss Browning. I don't quite understand. What meeting was this Sir James spoke to? I don't think he spoke at Oxford at the end of April. He generally goes down to Wiltshire then.'

She ruffled back the pages of a desk diary. 'What was the date of this meeting at Oxford?'

'April 30th, I think.'

She shook her head decisively. 'That's not possible.· He went down to Stancote on the 28th – he has a cottage there – and didn't return to London till the first of May.'

Margaret was overwhelmed with distress. She said, 'Oh dear, I'm really terribly sorry. My friend said it was Sir James Utley, and I wondered whether I could possibly ask him to come and speak to us. But if I've got it wrong—'

'Look, Miss Browning, Sir James doesn't in fact find time to do much for private societies, though of course he's always being asked.' She melted suddenly. 'It's the television, you see. People see him and then write in asking him. If you think you can interest him in your society, write to him and try. But I must tell you I think there's very little chance.'

She was a kindly creature, and for a moment Margaret considered the possibility of squeezing her further. But caution reasserted itself, and she rose in grateful confusion and bowed herself out. 'The odd thing is,' she said to Garrod afterwards, 'that the old thing liked my being smitten with her Sir James. She wasn't catty at all. Just kind to me and proud of the boss. I do think women are fools.'

She crossed the street to her car and opened the quarter-inch survey sheet. 'Stancote,' she said, 'Stancote. Ah, I thought so. Not far from Devizes. Back to the grass-roots. And I bet he goes to the cottage alone. And Stancote to Lodstone' – she unfolded another section of map – 'is, oh, easy. I must go and see Stancote.'

'Not much to see in Stancote,' said the cosy woman behind the bar. 'Nice, though, what there is of it.'

Outside the window the vast stretch of blue-green down fell away southwards towards Devizes. The road she had come by slanted across it, a ribbon of tarmac poured into a primeval furrow in the chalk. There were, besides the Rose and Crown, two brick farmhouses, a post-office and a bunch of thatched cottages. Stancote had, of its own, no church and no garage; for both it depended on Banstead-in-the-Vale, down below in the trees.

'There isn't a cottage empty, is there?' Margaret asked. 'I'd love a place like this to come to.'

'None that's empty, dear. There's one that's not lived in except in-between times, but you won't find that for sale. That's Sir James Utley's. You've seen him, I expect.'

'Oh, does he live here? I didn't know that.'

'Not live here, no, dear. But he comes here week-ends and the like, and in the summer he's here a lot. Comes all by himself and does everything for himself, and the place is as tidy as a church. He's a great one to talk when we do see him, though. Comes in here sometimes and makes us all laugh. Talks like a real old-fashioned Wiltshire farmer. I can't understand half of it, but my husband and some of the old men, they love it. But to see him there, with his beard and all, talking like that makes me laugh, I must say.'

'I suppose he's made a study of it. He's interested in that sort of thing, isn't he?'

'That's right, dear. But he is a Wiltshire man, you know. There's still Utleys in Banstead, sort of cousins of his, he says, and my husband remembers his father, though he died long before I come here. He's a proper Wiltshire man all right.'

A pink square man came through the door behind her, carrying a crate of beer in each hand. 'The lady was asking about Sir James Utley,' said his wife.

'Oh ay, all the ladies wants to know about him. Jimmy Utley when I first knew him, and his dad worked for Colonel Macrae at the Warren. He was always as smart as paint, they both were, Jimmy and Johnnie, and Jimmy, that's Sir James now, he still is.'

'Who was Johnnie, a brother?'

'That's right. They wasn't twins, Jimmy was the elder, but they was almost as like each other as twins and did everything together. Then Jimmy got a scholarship to Oxford, and Johnnie got one the year after, and soon after that their dad died, and we never saw much more of them, not till Jimmy was Sir James. Then he came along with his beard and that scar on his face, and bought the cottage here, and since then we see quite a bit of him. But he comes and goes to please himself. There's times we wouldn't know he's there, but for lights in the cottage, and there's times when he'll stop the car and have a glass before he even goes to open it up.'

'I was telling the lady how he makes us laugh talking old-fashioned Wiltshire.'

'Oh, that's good, that's really good. Not just the way of talking, you know, but all the old words he uses – I'd forgotten half of them, and the young chaps can't make head or tail of it. I asked him once why he didn't do it on T.V., but he said it wouldn't be much use, but he had recorded a lot on a tape-recorder for some society or other.'

Margaret said, 'What happened to the other one, Johnnie?'

'Well, I don't know exactly, but I know he's been in trouble off and on for years. He was sent away from Oxford for a start, that I do know, and then later we heard he'd been in gaol, though I don't know what he'd done.'

' "My erring brother," I've heard Sir James call him.' His wife imitated Sir James's public manner. 'But it's sad really, though of course he makes a joke of it, especially with them so fond of each other as boys.'

Margaret said, 'Does Sir James see anything of him now, do you suppose?'

'I couldn't say, dear. Johnnie's never come here to my knowledge.' She called to her husband, who had vanished into the public bar, 'Johnnie Utley's never come here, has he, since Sir James bought the cottage?'

He reappeared in the doorway. 'Not that I know of. I reckon Sir James would never say if he had, and I for one wouldn't ask. But I think he hasn't very long come out of prison. I tell you who'd know – old Charlie – that's if you're interested, miss.'

'No, no – it's Sir James who interests me, not the black sheep of the family. But it is sad, as you say, one brother being so well known and the other a bad hat. Oh well. You don't know of any cottage empty round here, I suppose?'

Husband and wife looked at each other and shook their heads. 'Was one down in Banstead, but that's sold. There's not much empty property these days.'

'That's true. I'm afraid.' She said good-bye and went out to her car. She had already identified the Utley cottage to her satisfaction as she came in, and now she had no doubts. It stood further out along the road, clear of the other houses; and although, like all farming villages these days, Stancote looked neat and prosperous, there was no mistaking the cottage that had had real money spent on it, and to a more sophisticated taste. It had a sleek and slightly spurious look and an air of keeping itself to itself.

An old man opened the gate and wheeled a barrow out into the road. He turned back to shut the gate and as he came back to the barrow her car slid alongside him.

'Morning, Charlie.'

'Oh – ah, good morning, miss.' He looked at her, struggling for the identification he felt he ought to be able to make. He was very old and scrawny, and she saw with relief that his glasses were pebble thick.

'You don't remember me, do you?'

'Well, miss, just for the minute—My eyesight isn't as good as it was, you know.'

'Never mind. You'll remember presently, you see if you don't. Tell me, Charlie, when did you last see Johnnie Utley?'

'Johnnie? Johnnie Utley? I don't know nothing about him, miss. Haven't seen him for years'. He shook his head defiantly. His faded blue eyes bored through the thick lenses in an effort to see her properly.

'Doesn't he ever come here? He did come here once or twice, didn't he?'

'No miss, no. I never seen Johnnie here, that's sure.' He put a thin but massive hand on the side of the car. 'You'll have to tell me your name, miss. It's clean gone from me, that's the truth.'

She started the car. 'Never mind, Charlie. It will come to you.' He still stood there as she moved off, staring after her with a bewilderment tinged with hostility.

'This was rash of me,' she wrote to Garrod that evening, 'but it may be some time before Sir. J. goes down to Stancote again, and by the time he does Charlie may well have lost interest.

'We are not by any chance involved in a Comedy of Errors or double act, are we? Two brothers, not twins (that would be too much to stomach) but very much alike and much of an age. The virtuous, successful one looking like a pirate chief with a

95

beard and scar and the wastrel looking (presumably) like big brother without these embellishments. I am much tempted to think there is confusion somewhere, especially when one remembers how easily Sir James's distinguishing marks could be artificially reproduced. And old Charlie was lying when he said Johnnie hadn't been to Stancote – probably lying under orders (whose but Sir James's?) and not much good at it, but certainly lying. The man I saw at the fire, for example, could presumably have been brother John dressed up, if he (or both of them?) had a mind to it.

'We must certainly find out more about Johnnie. I think this is where I bring in the other Charlie – Sir Charles Mayne to you. He could help us on this, though I don't propose to tell him everything – not yet, anyhow. I hope you don't mind my doing this.'

To Charlie Mayne she wrote, 'You said I might ask you for help if I needed it. May I come and talk to you one day next week? In the meantime, there is one thing you can do for me. You know Sir James Utley, the archaeologist and broadcaster? He has a slightly younger brother, John, who was sent down from Oxford and has since developed a criminal record. Could you please find out what you can for me about the history and present whereabouts of this black sheep? I promise I will do nothing rash until I see you. But I really should be very grateful for the dope on John Utley.'

But not telling everything to Charlie Mayne was, she knew, far from easy.

CHAPTER THIRTEEN

'What I can't understand,' said Charlie Mayne, 'is what all this has got to do with Lodstone. I take it it has something to do with Lodstone, because, cryptic as it all was, we were talking about Lodstone when we last met, and you give me to understand that the case is the same. But where a city rat like Utley – John, of course, not Sir James – comes in at Lodstone beats me.'

'I don't know myself,' Margaret said. 'I know there is an Utley-Lodstone connection, but I don't know what it is. If I know more about John, I hope I can find out. I asked you to help me with that because I've got no means of doing it myself, not really.'

'Does it occur to you that you are using me as Scotland Yard uses the local constable? Their chain of evidence against some big shot stretches all over the country. To forge one missing link in it they must know what happened to a particular car that left London on a particular date and has disappeared. So the call goes out. And somewhere in Northumberland or Caithness Constable Peabody, whose mind is really on local licensing offences, sees the car and reports it. He doesn't know what it's wanted for. No one's going to give him a medal, and he doesn't deserve one anyway for a piece of pure routine. But Scotland Yard can't get the big shot without Constable Peabody's help. Mind you, I don't mind playing Constable Peabody to your Scotland Yard, but I can't help feeling I'm wasted in the role. And to be frank, I badly want to know what's going on. So far as Lodstone is concerned, I can't find that anything is.'

'Have you tried to find out?'

'Don't worry. I haven't asked Robin. I have put out a few feelers, yes, but haven't touched a thing. Nothing seems to have happened there for months except a house struck by lightning.'

'A shop.'

'All right, a shop. But that's neither here nor there.'

'But isn't that always the way with Lodstone? You said that last time. You said there was always something going on under the surface, but always under the surface, with everything quiet on top.'

'All right. So I did. But it isn't your job to know what's going on under the surface. It isn't mine now, thank God, but it's even less yours. And I want to know for several reasons. Partly because I ought to be able to help. Partly because I'm pretty certain you oughtn't to be in anything like this at all, but I can't decide if I don't know what it is. And partly because I'm curious. So I tell you one thing. If you want my help, either you must tell me more or you must give me pretty sound reasons for not telling me. Which is it to be?'

'The second, I hope. Not the first in any case. Look. I stumbled on something by pure chance when I was staying at Lodstone in the Easter vacation. I had evidence, if you like, that something was going on. I didn't know who was involved, but I had good reasons – very good reasons indeed – for thinking that Constable Robin was, among others. This seemed so unlikely that I checked on your opinion of him. I'm sorry I was so damned disingenuous in my approach. It was silly of me.'

'It worried me. Not because I mistrusted you, but because if that was your standard of private investigation, I thought the sooner you stopped investigating the better. Perhaps I wronged you. But you were saying you checked on my views of Robin.'

'Yes – and found them at least not inconsistent with his being involved in the thing. I didn't want to tell you what the thing was – not yet, anyhow. For one thing, I had agreed not to tell you.'

'Agreed with whom? Not Robin?'

'Certainly not Robin. No, with this man who's in it with me.'

'There's a man in this with you? Well, that doesn't surprise me, come to think of it, and if he's dependable, I'm glad to hear it. Is he?'

'I think so. My present intention is to marry him some time, and I shouldn't do that if I hadn't found him pretty dependable.'

'Does he know of this intention on your part, or haven't you told him yet?'

'He has asked me to marry him and I've told him – well, more or less that I'll think about it, but not yet.'

'And in the meantime you've promised him not to tell anyone about this thing. Is he involved in it himself?'

'Like me, only incidentally. We both came in by pure chance. We hadn't met before. If you mean, can he have an interest in the thing, no, he can't. Like me, he's an outsider.'

'I see. You said "For one thing." What's the other reason why you can't tell me more?'

'It's because we don't—It's because I can't tell you or anyone else without starting something. You won't like the implication here, I'm afraid, but you'll have to take it on trust. If I told you about it, you couldn't leave it in my hands. No, I know you're no longer a policeman, but even so. And I'm not sure, until I know more myself, whether I want that. I'm afraid it's also true that if I was going to tell anyone, I ought to have done so months ago, and the longer I put it off, the more I shirk it.'

'You're quite right. I don't like the sound of that a bit. Have you told your grandmother?'

'No. She knows there is something. She has met the man. She is prepared to take it on trust for the present. As a matter of fact, she advised me to consult you.'

'And you come down here play acting with imitation breakdowns?'

'I'm sorry. I've said I'm sorry. That was very silly. Don't rub my nose in it.'

'I suppose it hasn't occurred to you that your grandmother could help you much more than I could? She knows all about Lodstone – much more than I do, because she knows much more what makes it tick. I told you I was no good with the working of people's minds. She's very good indeed. You ought to know that. I've no doubt she could explain half a dozen sets of facts about Lodstone that I have established at one time or another, but never really seen the underside of. Why don't you talk to her?'

'The second reason applies, don't you see? Even more strongly in her case. I feel I must go on with this. If she knew what it was, she would either worry a lot or feel compelled to take it out of my hands. And I don't want her to do either.'

'What it seems to come to is this – but correct me if I'm being unfair. You and this dependable man of yours have stumbled on to something that demands official investigation, but that for some reason you want to keep to yourselves, at least until you know more what is involved. You are therefore, in a half-baked sort of way, investigating the thing and will in due course decide whether to leave it alone or report it to the police. In the meantime you are probably running some degree of risk yourselves at the hands of those involved; and, what I frankly consider of greater importance, you are almost certainly suppressing evidence, or acting as accessories after the fact, or something. Despite this, you want me to help you by making an enquiry you are not qualified to make yourselves. Is that it?'

'I think most of that is probably logically unanswerable. But I don't think it's fair at all. I do want to find out more before I decide what to do. I don't myself believe that the risk involved is very great, but in any case I have been, and intend to be, careful. And I won't have what we are doing called half-baked. It is amateur but intelligent; and I am beginning to suspect that there are things here better not left to the professional. If you don't feel able to help us, we must do the best we can for ourselves. But it seems a pity.'

Charlie Mayne got up and said, 'Oh lor.' He walked to the door and shouted something to Karim. 'Does this man of yours know you can argue the hind leg off a donkey, regardless of who's right but preferably when you're wrong? Is he prepared to put up with it?'

'He says I have a tough mind and a nasty turn of speech, but that he loves me for my physical qualities.' Margaret noted with a slight twinge of uneasiness that she was coming to be rather proud of this and enjoyed repeating it. She was not sure why, but must remember to examine her conscience later and find out.

'He says that, does he? Well, there's some hope for him then. Have a Guinness,' he said as Karim came in and set down a tray of glasses and bottles with a swinging flourish. 'Coffee if you prefer it, but stout is much better for you.'

They drank peaceably, but Charlie Mayne frowned over his glass. At last he said, 'All right, I will accept your reasons for not telling me, though I accept them with a lot of doubt. I'll tell you about John Utley on one condition.'

'What's that?'

'Will you promise me here and now that you will let me know in advance whenever you go to Lodstone – when you are going, who you are staying with (if you are staying) and how long for? You can send a postcard, if you like, just giving times – needn't mention Lodstone. I won't interfere, but I want to know.'

'All right,' said Margaret, 'if you—'

'One more promise. Will you promise to tell your grand-mother of this other promise you have made to me?'

'Yes. I promise I'll tell you in advance of any Lodstone visit, and I promise I'll tell grandmother that I have promised this.'

'Right. Refill your glass, and I'll tell you what there is to know about John Utley.' He took some notes out of one pocket and his reading glasses out of another. 'Born in a Wiltshire village just over a year after his famous brother James. Father was a groom or something – genuine humble origin. Both boys were at a local school, but very clever, and both got scholar-ships to Oxford. James did very well there and never looked back. John got sent down for something pretty nasty. I don't mean strange sexual propensities or anything of that sort, but it was something his friends couldn't stomach, not just whooping it up or defying regulations. He was dishonest already at that stage, and I fancy it was some pretty raw financial work that they threw him out for. His mother had died early. Not much known of her, but she had a queer local reputation. His father died soon after he got to Oxford and luckily before he was sent down. So now he was out on his own, except for brother James, who was going from strength to strength. He got various white-collar jobs, including teach-ing. His school education had been good, and although the education authorities are aces on immorality, meaning sex, they didn't seem to mind a reputation for doubtful honesty.

'He was at a school when he ran into his first really serious trouble. He embezzled money he ought never to have been allowed to handle, and the Local Authority had to prosecute. There wasn't so much probation in those days, and he did a short stretch. More important, of course, he lost his job and

101

spoilt his chance of getting another. This was in the 'twenties, and jobs were hard enough to get without having a prison record before you were twenty-five. No one seems to know much what he did for a bit after that, but at least he kept off the police records. He reappeared in the 'thirties with quite a serious false pretences charge against him, and this time he got a year. After he came out he had a near miss with a kindly jury (who of course didn't know his record) and then another conviction and a bigger sentence. When the war started he was an established professional swindler, but like others of his kind he got himself into the Army and served the whole war, if not with any distinction, at least without getting into trouble. There were, of course, opportunities, particularly in the later stages of the war, for men like John with keen business propensities and no scruples, and he no doubt made the most of them. At any rate, a few years after the end of the war, when James was just beginning to hit the headlines, John was in business in quite a big way, in scrap and Army surplus stores and all those other fringe trades of the time, in which you either emerged as a prosperous manufacturer in a seller's market, headed straight for the Honours List, or else overstepped the mark and went to prison. With John you could have guessed which it would be. This time he got three years.

'That was the end of him as a business man. When he came out he seems to have lived obscurely for quite a long time, probably on the edge of the law, but at least keeping out of trouble. He is known to have been in touch with James at this time. James was by now a well-to-do bachelor, and is reported to have helped John quite a bit. He even set him up in a small business, but John's dishonesty was too ingrained, and although there were no criminal proceedings, there was a pretty shady bankruptcy, and even that was made possible only with James's backing.

'There have been no convictions since, but I gather that during the past year or two they have had their eye very much on our John. This bit is off the record, of course, but there seems to be the idea that John has recently been operating, though in a fairly small way, the nastiest of trades, but will be unlucky ever to be caught at it.'

'Blackmail?'

'Something of the sort. Anyhow, squeezing rather than swindling.'

'What does he look like, do you know? I am told the two brothers used to be very much alike.'

'I did see a photo. Very ordinary looking, like so many of that type. I'm trying to think. One knows Sir James's face, of course, but he has that beard and scar. I should think there probably is a likeness, but the face itself is not at all distinctive, so that Sir James's extras would probably swamp any resemblance, even if you saw them together. James isn't the first man who has built up a naturally uninteresting face into something better suited to an acquired character.'

'Is the scar genuine? Grandmother said that he explains it as an air-raid injury.'

'My dear girl, I don't know. I'm not a doctor, and Sir James hasn't got a police record. All I can say is that he certainly emerged with the scar after the war, though he was never a fighting man. The beard came a bit later, when he started to be noticed. I should say that without them James might well look quite like John, but with them he probably looks completely different.'

'So that if John provided himself with similar extras artificially, he might well be mistaken for James?'

'Ah. That's interesting. Yes, I should say he might.'

'Constable Peabody, you have earned your sergeant's stripes by this day's work. You may take it from me that the Chief Constable will hear of this.'

'I hope he won't indeed. Have you met Colonel Watkyn?'
'No.'

'Like something in a book. Never been a policeman in his life, and if you ask me never will be. Good old Army type. He'd call you "m'dear" and probably tell me afterwards you were a nice gel. He's driving the regulars mad.'

'I think I must have met him after all. But I won't tell him if you'd rather not. Still, I am extremely grateful to you for getting all this – and for letting me have it. Oh – one more thing. Where can John be found? If they've had their eye on him for the last year, they must have an address.'

He looked at her for some time before he answered. 'I know where he lives, of course. You don't want to go after him, do you? The man's pretty nasty, you know.'

103

'But not violent.'

'No, that's true. That type never is. They suffer violence in the end, a lot of them, and it generally serves them right, but they don't use violence themselves. I tell you what. I'll make one further condition. Will you promise not to go after John unless you take the dependable man with you?'

'Yes, indeed. I don't think I should anyway.'

'Glad you've got some sense at least. All right. John is reported to be living at 4 Thistleton Gardens, near Victoria.'

'Thistleton Gardens? They're quite respectable, you know – at least, they're not a slum or anything like it. There'll be quite a rent to pay there.'

'That so? Well, there you are. John must be doing quite well for himself. I still very much want to know how all this joins on to Lodstone.'

'So do I. I'm not holding out on you there. I have told you – I know there is a connection, but I don't know what it is. I hope one of these days I shall be able to tell you.'

They walked, as before, down the immaculate drive, but this time the car was where Margaret had herself left it. She said, 'Do you mind my not bringing the car up to the house? I couldn't bear to spoil the gravel.'

'Good God. Is it as bad as that?'

'It's not bad at all. I love this sort of perfection. I could never do it myself, but it appeals to me tremendously. I could live with it, but I'd have to have it all done for me. Like slaves to build the Parthenon.'

'Yes. You're very like your father. You hardly remember him, do you?'

'Not really at all.'

'You'd have had God-awful rows, the two of you, if he'd lived. But it would have been an experience for both of you. Perhaps after all you've been better off with your grandmother.'

'That's what the dependable man says.'

'Does he? Bring him with you next time. And don't forget that postcard.' They parted amicably.

CHAPTER FOURTEEN

Even with everybody moving into Messleton market, Garrod had a strong feeling that his car should not be there to be identified. He came at the town from the opposite side, left his car in a lane and walked to the main road. Ten minutes later he filtered slowly out of a packed bus in the market square, lost among the tweed caps and plastic mackintoshes. It drizzled steadily in a mild, unmoving air.

There were two Land Rovers in the main car park, but long-range inspection showed that neither of them was Valance's. He walked down the High Street, watching approaching faces carefully, and made for the outlying car-park on the Lodstone road. A sense of discovery and adventure possessed him, but he did not, on consideration, feel in the least like king of the wild frontier. It was more being one in a crowd, a stranger with his cap pulled down in front and a purpose of his own. For a moment he wondered whether he was Lemmy Caution, but this too he rejected on examination. He did not feel tough, and the exhilaration he experienced was native and spontaneous. It occurred to him that he could do with a pint, but he did not want bourbon.

The George was out of the question, and he did not in any case fancy the Messleton version of café society. He tried the Swan, which was dark and steamy with crowded mackintoshes. The beer was good, but a second would taste better elsewhere. He moved on, drifting luxuriously through the shoppers and stock-dealers to the market proper, where he bid unsuccessfully for a lot of heifers whose air of gentle bewilderment appealed to him. They attended the event placidly, like a consignment of Circassian virgins under the hammer in imperial Rome, and he considered the feasibility of herding them up Holywell and across the traffic lights into the Broad.

At the Woolpack the beer was better. His sense of remoteness increased, but unrest drove him back to the street and headed him for the top of the town. The rain had stopped, and the air smelt of damp awnings. She came out of a chemist's shop just in front of him and stood for a moment on the edge of the pavement, watching the traffic with a kind of golden impersonality. It was like a full moon emerging suddenly on a night of moving cloud. The idea of speaking to her never entered his head, nor was there anything he wanted to say. She had said they would not meet, and a meeting was beyond the capacity of his thought. His sense of loss was inviolable.

She moved off with her shopping basket on her arm and the dark crowds drifting and melting about her undeviating course till she was out of sight. It did not occur to him to follow her any more than it had occurred to him to speak to her when she stood in front of him.

He bought another pint, but did not notice the name of the pub. As he came out, Valance's Land Rover went up the street, moving slowly through the traffic towards the George. He walked briskly to the edge of the town, where the outgoing traffic piled up at the bridge, and spoke to the driver of a stationary cattle-truck. He said, 'Can you drop me half a mile out? I had to leave my car on the road.'

The man nodded towards the near-side door and he climbed in as the truck moved off again. It occurred to him that he had never thumbed a lift in his life, but today every man was his brother. The driver, intent on the traffic ahead, said, 'Had a breakdown, then?'

He nodded, though the man could not see him. 'I can manage it, but I didn't want to wait, and got a bus in.'

'Say where.'

Presently he said, 'Anywhere here. The next bus-stop will do fine.' The truck, with its load of warmth and sodden beasts, moved on again as he shouted his thanks. The air was sweet but startlingly cold, and he walked briskly towards his car, still full of an overriding detachment. He did not turn back to the road, but drove on into the lanes, turning left-handed in a wide circle with an unquestioning certainty that hardly bothered to read the signposts till he came out on to the Ebury road. There he turned left. The trees were rusting with autumn and the level roofs dark with the recent rain. The sky behind was dead white, throwing up tower and tree-tops in hard silhouette. He turned the car into a gate-

way, daubed a handful of mud over the rear numberplate
and began to walk up the hill.

When the Straightways signpost was in sight, he climbed
over the first gate on his left and began to work his way
across the fields parallel with the farm-track. Valance and
his friends always met at the George on market days. There
was nothing special in that. With the possible dog or farmhand he was not concerned. So far as Straightways was concerned, he knew it was only Valance that mattered.

He came in along the hedgerows, working his way towards
the farm buildings. A dog barked and he stopped and listened.
A moment later it barked again, a single bark with a wavering
carry-over that was not quite a howl. He walked on quietly,
listening for the dog. The interval was longer, but the bark,
when it came, was a long-drawn-out, throaty affair and slightly
muffled. The dog was alone in the house. There might be
hands, but probably away from the buildings at this time of
day. There was no one in sight, and today no tractor worked
in the Straightways fields.

The buildings were of that bare-faced utility characteristic
of the most efficient agriculture in the world. Even the farmhouse, which might offer some graces, was a red-brick box
with shut windows. By the mere grouping of the buildings
an effect was achieved: like all farmyards, it was worth looking
at, and it smelt reassuringly of dung. But the detail was
uncompromisingly ugly. The dog still barked like a minute-
gun, but did not seem to know he was there. At two different
places water dripped audibly into corrugated iron butts.

He leant on the gate where the track entered the yard and
let his mind go back to May Morning, when he himself had
passed by on the road with his green uniform and his sleeping
celebrity. A tractor had pulled into the yard with Valance at
the wheel and a trailer, rubber-tyred but still sprung like a
farm cart, jolting over the track behind it. There had been,
probably, a tarpaulin thrown over the trailer, and an in-
conspicuously dressed little man had lain flat on his back and
smiled slightly and sightlessly at the underside of the tarpaulin. Valance had got down and looked round. The place
was utterly deserted, but would not remain so for long. Hands
would arrive on bicycles or motor-bikes, delivery vans or
salesmen might come bumping over the track. The little man

must be got rid of promptly and permanently. To dig was not difficult, but to dig deep was laborious and to dig shallow unsafe. Besides, the surrounding fields – Garrod looked round slowly at an unbroken ring of plough – almost certainly were under crops, and you cannot put even a little man under a standing crop and expect to harvest over him in a few months' time.

There remained the buildings. The Dutch barn, now full to its roof, had been near empty on May Morning, but its floor – Garrod walked over and looked at the foot of the stacked bales – was brick, and brick paving can no more be disturbed and replaced without trace than standing corn. The milking shed, like all milking sheds now, was all concrete and steel and power points. You might as well try to bury a body in an operating theatre. He walked across the yard to an open-sided shed, where farm machinery stood between stacked fencing and a carefully tarpaulined mound. His foot caught an oil-drum, which rang like a bell. The dog began to bark hysterically in the shut-up house, but he thought he had found what he wanted.

The shed was being progressively floored with concrete. There was sand and ballast in the yard, and the tarpaulin covered stacked bags of cement. Valance or one of his men had evidently cleared the shed of machinery a section at a time and put down a roughly screeded concrete floor in the cleared section. He counted five sections already done. The joins were visible, but it was impossible to tell when each section had been laid. He reckoned there were four more to do. He wondered how often the process was taken up, and which section it was that had, in part at least, been put down hurriedly over disturbed earth early on May Morning. He wondered whether by now Valance remembered which section it was. There was nothing to show, but in his present mood he had no doubt.

He sat on the tow-bar of the tractor and thought about the small room at the George which Valance and his friends generally had to themselves on market days. The air would be dark with smoke by now, and the chrome cocktail-shaker would have gone the rounds three or four times with the particular sweet poison they favoured. Valance and Stallard would be in good voice and Belling and Marston in good heart. Only at the centre of the circle there was rest and golden silence. Out here, on the extreme perimeter, their guest was silent too, silent under a foot of scrabbled clay and six inches of roughly screeded concrete. He was Stallard's and Belling's and Marston's guest, not only Valance's, though Valance was personally charged with his entertainment. Whatever else they had in common, they certainly had the little man. He wondered whether they had other guests of the establishment, whether Stallard's or Belling's farms stood the more securely for a similar time-honoured addition to their foundations.

He had had, he was now ready to admit, too much beer. He leant his head against the cold dirt of the tractor body and thought it was time to be going. Valance, certainly, would come to Straightways from the village, not passing his car, and on a morning like this the Land Rover would give plenty of warning that it was on the way. But it wasn't sensible to play hide and seek over the hedges when he could walk out as collectedly as he had walked in.

He got to his feet and sat down again silently and at once. a boy was standing in the yard, not Valance certainly, probably a farmhand. He must have come in from behind the milking shed, and he had come silently and under his own power. He had not, at a first quick sighting, looked formidable, but he was for the moment in charge, and he was between Garrod and the way he wanted to go. He lifted his head cautiously and had another look.

The boy was harmless enough in himself, as was, almost certainly, the dog. But neither lacked a voice, and the boy had speech of a sort. They were witnesses and he saw now that one had called the other. The dog still barked, though no longer continuously, at an unseen intruder. The boy, who must have been silently engaged much nearer than Garrod cared to think, had come to see what the dog was barking at. Finding all quiet, he walked to the back door of the farm house and called, 'Jet! Hey, Jet boy.'

The barking stopped and there were sounds of frustrated emotion inside the house. 'Quiet! Quiet there! Quiet, Jet boy!' He turned back into the yard and stood there, uncertain and not by nature a quick decider. Garrod wondered what he would do if the boy decided on a tour of inspection. He might hope to dodge him round the cement stack, but in that complete silence he would be very lucky not to be heard. He knew that he could with perfect impunity walk out into the yard and say, 'Ah, I couldn't find anybody. Is Mr Valance at home?' The boy, who was a very ordinary boy, would let him talk himself off, and would later tell Valance whatever he was told to tell him. Whether Valance would believe it or not was another matter.

The odd thing, which he had already faced on other occasions, was that it was not primarily fear that made him keep out of Valance's way. Even if Valance was murderously inclined, he would not shoot an enquiring stranger in the presence of his hired hand.

He did not want Valance to know he was there because secrecy was an essential part of the process of discovery to which they were committed. Only if the knowledge was secret knowledge could they judge it for themselves when they had it. He did not even believe, now, that the knowledge could ever be complete unless it was secret. The police could take up the concrete floor under his feet and bring up the little man, or what was left of him, and put Valance on trial for his murder or disposal. But the little man was no longer of central importance. Even Margaret had not taken much notice of him, except to be irritated by him, when she found him, and no one seemed to have missed him since. If his blood cried from the earth for vengeance, it cried in a very faint voice. To know how and why he had died had become much more important than to exact retribution for his death; and to confront Valance and his friends might precipitate retribution, but could never, he knew, exact the knowledge.

The boy turned and walked into the milking shed. His boots rang hollowly on the scrubbed concrete as he went round it. Then he came out of the door, facing Garrod, and began walking across the yard towards the machinery shed. Half-way across he stopped, turned and listened. Then he went over and opened the far gate, propping it open with a brick. The Land Rover was coming down the track.

Garrod got up from behind the tractor, and with the boy watching the track opposite melted out of the shed and round the corner of the house. He looked back and found the boy still facing away from him. He ran along a low wall, unlatched a wire gate and hooked it behind him and plunged round a corner into a statuesque assembly of waiting chickens. They cackled and scattered along the wire walls of their enclosure, and behind him the Land Rover, driving fast in a low gear, roared into the yard.

Baffled like the chickens in his efforts to escape he doubled back to the gate and shut it behind him as the car manoeuvred to a halt. He went over the wall and this time found himself among cabbages. The chickens had stopped cackling and in the yard the engine roared and stopped. Inside the house Jet barked in a muffled but mounting excitement, but the voices were audible in the yard.

The boy said, 'Jet was barking a bit, so I come up to see.'

'It's the car,' said Valance. 'He hears it coming and he's been shut in since morning. I'll go and let him out.'

'No, it was before he was barking. I come up but I couldn't see nothing.'

Masked by the end of the shed, Garrod emerged cautiously from his cabbages and crossed a gateway into a field. Here the bank afforded solid cover. He moved over a short distance and then, raising his head cautiously, looked into the yard. He must have missed some question of Valance's. The boy said, 'Only just before you come. There wasn't nothing about I could see. I come up and looked.'

Valance stood barely three yards from the bank and Garrod saw him in profile. He was no more than a medium-sized man, slightly built but agile. His arms hung limp, and he swung his head slowly round the grouped buildings. It occurred to Garrod that he had been drinking, and he remembered the strength of the sweet mixture poured out of the chrome cocktail shaker.

Valance said, 'All right, all right. You get along back; I'll see to it.' The boy went off, as he had come, behind the milking shed. For what seemed minutes Valance stood where he was. His head slewed slowly from side to side. He seemed to be listening. Then he walked quickly into the shed, and Garrod half lost him among the machinery. He stopped on what might be the third section of new concrete. He said something inaudible and Garrod thought he raised his hands for a moment and dropped them again. Then he turned and came out into the yard. His face was still pale, but he smiled

111

and his slant eyes were wide open and staring. He breathed rather quickly through parted lips. Some strong emotion worked in him, but he looked neither guilty nor furtive.

He turned towards the house and said, 'Coming, Jet boy.' He went round the corner, feeling in his pocket for a key. Garrod turned and ran. It was a long time since he had run at full stretch. He wondered whether the muscles would stand up to it, but he covered the width of the field in a comfortingly short time. He flung himself over the gate and heard, as he dropped into the shelter of the bank, the jubilant barking of the liberated Jet.

He ran on in the shelter of the hedge and at the next gate turned and made straight for the road. He scrambled breathless into the driving seat, started and backed the car and drove hard towards Ebury. Where the roads met he hesitated and drove on. Then he changed his mind, stopped and backed to the Messleton turning. He put the gear-lever into first, but a blue arm came suddenly in through the driving window.

'Excuse me, sir,' said a pink young constable, 'but your rear number-plate's completely obscured by mud. Looks almost as if it was done on purpose. I'll have to ask you to clean it.'

'Oh, sorry. I'll give it a wipe.' He climbed out. 'Yes,' he said, 'completely covered. Boys, I expect.'

He cleaned it painfully with a handful of grass while the constable watched. For the moment his frontier days were over.

Chapter Fifteen

When the road reached the highest point of the down, Margaret stopped the car and got out. This golden weather, when it came, was for her the last perfection of the year. Whatever you made of it, the spring was never comfortable. Even the summer, which in the native English tradition was uncertain and impermanent, had its own restlessness. There was always the obligation to make the most of it while it was there, to get into the country while the daylight lasted, or to get your holiday in at the right time, or to get yourself properly sunburnt before you went home. By now all this seasonal opportunism was over. There was nothing to look forward to but the winter and therefore nothing required of you but to enjoy the sun, while it lasted, with your clothes on and your mind at peace.

A haystack between the roadside and the southern slope offered, and on inspection provided, the perfect place from which to contemplate perfection. She muttered an apology to the farmer and pulled out a handful or two of hay to make herself comfortable. A village in the valley sent its wisps of cottage-smoke, in the traditional manner, straight up in the slightly misted air, and all round her the tops of the downs were bare and silent.

This was the Utley country. The village below was not Banstead, but it was the sort of village Banstead was. Jimmy and Johnnie had been children together in Banstead in the unimaginable world before the Kaiser's war. She wondered whether you could ever lose a childhood like that, and what it meant now to Sir James with his popular academics and his London house and his expeditions to the Amazon Basin. It struck her suddenly that the knowingness and the dropped eyelid were a very village quality. She could imagine him as a preternaturally bright village child, with just that expression on his face, taking the rustic mickey out of the gentlemen from London down for the shooting.

113

It was Johnnie (the town rat, Charlie Mayne had called him) who had really sold his birthright and Jimmy who had got the best of both worlds. He had got it publicly, as it were, by combining sophistication with a working insight into simpler minds. He had also, she now suspected, got it privately by retaining, somewhere in his own mind, the simple man's view of the sophisticate. It was an intriguing picture, and she found it endearing. She wondered whether she would ever meet Sir James in the even slightly normal circumstances that would give her a chance to see whether it fitted the man as he was.

Banstead, when she had torn herself from the haystack and found her way to it, was inevitably less perfect than a village seen in a golden haze from a lark-ridden hilltop. It had spread a good deal since Sir James had first known it, and the additions were often sad. But church and pub and big house (she imagined the Warren, where Jimmy's father had worked for Colonel Macrae) were still in position, and she was not one to object to petrol pumps on the green when she badly needed four gallons to get her home.

She paid for her petrol and said, 'I'm looking for a Mr Utley. Can you tell me where I can find him?'

'There's two Mr Utleys. There's Bob, up the Stancote road, and there's Fred. He's in Devizes, but his wife keeps the shop. Which of them was it you were wanting?'

'Are they relations? I'm really looking for relations of Sir James Utley. Perhaps they both are?'

'They're cousins. I've heard Sir James Utley's a Banstead man and related to them, but I don't know much about it. You could ask Mrs Utley at the shop. Is it for the papers?'

'That's right – a bit about his early history and his family and all that. There's a lot of interest. He's an interesting person, isn't he?'

The man grinned suddenly. 'You'd better ask the wife. She's always on about him. All I ever watch is the football and the boxing. He stays up at Stancote, you know – got a cottage up there. They'd tell you all about him there.'

'Yes, but Banstead's where he was born and brought up, isn't it?'

'I've heard so, miss. I don't know, to tell the truth. You try Mrs Utley at the shop. She'll tell you.'

114

The shop was no longer the splendid confusion of lines it would have been when Jimmy and Johnnie spent their pennies there. It was now groceries, soft drinks and a deep freeze. Everything was packaged and stood on plastic shelves.

'My husband won't be home till this evening,' said Mrs Utley. 'What was it you wanted?'

'I am writing a piece on Sir James Utley, and I wanted to speak to someone about his family and early life here. I believe your husband is a relation of his, and I thought he might be able to help me.'

'Oh – well, he is a relation, I know, but he's a lot younger, and I don't think he ever knew him when he lived here, not to remember. I know. You'd better talk to Auntie. She's always talking about him, and she'll enjoy telling you. She's an old lady, you know, and you'll have to let her tell you her own way, but she's wonderful really.'

'That sounds perfect. If you're sure she won't mind.'

'Mind?' Mrs Utley laughed in a slightly sinister fashion. 'You're not from T.V., are you?'

'Well, no. No, I'm a journalist really – I write for the papers, you know.'

'Oh well. She'll be disappointed, but it can't be helped. She'll tell you all right. Come through here, will you? One thing, she's not deaf. Not that that matters much.'

The interior had not been modernised as much as the shop, and they passed through a bead curtain into a tiny cluttered room resolutely cleared of both dust and oxygen. Auntie and a very large television set faced each other across one diagonal with upright bamboo chairs occupying the neutral corners.

'The lady wants to talk to you about Sir James Utley,' said Mrs Utley, making rather breathlessly for the door. 'I'll bring you a cup of tea presently,' she said to Margaret and vanished with a swish of beads.

'Are you going to interview me?' said Auntie.

'Well yes, I suppose—'

'Like in Tonight?'

'Well, no, you see—'

'I can tell you all about Sir James Utley when he was here. Jimmy he was then, and Johnnie was the younger one. My Uncle Jack, he was their grandad, see, he used to say Jimmie would come to no good, too clever by half he was, Johnnie was the one we all liked. But Cousin John wouldn't have it, he was groom, see, with Mrs Vickers, he said Jimmie was the good boy, but the two was always in everything together, and the dead spit of each other, and I always say no one ever really knew which of them had done it.'

Margaret took a deep breath but got less benefit from it than she had hoped. She said, 'But Miss Utley—'

'Mrs Sykes. I was born Utley, of course, my dad and Jack were brothers, and the elder boy was called after his grandfather, see, and the younger after his dad, though he was never the favourite, like I said, he preferred Jimmie, still he was a good father to them both so much as he was allowed to be. But I've been widowed nearly thirty years now, and one forgets.'

'Yes, of course, I'm sorry. Your father and – and Jack Utley were brothers. And John Utley was Jack's son and your Cousin. He was groom – with Mrs Vickers, you said? Was he ever at the Warren?'

'Only in the old Colonel's time, that's after Mrs Vickers married again and went to live in Chippenham. It was John who preferred Jimmie, but Uncle Jack, he said he was too clever by half. The mother we never liked, but of course she brought them up and John was out at all hours, grooms were then, you know, though the old Colonel had his motor at the Warren, which John could never manage, always having worked with horses.'

'The mother – that was Jimmie and Johnnie's mother – your Cousin John's wife – you said you didn't like her. She's dead, isn't she? What was wrong with her?'

'Well – of course John ought never to have married her. A fine big man he was, and fair like all the Utleys, and wonderful with horses, but she was a Somerset woman, that's what we were told, small and dark as a mole, she was, and quiet and always smiling, and she had John properly to rights from the start, he couldn't cross her in anything. Of course, she was clever, that kind always is, and we couldn't do nothing, but it wasn't right his marrying her from the start.'

'Jimmie and Johnnie were both clever, weren't they? Do you think they got their brains from their mother?'

'She said so, I dare say, and John wasn't contradicting her.

116

As I say, he was a good father to those boys, but they were like foreigners almost, I used to think half the time he didn't know what they were thinking about, any more than we did the mother.'

'What happened to Johnnie? We know all about Jimmie, who's now Sir James. Is Johnnie still alive?'

'Oh yes, Johnnie's still alive. But he's never had any luck, Johnnie. They sent him away from college when Jimmie stayed on and did well, and he's never had a proper chance since, I don't reckon. He was the younger, of course, though there's not much more than a year between them. We don't hear of him much, I don't think he's been here for years. We always liked him the best.'

'Both the parents are dead?'

'Oh yes, John died soon after the boys went to college, he died of pneumonia that terrible winter we had, but it didn't seem he ought to have, he'd been out in all weathers all his life and hardly had so much as a cold, but he seemed to have no heart left, and he went down sudden and was dead in three days.'

'His wife was already dead?'

'That's right, we just heard she was dead and didn't even know she was ill. Kept herself to herself to the last, as she always had, and the vicar took and buried her on the south side, where all the Utleys were, though there were some objected, and she hadn't been near the church that we knew of till she came to be buried there. Of course, we all hoped John would marry again, but he never made no move, he seemed to lose all heart really, with all the time she'd given him.'

'You said she came from Somerset. What was her name, do you know?'

'John always called her Meg, her real name was Margaret, see, but I never heard what her maiden name was, he married her there and brought her home, and Jimmie wasn't born till a year after they come home, so there was no need for him to have married her. He must have met her when he was away with Mrs Vickers' horses, as he was sometimes, but the first we knew of it was when he brought her back and told us they was married. I'll never forget the shock it gave us, her being her, though of course it was no good talking to John about it,

117

he wouldn't hear a word against her, and in any case what was done was done. And then next year I married Alf Sykes, and we never saw much of John from that time on really, except the once when my brother Harry, that's Fred's father, got married, and they both come to the wedding breakfast with the two little boys, but she wouldn't come in the church, nor let the boys come either, we thought, anyway they never come, only to the breakfast, and then she was smiling very pleasant at everyone but didn't say much.' ·

Margaret said suddenly, 'Was there a photo – taken at the wedding, I mean – with the two boys in it?'

For a moment Auntie stared blankly in front of her. Then she opened her mouth and screamed. 'Eileen!' she yelled, 'Eileen!' The effect in the small room was shattering, and Margaret shot to her feet, but the beads jangled quietly and Mrs Utley was at her side with a cup of tea. She handed Margaret the cup and said, 'What is it, Auntie?'

'Lady wants to see the album.'

'Oh yes, with the old photos. I'll get it. You drink your tea while I find it.' She swished out, and Margaret repeated her question, less from hope of a direct answer than to observe the formula of evasion. 'Mrs Sykes,' she said, 'what was it you had against John's wife? What was wrong with her?'

She shut her mouth suddenly and made little mewing noises, rocking slightly in her chair. 'Well,' she said. She mewed again, visibly torn between strong feelings and an equally strong instinct not to give them words. 'She wasn't the right sort.' She raised her voice suddenly. 'She wasn't the sort I'd ever care to have anything to do with, let alone to have John marrying her. She—'

The beads jangled and she stopped suddenly. Mrs Utley produced the classic album, brass-bound, with pages slotted in arbitrary shapes. Auntie took it and flapped over the heavy pages. From what she could see, Margaret thought the early pages must be late Victorian. After a time carelessness, coupled with a change in the shape and size of the photographs themselves, had let the formal arrangement go, and there was a jumble of prints loose between the pages. 'There,' said Auntie, and Margaret found herself suddenly looking into the end of an era. This must have been just before the war. Give them another year or two, she thought, and some of

118

these men would have been casualties and some of them in uniforms that already looked as dated as chain-mail. But this was the last of the golden years; and even the appalling costume of the time could not altogether obscure a genuine grandeur. The Utleys were, as Auntie had said, big fair men, indelibly Anglo-Saxon with their full moustaches and light eyes, and the women mostly matched them. It was all classic Wessex.

There was no need for Auntie to point out Meg and her sons. Apart from whatever other differences there were, in appearance alone they were, as she had said, 'like foreigners almost,' a dark enigmatic corner in this group of blond extroverts. The two small boys looked, as she had been led to expect, very much alike, dark and watchful, but impervious, like so many children, to the camera's penetration. The mother was different.

She stared full into the lens, ignoring alike the earnest technician behind it and the whole group of innocent subjects around her. The eyes were alight with mockery, compelling Margaret, across the backward chasm of time, to share some tremendous, unexplainable joke. The mouth was immediately familiar, small, full and turned down at the corners in a knowing, secretive smile.

With mechanical politeness Margaret acknowledged Auntie's introductions to the family, noting only incidentally that in Alf Sykes she had run true to type, Alf being as blond and straightforward as her Cousin John, who had imported his dark mystery from Somerset. She had no wish to press her question further. Whatever the undercurrents of feeling, Meg could never have been anything but an intruder among the Utleys: and it could not have helped that she seemed to have evolved her two sons by some private alchemy without any help from her big fair Utley husband. Whatever her stock, it must have been rich in dominant genes.

The air of the shop seemed almost heady after Auntie's pressure-tank. 'You've done her good,' said Mrs Utley. 'She likes to talk, as you can see, and someone fresh is an excitement for her. I think she half expected to see herself on the screen, but she'll get over it. I hope she told you what you wanted to know.'

'Oh yes, indeed. She seems to remember everything. Tell

119

me, Mrs Utley, do you know why they all had it in so for John Utley's wife, Meg, that's Sir James Utley's mother? I can see she was an outsider, and very different from the family to judge from the photo, but your Auntie talks of her as if she was quite beyond the pale. What really was the trouble, do you know?"

'I don't really. I know the way she goes on about her, and Fred's father is almost as bad. Of course, she was dead before I came here. I've often thought that Auntie wanted to marry John herself, they were only cousins, after all. But it wasn't only that. They were all against her. One thing I do know. Her husband adored her. Of course, I never saw him either, but from what they tell me – not the family, of course, they wouldn't have it – he as near died of a broken heart as anyone ever has. But her – there's nothing too bad for them to wish on her, from immorality to black magic. And of course, they say the boys weren't John's, though they can't put a name to any other man that ever came near her. They were too different, if you ask me. I married an Utley myself and even now it's not always easy. Fifty years back it must have been shocking. But don't go putting that in the papers, or you'll have me in real trouble.'

On the south side of the church Margaret found many Utley graves, but none of Margaret, wife of John. There was a green mound among them, hardly bigger than a child's, that might have been it. But wherever Sir James's mother lay, no stone pinned her down.

CHAPTER SIXTEEN

'I wish you wouldn't go snooping round Straightways, especially with half-a-dozen pints of beer inside you. I've promised Charlie Mayne not to go after John Utley without you. I wish you'd promise not to go after Valance and his lot without me.'

'I find this solicitude in you rather disturbing. When we were at the Ram you told me quite cheerfully you'd leave all that to me. I admit it gives me a pleasantly warm feeling to have you worrying about what I do, but it also leaves me slightly apprehensive. I had to go to Straightways. I might have to go again. If I did have to, you wouldn't really want to come, would you? I can't be king of the wild frontier with you on my gun arm. The heroine is better employed back at the old ranch-house than riding with the hero.'

'Yes, but as often as not she finishes off by shooting down the bad man with someone else's gun. Admittedly she drops the gun, covers her face with her hands and collapses on the hero's shoulder immediately afterwards, but that's too late to save the bad man. It's the surprise element that gets him. She never misses.'

'I admit that. I often wonder why the implications of this are always wasted on the hero. If he'd only use his head, he'd be off into the sunset in a flash. But he never sees it.' He took his hands off the wheel of the stationary car, turned and pulled her towards him. 'I really do love you quite surprisingly, Margaret, but don't ever make me promise not to do anything without you.'

'Well—'

'I mean within reason.'

'I should hope you do mean within reason.'

After an interval he said, 'You're not as young as you were, are you?' She shook her head, her mouth close to his. 'Well,' he said at last, 'that's all to the good, isn't it? What about Johnnie the town rat? Shall we go after him?'

121

'We must, I think. Thistleton Gardens seem a far cry from Lodstone. Farther still from pre-war Banstead, if it comes to that. I can't think why Johnnie turned nasty in this sort of way. They must both have been happy as children.'

'Happy at home, from what you say. But against the outside world, surely. They must have adored Meg, and they must have known how she was treated. That sort of thing could work several ways. But whatever Meg taught her sons, it can't have been to love their neighbour. My bet would be that Johnnie, the one they all liked, was the simple one. He may have got to Oxford, but he probably lacked sense. Neither of them was a man of violence, but Jimmie had the subtler approach, whereas Johnnie simply went crooked. Probably nothing to choose between them morally, at least to begin with; it was a matter of efficiency. We know Jimmie helped Johnnie up to quite a late stage. Later, by all accounts, Johnnie deteriorated fast, as such a character would be apt to do; and probably at some point Jimmie refused to play any further. But of course it's all speculation. Jimmie is now the enigmatic Sir James, and Johnnie we haven't even seen. Or have we? Have all our beards been real beards, I wonder?'

'Let's go and beard him in Thistleton Gardens. I think we ought to have a look at him.'

'Yes, I think so. I can't see why not. If we have to talk to him, we can always tell him your story about the early life of his famous brother. If Johnnie's half the man I take him for, we might well get a substantial low-down on his famous brother. Anyway, it's worth trying.'

Thistleton Gardens, they judged, had seen better days, but it had also seen very much worse. As with so many other originally respectable but since abandoned parts of London, the money was coming back. The money, not the style. It was the new sort of money, that carried no social implications of any sort, but could afford several coats of paint and some modern plumbing, and asked nothing better than to be left to itself. Sometimes it had prams and families, sometimes it was arty and peculiar, sometimes it was simply speculative, and did a steady business letting tiny subdivisions of once substantial rooms. But it was all, generally speaking, reasonably legitimate and respectable. Thistleton Gardens were not the slum they had at one stage threatened to become.

No. 4, like all the rest, had a portico of stuccoed brick. What the agents called semi-basement windows peered up from behind railings and a low mound of exhausted earth that had been, and could still be, a flower-bed. The door was glass-panelled but opaque, and had four bell-pushes beside it with slip-in card holders for names. Three of the four had cards, but none of the cards had the name Utley on it. They hesitated.

The man was so dark and nondescript and evasive that for a moment Margaret thought they had found the missing Johnnie. He came silently up the path behind them and spoke suddenly from the bottom of the steps. He said, 'Excuse me, but are you by any chance looking for Mr Utley?'

Garrod said. 'Yes, are you?'

He hesitated, looking from one to the other of them as if he was trying desperately to make up his mind about them. Finally he nodded. 'That's right.' He smiled with a dreadful assumption of confidence. He was a respectable little man, but much battered. 'But I haven't seen him for – oh, some time now. I come along occasionally in case, but I haven't seen him. I wondered' – his face worked suddenly and shockingly and then straightened itself out – 'I wondered if perhaps he had gone away altogether or – or something.'

'Did you want to see him?'

'No, oh no – at least, well, he asked me to come, you know, so I thought I'd better try to find him. But it's some time now, and I haven't heard. Only I come occasionally, just in case. Did you – had you business with him?'

'Of a sort. When did you last see him?'

'In the spring, quite early in the spring. And now I see his card's gone. It was on the bottom bell – he had the downstairs rooms. But I think the landlady must have taken it away, and of course I wondered – well, what had happened and whether he'd be back.'

Garrod said, 'I shouldn't worry any more if I were you. I don't think he will be back,' and Margaret was surprised at the kindness in his voice. The little man's face crumpled like a child's at the sudden promise of something too good to be true. He said breathlessly, 'Do you think so?'

'Yes, I think so. I can't swear to it, but I'd be surprised if he does.'

'You're not the police, are you?' He looked at Margaret doubtfully, trying to see her as a policewoman.

'No, we're not the police. But we are interested in Mr Utley. Do you mind telling me what he – whether he has always looked much the same since you have known him?'

'Oh yes, I think so, always. It's not long, I suppose, really.'

'You've never seen him with a beard?'

'No. You know, I've really only seen him twice.'

'Well, that ought to be enough. Thank you for your help. And as I say, I shouldn't worry any more about him if I were you.'

The little man suddenly turned his face away from them. Then he turned his body after it and scuttled down the path and out of the gate.

'Poor little sod,' said Garrod. 'I've never actually met one before, I mean not as such. One does occasionally wonder how many of one's respectable friends may not be in the same case. But this one was very small game. I don't warm to Johnnie somehow, do you?'

'What do you suppose this one had done?'

'Probably a bit of mild embezzlement, but quite possibly nothing illegal this time at all. I should think quite likely he'd been in prison and the boss didn't know it, and wouldn't like it if he did know – and of course, our Johnnie knew. Something of that sort. Not the big stuff, but a man like that will probably pay steady weekly money rather than risk losing his job. It's an easy game really, once you know, but mean stuff. Anyhow, that completes the picture of Johnnie Utley. The police aren't far behind him, but it's the hardest thing in the world to catch up with. I wonder where he's got to?' He suddenly leant forward and pressed the second button from the bottom, and a bell rang audibly on the ground floor, somewhere through at the back. The card said 'Mrs Campbell,' but for a long time nothing happened. Then a door opened and shut ponderously, and a pair of feet dragged themselves by reluctant stages towards the front door.

'Dinna ye hear them?' said Margaret. 'The Campbells are coming.' Then the front door began to open.

As it opened more fully, the effect became impressive, like a ceremonial unveiling. Mrs Campbell was statuesque, but in a ruinous modern style.

Garrod said, 'Mrs Campbell?'

'Yes.' It was difficult to see where she spoke from.

'We're looking for Mr John Utley.'

'So am I.'

'We thought he might be able to help us.'

'I know he can help me. He owes me six weeks' rent. A fortnight owing when he left, and four weeks in lieu of notice – that's presuming he has gone. Some of his stuff is still here, but it's not worth one week's rent, let alone six. How do you think he can help you?'

'Well – we wanted to ask him some questions—'

'So do I. Oh, indeed I do. There are quite a lot of questions I should like to ask Mr Utley. But my own feeling is that I shall have to guess the answers.'

She and Garrod looked at each other, Margaret noticed, with a curious sort of truculent mutual approval. Garrod said, 'May we come in?' and she moved slowly back, still holding the door. They came rather self-consciously into the hall and she shut the door behind them. Then she moved off towards a door at the far end, and they tiptoed after her. She walked with elaborate unease, as if nothing moved in its expected channel, and she had continually to improvise.

The room was ordinary, but comfortable and unexpectedly civilised. She turned to face them, but did not ask them to sit. She said, 'You'll have to tell me your business.'

Garrod said, 'We came to see Mr Utley. We are enquiring into a matter that has arisen elsewhere, and we think he may know something about it.'

'This is a private effort, isn't it? You're not professionals.'

'It is, yes. No, we're not.'

'You're not – well, personally involved with Mr Utley, I take it?'

'We're not, no. We've just met one of his personal involvements outside.'

'I know, and he's not the only one. That's what puzzles me.'

'You say he left nothing of value.'

'He had only one thing of value, his camera, and he took that with him. He left what they call personal effects. In his case that means one or two bits and pieces of clothing, shaving things and a make-up box.'

'Did he take his beard?'

125

She hesitated and drew back the corners of her mouth. Margaret realised that she was smiling, but it did not look like a smile. She said, 'You've seen him with a beard?' ·

Garrod nodded. 'He had one in his box, hadn't he? Is it still there?'

'All right. He was clean shaven – you know that. He had a small beard in his make-up box. I have once seen him wearing it, when I wasn't supposed to. There is one in his box now. He may have had a spare, of course.'

'When you saw him with his beard, was he – well, made-up otherwise?'

'You mean was he got up to look like Sir James Utley, don't you? Well, he was, and it was very successful. I suppose he must have been a relation. I have never seen Sir James except on television, of course, but I should think that the likeness must have been very strong.'

'Including the famous scar?'

'Oh yes – there was the make-up, you see. I don't see what else he used it for.'

'You only saw this once?'

'That's right. He didn't do it often, or I should have known. That time I got the impression that he was trying it out.'

'You've been very helpful. You could just have shut the door on us.'

'I liked the look of you. I still do. So far as Mr Utley is concerned, I am glad to help you.'

'Is there anything we can do to help you?'

'I don't think so. I'd like to know one way or the other, of course, and I'd like my money, but I don't expect I'll get it.'

Margaret said, 'Do you mind telling us what he was paying?'

'Six. It's only the two downstairs rooms with a small cooking-place and the use of the etceteras on this floor. But rooms are expensive round here.'

'So he owes you thirty-six pounds – or guineas?'

'Pounds. That's if he doesn't come back. If he does, he owes me all the rent to date.'

Garrod said, 'And he hasn't paid since April?'

'I didn't say that.'

'No, I got it from the personal involvement. I gather he hasn't been around since then.'

'All right. No, he hasn't.'

126

'You said you would help us. Is there anything else you can do to help?'

'There is an address. I don't know if it's any good. I have written to it and got no reply. But I know he used it himself once. Never mind how I know. As I say, I have had no reply from it, but you might like to try it.'

'Yes please, I think we should.'

'The address is 23 Milton Road, Barton Woods.'

'Barton Woods? That's a suburb, isn't it? Up in North London somewhere.'

'It's up the Northern Line Tube, but I haven't been there.'

'Mrs Campbell,' said Margaret, 'was Mr Utley always here? I mean, did he live here and go away occasionally, or was this more or less a convenience to him? Or didn't you know, really, whether he was here or not?'

'I knew pretty well. I didn't know, naturally, exactly when he came and went, but when he wasn't here I think I generally realised it within a day or so. You know how it is – lights, movements, doors. Then presently I'd gather he was back again – I might even see him. It was no business of mine, you see, as long as he paid the rent.'

'But he was away quite a lot?'

'Oh yes. He was away almost as much as he was here, I should think. That's why it took me some time, you see, to make up my mind that he wasn't coming back. I still haven't cleared the flat and re-let it, but I'm going to now.'

'There aren't any books or papers, are there?'

'You mean private papers? Nothing at all. He must have kept all that sort of thing on him. Or else he kept it somewhere else. There was nothing – nothing personal about at all, if you know what I mean. There were odd things in the drawers, of course, but nothing to show. And it was always very clean and tidy. It didn't look lived in at all really. You could go in there when he wasn't there, and you'd think it was an empty flat.'

Margaret and Garrod looked at each other and made a movement towards the door. 'Well, thank you again,' said Garrod. 'It's been very helpful indeed. We'd better try Barton Woods, I think. If he's there, or if we get a line on him, shall I let you know?'

'Yes please. You know where I can be found. I haven't asked your names.'

'They wouldn't mean anything to you if we told you. We're only ordinary people who got involved by chance.'

'Separately or together?'

'Separately, in the first instance. Now we're hunting in couples.'

'Yes,' said Mrs Campbell, 'I can see that. That's one good thing Mr Utley's done, anyhow.'

'Yes,' said Garrod, 'it is, isn't it?'

She conducted them tentatively to the front door and opened it for them. It shut the moment they were outside it. No one hung about the steps waiting to see them go. The semi-basement windows, blinded with white curtains, looked up blankly at the railings.

'What an odd place,' said Margaret.

'What an odd woman. Very intelligent indeed, and not ill-disposed, but sort of ironically detached. It's her physical trouble, don't you think? A sort of enforced passivity she has schooled herself to accept. I don't know what the trouble is – something nervous, I imagine. But the mental attitude is very striking. I liked her, didn't you?'

'You took to each other, didn't you? I saw it happen. Oh well – so long as it's only the Mrs Campbells.'

'Oh, it's not, indeed. My charm is universally acknow-ledged.'

'Well, turn it down for a bit. It's wasted on me. What are we going to do now? Try Barton Woods straight away? What sort of a place is it, do you know?'

'Between-wars development, I think. Rows of little houses with fancy names, but all exactly alike. This was before the days of artistic town-planning.'

'Yes. Milton Road. Nowadays they'd dig up an old field name and call it Jordan's End or Pargeter's Piece or something. I bet 23 is called Alaska or The Firs.'

'Bah. None of your intellectual snobbery. Let's go and see for ourselves.'

CHAPTER SEVENTEEN

'Milton, thou shouldst be living at this hour,' said Margaret; 'what number have we got to?'

'Two-hundred-and-thirty-nine on our right now,' said Garrod, 'and we came in at the top. Two-hundred-and-thirty-five is not two-hundred-and-thirty-five, but Elmhurst, and it has a red door, which I find faintly shocking. There are brave spirits in Elmhurst that will not be confined. Is this really worse than the old-fashioned slum, or is it only intellectual snobbery to think so?'

'Not worse in itself, obviously. The danger is in complacency. No one is content in a slum. To be content with this is just possible, I imagine, and that would be to be damned indeed. Are we looking for a clean-shaven man called John Utley, do you think, or a bearded man called Sir James Utley?'

'Or a clean-shaven man calling himself John Jones, or a bearded man calling himself John Utley, or any other combination? A hundred-and-thirty-five, and still they come. Let's stop a moment and consider this.' He pulled the car in to the pavement between an ornamental lamp-post and an appallingly mutilated elm-bole, stripped of everything but a sporadic rash of twigs. 'This is the last elm in the hurst. If we had any regard for propriety at all, we should go down on our knees to it and ask its forgiveness for what it has seen and suffered. I'm not certain, but I think we must be looking for John Utley, though whether bearded or shaven I can't say. The Campbell wouldn't tell us how she had got this address, but she said Johnnie "used it." She probably saw a letter addressed to him there or something. But it must have been to John Utley, or it wouldn't have meant anything to her. John Jones of Milton Road might be anyone. John Utley of Milton Road is his mysterious tenant in another guise, and her curiosity would be roused enough for her to remember the address.'

'But she has tried the address and had no reply.'

129

'No more may we. But we may as well try, and I think we can only try for a John Utley.' He started the car again. 'As a matter of fact, it might be better to start next door, as it were in a spirit of innocent enquiry. Don't tell me that in a road like this one doesn't know the neighbours. Which are our best informants – twenty-one and twenty-five, who hear things, but see only the garden and the milk-bottles, or twenty-two and twenty-four across the way, who can't hear much, but can look straight into front windows and see who comes to the door?'

'Start across the way and let them direct us to the right side of the road. We can still cross the road and hit twenty-one instead of twenty-three. But if we start at twenty-one, it is difficult to misunderstand them so grossly as to cross over to twenty-four.'

'Quite right. You are naturally fit for treasons, stratagems and spoils. I have noticed it before, and with some misgiving. It's me that can't deceive a two-year-old.'

'Never mind. Your capacity for self-deception is bottom-less, and that's half the battle. There is thirty coming up on our left. Slow down a bit and make the car look puzzled, as if it was groping its way through a forest of uncertainty.'

'How you grandiloquise. A forest of uncertainty. But there – I slow down, as you say. I hesitate. I wonder if – no, let's try further down. I cannot see the hurst for the elms.' The car wandered uncertainly to a halt outside twenty-four and Garrod got out and looked about him. Twenty-four was called Deepdene. The lace of its curtains was white but opaque. Followed by Margaret, he pushed open the little gate and walked hesitantly up the path. There were no signs of life, but somewhere at the back they could hear the steady throb of dance music. The bell-push woke a peal of muted bells inside the front door, but he wondered whether this could compete with the more vibrant stuff that filled the kitchen. Then a door opened at the back of the house, bringing the sound of revelry nearer. A moment later a face appeared inside the door, and Garrod and the face peered at each other through the distorting filter of the leaded glasswork at the top. The fact that this was embarrassing and unsatisfactory seemed to occur to both simultaneously, and both faces bobbed back to a safer distance. Then the door opened briskly and she said, 'Oh, I'm sorry. Were you ringing? I didn't hear.'

She was overalled and her head was swathed in a working turban of parti-coloured silk. The effect was neat and gay, but not glamorous. The music was much louder now, and Garrod had to raise his voice above it. He said, 'I'm awfully sorry to worry you, but can you tell me if a Mr Utley lives round here?' I think it's in this road towards this end, but I haven't got the number.'

She said, 'Utley? Just a minute.' She turned and slopped off down the hall. Her slippers had been trodden right down at the heel and spoiled the overall and turban. The music dipped suddenly to a tuneless rhythm, leaving a hitherto unnoticed background of moving domestic machinery.

A child's head spoke up suddenly round the top banister. It said, 'I'm ill in bed.'

'Are you?' said Garrod. 'Bad luck.'

'My dolly's ill in bed too.'

'I expect she caught it from you.'

'Yes. I've got spots almost all over. I'm very infectious.'

A waft of warm stuffy air streamed out of the open door, and Garrod found himself shutting his mouth and breathing resolutely through his nose. The mother reappeared and said, 'Get back to bed, Nina' in a hopeless, perfunctory sort of way that neither she nor Nina expected to have the slightest effect. 'I'm awfully sorry,' she said, 'I had to turn the washer off. Who was it you wanted?'

'A Mr Utley. We were told he lives in this road, towards this end, but we haven't got a number. John Utley, it is.'

She reflected. The child's head slid slowly down the banister to the level of the top stair and stayed there, detached and silent. The music checked and then broke out again in a wilder rhythm. Finally she said, 'There's a Mrs Utley.'

'Oh well, if there's a Mrs Utley, there must be a Mr Utley, surely.'

She seemed doubtful of this, as if the marriage laws had been suspended in Barton Woods. 'I don't know, I'm sure. You could ask. Mrs Utley lives across the road there. The house with the green door. Oakdene, they call it.'

'Not the Firs?' said Margaret.

'Not that one, no. The Firs is two doors along. Of course, they're all numbered.'

'Do you know where there is a house called—'

'Well, thanks very much,' said Garrod. 'You've been most helpful. Sorry to have worried you.'

'Alaska,' said Margaret.

'Alaska?'

'A house called Alaska.'

'No, I haven't seen one. Not in this road, anyhow. That may be in the next road.'

'Shakespeare Road?' said Garrod.

'No, Marlowe Road, that is.'

'But there is a house called Alaska?' said Margaret.

'I really couldn't say, I'm afraid. I don't think I've seen it.'

'Never mind,' said Garrod, taking Margaret firmly by the arm and pushing her towards the gate, 'thank you very much indeed.' The door shut, and a moment later a solo trumpet soared magnificently from the back kitchen.

'How deep was my dene,' said Garrod. 'But you and your ridiculous questions – Alaska, indeed,'

'You're only angry because you got Shakespeare wrong. Marlowe left you standing.'

'Well, it is a bit advanced, isn't it? Some literary Councillor on the Highways Committee in the early 'twenties. There is probably a dual carriageway called Beaumont and Fletcher. Let's leave the car here.'

They crossed the road and, ignoring the Oakdene on the gate of twenty-three, plunged boldly into twenty-one. Garrod looked back over his shoulder. Nina's head had transferred itself to the first floor front. 'She is even now calling out to her mother that we have gone into the wrong house,' he said. 'Blow, trumpet, blow. Make her work for her triumph. I don't think the mother will come after us. Oh, I beg your pardon.'

Twenty-one was standing in his open doorway watching them critically. He had a fuzz of mouse-grey hair brushed up all round a shining dome of scalp. He wore a cardigan instead of a pull-over and pince-nez instead of horn rims. Hardly checking in his stride, Garrod thrust out a hand and advanced on him cordially. 'Mr Utley?' he said.

He did not appear to move at all. He did not put his hands

behind his back, but his right hand remained suspended in front of him, just below the waist-band of his trousers. Garrod looked at it, hesitated and let his own drop. He continued to advance and twenty-one still stood on his doorstep. They finished face to face, motionless and silent. With admirable tenacity Garrod smiled genially into the colourless eyes and said, 'It is Mr Utley, isn't it?'

Twenty-one shook his head. 'My name's Webb-Partington,' he said.

'Oh I say, I'm awfully sorry. They told me across the road this was Mr Utley's house, and I'm afraid I assumed you were the owner.'

'I am the owner. My name's Webb-Partington, not Utley. Did you see the child?'

'The child?'

'Nina,' suggested Margaret.

Mr Webb-Partington nodded, waving his halo of hair like a sea-anemone in tidal waters. 'What's the trouble, do you think? Come, come, you can't deceive me. That's what you've come about, isn't it?'

'Well—'

'All right, all right. I'll respect your discretion. But if you want my opinion it's small-pox.'

'Mr Webb-Partington,' said Garrod with immense seriousness, 'this may be most valuable information you have given us. The matter must be reported immediately. You are yourself in no doubt?'

He shook his head with equal gravity. 'Very little, I am afraid. I have been keeping her under constant observation and have a complete case-history which I have compared with the authorities. You may care to see my notes.'

'Not for the moment, Mr Webb-Partington, though I shall certainly have to ask you to place them at the disposal of the Authority.' A light of transcendent happiness spread slowly over Mr Webb-Partington's face, and he giggled slightly. 'But for the moment you will appreciate that immediate action is imperative. Now will you complete your willing help by telling me which Mr Utley's house is.'

'Trouble spread there, has it? Could well be. The children play together.' He beamed on them in pure benevolence. 'That's next door, number twenty-three. You won't find Mr

Utley there, though. Haven't seen him for some time. But he's never there much at the best of times. But you'll find Mrs Utley – er, ready to help. I'm sure. Charming woman, as a matter of fact.' He passed his body hand back over his scalp, smoothing down the grey tufts, which stood up again soft but persistent behind the moving fingers.

Garrod said, 'Mr Utley, now. Small, dark man, isn't he, quietly dressed, clean-shaven?'

'That's the man. He is a great deal away – I suppose his business detains him – but too much for an intelligent, companionable woman like Mrs Utley. She gets lonely, you know. And the money's pretty short, too. I can tell that. It's not fair on her. I do what I can to help. I'm a bachelor, of course, and not pushed for cash.' He passed his hand over his head again, and Garrod had a dreadful feeling that he was going to lick his lips.

Garrod nodded hastily. 'I won't worry her more than I can help,' he said. 'Thank you very much, Mr Webb-Partington. You will of course be hearing from the Authority very shortly.'

They went to the gate. Margaret said, 'These observations of yours, Mr Webb-Partington—'

He nodded his head towards the upper window, where the edge of a gauze curtain barely concealed the object-glass of a sporting telescope. 'Ah yes, I see. Excellent. Good-bye then, for the present.' He saw them to the gate and walked back to his front door springing slightly at each step on the ball of his foot, as though he trod on air.

Garrod rang the bell of number twenty-three. 'Mrs Utley?' he said. Then, sensing rather than seeing a disturbance in the side-window of twenty-one, he said, 'May we come in? This is my assistant, Miss Harbottle.'

She was a pale, wary woman, above the average height and carrying no weight at all. She looked from one to the other, puzzling over Margaret as the little man in Thistleton Gardens had puzzled over her. Then she let it go and spoke to Garrod. 'Where is he?' she said. 'Do you know?'

'We were hoping you could tell us that.'

'You're not the police, are you?'

'No.'

'Then what do you want him for?'

'We think he may be able to help us—'

'In your enquiries. I know. That's what they always say. You even see it in the papers when they are after someone. But you're not the police. I didn't think you were, anyhow. So what's going on?'

'Mrs Utley—'

'That's nice of you, but please don't bother. My name is Chennell, as I expect you know – Martha Chennell. Johnnie and I never married in our lives, and I can't see us changing our minds now. Do you know the police have never come here? I've been waiting for them, of course, and just recently almost hoping they'd come. But I'd like to know how you got here.'

'From Thistleton Gardens. Mrs Campbell knew. I think she'd seen a letter.'

'Prying old bitch. She wrote here asking for her rent. She's got a hope. But she shouldn't have told you. If she did that, she'd tell anyone.'

'As a matter of fact,' said Garrod, 'I don't think she would. That's only my guess, of course, but I think she told us just because she knew we weren't the police.'

'You still haven't said what you are.'

'We're' – he spread his hands – 'we're nothing. Just ordinary people. We got mixed up in something by mistake and want to get to the bottom of it.'

'If I believe that, by God there aren't many that would.'

'I don't think it makes all that difference whether you believe it or not. We're not working against you, nor for the matter of that particularly for you. We're working for ourselves. But it may help everybody to get everything cleared up.'

She said, 'Come into the kitchen. The children are at school.'

The kitchen was poky but not at all unpleasant. It was orderly, and they felt that the children would get home to a substantial tea. They pulled out chairs and sat round the table. Garrod said, 'When did Johnnie last go to Lodstone?'

'Go where?'

'Lodstone.'

'Never heard of it.'

'Well then, when did he last see anything of his brother, Sir James Utley?'

'To my knowledge, not for several years. But I've sometimes wondered whether he hasn't seen something of him fairly recently. He hasn't said so. But he doesn't tell me everything, of course. Only he's been a lot more interested in him during the past year or so. Used to watch him on T.V. and be sarcastic about him. He seemed to be working up a hate against him for some reason or other. I think – I thought – I don't know, but I got the idea he was hoping to get him to help him again with money. He used to, you know, and then there was some row and it stopped. And there've been times when we could have done with it, I can tell you. Then a few months back he started talking as if things were going to improve. Nothing very definite, but I'm pretty certain he had it in mind that there'd be a bit more coming in. He never said it was anything to do with Sir James, but I got the impression it was. You know how one does that? He'd mention Sir James, and then the next moment he'd talk about this – this idea he had, whatever it was, and I got the impression that one had reminded him of the other. But there was never anything more definite than that.'

'Have you ever seen him get himself up with a beard to look like Sir James?'

'Not for years. He doesn't look like him so much now, you know. He used to, of course, but things have changed him – it would change anyone, what he's been through. They don't look half so much alike now.'

'Do you mind telling me when you last saw him?'

'Not for – oh, months now. Mind you, he's always been away off and on, even when he wasn't in trouble. But I don't think ever quite so long as this. I thought perhaps he was in trouble again, but there's generally those who would let me know – only I'm not quite certain whether they'd know where to find me here. I've seen nothing in the papers, but it wouldn't necessarily be in.'

'Have you been here long?'

'About three years. But as I said, nobody knows of it much, not even the police, I don't think. He's never been in trouble since we came here.'

'What does he live on?'

She shook her head. 'Next question, I don't mind who the hell you are.'

'How have you been managing since he left?'

She shook her head again. 'Not that either.'

'Why did he have those rooms at Thistleton Gardens? They were quite expensive.'

'He needed them to work from. He wouldn't work from here. There's the children and all, you see. He liked to be able to get here without his – his work following him.'

Garrod got up. 'Mrs Utley – oh, all right, Miss Chennell, if you prefer it – you really don't know where Johnnie is now at all?'

'No. I don't know at all. He'll be back presently – he always is.'

'If we find out anything, do you want us to let you know?'

'Nothing Johnnie wouldn't tell me himself.'

'All right. Nothing he wouldn't tell you himself. I mean, supposing he was in trouble again and couldn't manage to let you know – that sort of thing?'

'Yes, I'd want to know that, certainly. You must go now. The children will be back any minute and I'm no good at explaining things to them. They always know.'

They went back to the car, followed every inch of the way by Twenty-one.

CHAPTER EIGHTEEN

'I'm tired,' said Margaret, 'and I'm a bit depressed. Do you think we could possibly go out into the country for a meal before we go home?'

He nodded. 'I'll keep driving in the right direction. There must be an end to this somewhere. Then we can stop and look about us.'

Presently she said, 'Is that what we're all heading for? It terrifies me.'

'Martha Chennell?'

'Martha Chennell. Johnnie will come home. Johnnie always comes home. It's only a matter of keeping going, somehow, till he does.'

' "Thou needst must come back to the heart's place here I keep for thee." That sort of thing?'

'That? That's nothing. All Browning had in mind was a gormless but devoted little woman ready to forgive what little she understood and in the meantime living quietly on a small income from Consols helped out by a little sewing. Martha knows everything. She knows Johnnie's vermin. She has no pretensions of any sort, either for him or for herself. She'll even take money from that horrible little loony next door. It's all stripped right down to the bone, and the bone, when you come to it, has a sort of dreadful integrity. And they're not even married.'

'What do you suppose you would do if I came in one day and said, "I have decided to resign my fellowship in order to better myself. I am setting up as a small blackmailer, but the prospects are good. I am sure, if you will only stand by me, that we cannot fail to find success and happiness"?'

'I can't answer that. It's not only hypothetical – it's non-sense. I mean – what I should do at the moment, of course, is simply disbelieve you. If you were suddenly arrested and convicted on irrefutable evidence of something ghastly, I should nearly go round the bend, of course, but it wouldn't be all direct personal loss. It would be to quite a large extent intellectual shock, like discovering that the Odyssey was written by a mediaeval monk or that the *Mayflower* sank in mid-Atlantic. Exactly what degree of moral turpitude, God bless the phrase, you would have to confess to to make me wash you right out of my hair, I can't say. If you had been blowing safes, I might feel, if anything, rather pleasantly excited. If you had been defrauding the widow and orphan or molesting little girls, I might well have doubts. If you had been selling your country's secrets to the enemy, I should phone Scotland Yard at once and come and jeer at you in the dock. I wonder where one gets one's scale of values? But that's not the point, I don't think. We haven't been married, or as good as, for years. I should still be able to admit doubts and make a decision. But not Martha. Martha's committed to an absolute loyalty. The fact that he's a rat and she's a tart is irrelevant. That's what I meant when I said is this what we're all coming to. How can you decide whether to commit yourself when the commitment is apparently progessive? It's like borrowing at an unknown rate of compound interest.'

'I'm not at all sure about this, but I should say it's either a conscious act of faith or an act of passive acceptance, like being born in the first instance. Nine times out of ten it just happens. You think too much.'

'I'm tired. Let's not talk for a bit.'

It seemed unreasonable of him, when she was so tired, to insist on what he called a reconstruction of the crime. 'He can't still be there,' she kept on saying, and indeed she was fairly certain she knew where he was, only for the moment she couldn't be clear about this. There were men with guns walking with elaborate unconcern across the fields on either side of them, but Garrod seemed able to duck out of their sight and made her do the same. There were engine noises that might have been tractors behind the hedges. She could not see what was making them. A dog barked frighteningly across the fields behind them, but she knew, because Garrod had told her, that it was shut in an empty house. They hurried on towards an objective she did not want to reach, though sometimes she could hardly lift her feet over the crumbling, tenacious furrows. If he would only carry her over the plough, she would feel less frightened, but he went steadily ahead and did not look to see how she was getting on. He said, 'There's Lodstone,' and she saw the village down in the valley, a jumble of roofs with smoke coming slowly up from the chimneys. It didn't look like Lodstone, but if this was the way he wanted to reconstruct the crime, she supposed it was all right; and it was a nice village, less frightening than Lodstone. Where their track crossed the farm road, she looked along the bank but could see nothing. 'It was here,' she kept saying to him, almost crying because he did not seem to believe her, 'it was just here.'

They turned and walked over to the bank and she saw someone sitting there. She could not see clearly at first, but when they got closer, she found it was a small, dark, smiling woman in a silk frock. Her mouth had a little smile on it and her eyes stared straight into Margaret's, challenging her to share a joke which she could not explain because she had been too long dead. There was something missing, Margaret knew, and then she remembered and looked down at the small woman's feet. There were two sleek, black objects there, and she found they were cats, crouched comfortably against the silk skirt, but quite cold and stiff. Then a tractor engine roared suddenly behind the hedge, and Garrod said 'Run!' She tried to run, but could not move her legs. She clutched at him, and found herself staring with sick relief at the dashboard lights. The engine roared once more and stopped. The car was still.

He turned and looked down at her, smiling. 'You've been asleep,' he said. His arm, free of the steering, came comfortingly round her. 'Jacob,' said Margaret, 'oh Jacob.'

'What's the trouble?'

'It was a dream. Don't talk to me for a moment. I must go back over it.' She shut her eyes again, and he waited, motionless and silent. She went over the dream in her mind and then followed the events of the day, remembering what everyone had said in their scattered and fugitive conversations. Then she sat up. They were on a dark empty road, but she could see in the driving mirror the lights and sign of an inn fifty yards behind them. She said, 'When did you first see that the body was Johnnie's?'

'I still don't know for certain. In fact, I've really no evidence at all. Only from what you say the body might have looked about right, Johnnie's obviously mixed up in the Lodstone business and on today's evidence he hasn't been seen since before May Day. But it only looks like it – I don't know.'

'I do. I saw him, and I know. Of course, I saw him before we knew he existed, and when you discover a person's existence, it doesn't easily occur to you that he may already be dead. But it was the likeness, you see? When I saw Sir James on television I felt his face was vaguely familiar, and then when I saw the photo of his mother, the obvious likeness between her and Sir James somehow satisfied me. I felt, "Aha, the family look" – it is a look, you see, particularly about the mouth and eyes, rather than anything in the features – and I somehow overlooked the fact that Sir James's face had rung a faint bell before even I saw the mother's photo. The odd thing is that I saw Sir James asleep in your car almost within minutes of seeing Johnnie's body, and there was no likeness at all. There was the beard and the scar, of course, and his eyes were shut. But mainly because he was asleep – I'm sure of that. The sleeping man was merely a blank. The dead man looked very much alive. It was when I saw Sir James on television that I felt the jolt, but by then the connection was too difficult to make. It was the mother's face that formed the link. It did remind me of Sir James, but what it really reminded me of was Johnnie's face on May Morning. But it took a dream to prise it out of my subconscious. Poor Martha.'

'There's always the little man in Thisleton Gardens and his fellow victims. I think Martha can look after herself. Look, there's quite a nice-looking pub back there. Let's go and eat, and then we can talk things over.'

'There's only one thing that worries me still,' he said later. 'This business of false beards. There has been some masquerading at some point – Johnnie masquerading as Sir James, that is. That's no longer a complication, is it?'

'Not possibly, no – so long as we assume that Sir James's scar is genuine. The body had no scar. If Sir James's scar won't come off, the body was Johnnie's. Even apart from that, Sir James had been very much in evidence since May Day. Johnnie might be able to impersonate him on the isolated occasion, but he could not take over his public role, archaeology and all. No. It's Johnnie under the concrete at Straightways, if that's where he is.'

'Which doesn't look very good for Sir James.'

'I don't think it does. I remember two things people have said to me during this business, one about Sir James and one about Johnnie. My grandmother said that Sir James might be unexpectedly ruthless in defending the position he had built up for himself. And then later Charlie Mayne said that people like Johnnie never used violence, but often suffered it in the end, and generally asked for it. You see what it rather adds up to, especially if you accept Martha's account of Johnnie's hopes of touching Sir James for a further contribution?'

'Yes. Yes, I do indeed. Johnnie, the one-time confidant, gradually going adrift, despite a good deal of rescue work by the successful Jimmie. Then a complete break, with Johnnie finally shouldered out of the way while Jimmie becomes Sir James, with everything handsome about him. Then Johnnie, on his way down the slide, comes to see how much people will pay for a little discretion. Finally and fatally, he decides to try this on successful brother Jimmie. Whether it was something he knew from the old days, or whether he got hold of something new, we can't say. That may have been where the false beard came in. There is nothing more revealing about a person than to be mistaken for him. Whatever it was, Johnnie tries the touch on Sir James, knowing very well – but still not quite well enough – how much his new-found position means to him. But he has mistaken his man. The brilliant and successful Sir James is a different proposition from the easy-going big brother who indulged him so long before he finally pushed him aside. So instead of a bit more for the Oakdene housekeeping, Johnnie gets what looks like a hole in his chest and a load of concrete on top of him to make all fast. But where the devil Valance and his lot come in, not to speak of Police Constable Robin, I'm damned if I know. Johnnie may have gone to Lodstone on Sir James's trail, but we still don't know what took Sir James there at all. We know he went there privily, using the Stancote cottage as a covered approach. We know he was there on two particular occasions. But we don't know why.'

'There is one thing, though. Don't you think that whatever Johnnie had got hold of about Sir James, the secret lay at Lodstone? As you say, Sir James kept his visits there pretty dark. And whatever happened in the end, it looks as if Johnnie was killed when he followed him there. My own bet is that once we know what took Sir James to Lodstone, we'll know what Johnnie had on him and why he got killed. The rest of the story, in fact.'

'You're very probably right. So the hunt comes round full circle to its original starting point.'

'And in the meantime it's term again in three days' time and I start my final year.'

'Lor, so you do. You'll have to work this year.'

'I always do work. My grandmother's only expressed apprehension about you was that you might interfere with my work, but I assured her it was all right.'

'You are too ready with your assurances. And the trouble is, I think you mean them. I sometimes wonder whether I have done more than ruffle the surface of your serenity. Not that I want to make you less serene,' he said quickly, 'but I'd like to feel I had made a lasting impression. Now let's for home. We have done a lot today.'

They were nearly into London again when he said, 'You've still got no regrets.'

'About what?'

'Well – anything to do with me, of course. But what I actually meant was what we've done in this business – and what we haven't done. I mean – supposing we are right in our general thesis that Johnnie was a blackmailer, and tried to blackmail Sir James and got bumped off for his pains – is there anything here to make you wish that you'd raised the roof on May Day and had the whole thing out in the open?'

'No. No, there isn't, on what we know or suppose so far. You remember you were asking this afternoon what you'd have to do to make me reject you completely? Well, getting rid of a blackmailer definitely wouldn't qualify. I'd much rather you didn't – I'd much rather not have anything under our concrete. It would be too much for my peace of mind. But it wouldn't make any real difference to my feelings for you. Mind you, there'd be your guilty secret to be taken into account too. I suppose it could be that what the blackmailer knew about you was something I couldn't myself stomach. I suppose then for you to bump him off might make it worse, not better. But if I already knew and had accepted your secret, I'd back you all the way in your efforts to keep it. And that being so, I'm not bursting to send anybody down for getting rid of Johnnie Utley. I'm sorry for his Martha, but her Johnnie's dead anyway. The only thing that could possibly make me change my view would be what I said just now – if Sir James's secret was something I felt justified no defence. I'm very doubtful of the rights and wrongs even there, but I know it might in fact change my attitude to Johnnie's death. Only it would have to be something in Sir James that I could not myself in any circumstances forgive.'

'Which I myself find hard to believe. Don't you agree?'

'Yes, I think I do. The more I have learnt about Sir James, the better, on the whole, I like him. I still think his T.V. personality is pretty spurious, but aren't they all? And I've had the feeling, ever since I went to Banstead, that whoever eyes he is pulling wool over, he isn't pulling it over his own. I think he is consciously and deliberately taking the great dumb public for a ride and enjoying every moment of it, and I rather warm to that. And there's his mother. My namesake, Meg. I rather fell in love with her. Of course, she was Johnnie's mother too, but I know which her favourite was. They couldn't stand Meg in Banstead, but they all liked Johnnie. Not me. I'm all for the Somerset mystery, as dark and quiet as a mole, she was (Margaret's voice suddenly and startlingly echoed Aunty's) against all the blond extrovert Utleys. And if Jimmie was her choice, he's mine, whatever he's done to Johnnie.'

'Good. I'm very glad you feel like that. For what its worth, our consciences are still clear, subjected always to further information on what Sir James did at Lodstone.'

'Yes. What's the next step then?'

'You're still in the hunt?'

'Oh yes. Our hypothesis may satisfy our consciences, but it remains a hypothesis, after all. We still haven't got the whole truth.'

'Glory be, what a woman. You frighten me at times. But I've said that before.'

'Yes, you seem to live in a state of perpetual terror. But what I say is nothing new, surely? We think we know who the body was, but we know precious little else. And we agreed to find out.'

'Yes, all right. So we turn back to Lodstone.'

'There are two people we can profitably go to again, I think – or rather, I can. One is Charlie Mayne. The other is my grandmother. Charlie Mayne told me she knew far more about Lodstone – and especially Lodstone under the surface – than he did, and strongly advised me to put the thing to her. You know why I haven't up to now. But I think we've reached a point now where I might. I might have another go at the vicar, too, but I doubt if there's much to be gained there.'

'All right. We've both plenty to do, and it seems to me that if anything time is on our side. What we know cannot be undone, and the longer we seem to do nothing, the easier it may be to act when we want to. So back to Oxford for the present. And then, when we're ready, back to Lodstone. Agreed?'

'Aye, aye, sir.'

They picked their way back into autumnal London.

Chapter Nineteen

'Your father used to say that for him Oxford was always in mid-October. It is the freshman's vision, of course – golden, but damp and rather aloof. In those days the early mornings smelt of kindling and coal-smoke. Now I suppose it is all gas-fires or central heating. But I don't imagine that matters.'

'I think it is certainly one of the two great times. It's a bit solemn to think this is the last Michaelmas Term I shall see from the inside. The other great time is the end of the summer term and Commem. What that must be like the last time round, with schools over and nothing ahead, I can't bear to think. But there's plenty to do before then, heaven knows.'

'I formed the impression before you went back that of your twin distractions one at least was in abeyance. I don't know about Mr. Garrod.'

'He's in abeyance too, in a sense. So far as the Lodstone business is concerned, we have reached a certain stage and are in no hurry to go further. We think we know, in general, what happened and who was involved. We don't altogether know why. But what we know at least satisfies us that there is no hurry about knowing the rest – though we still feel we want to know it some time. Charlie Mayne said that he knew what went on on the surface in Lodstone, but never really knew what went on underneath. He said you'd know a lot more about that than he would.'

'Yes, I must say, that on the whole agrees with my impressions both of Charlie Mayne and of Lodstone.'

'Grandmother – what is this under-the-surface business at Lodstone? The vicar in a distraught moment spoke of some sort of evil influence at work; but I thought he either didn't know much about it or rather avoided facing it.'

'You haven't told me the surface events of your particular case. I don't think you can expect me to offer a diagnosis without describing the symptoms.'

146

'Well, here's one set of events. There was a young man who opened a wireless and television shop in the village and had a row with one of the farmers, who refused to pay him for a job he had done. The young man threatened to sue the farmer. He seemed to have the right on his side, but everyone told him not to go on with it. The vicar gave him the same advice, if for no other reason, as a matter of Christianity. Whether he was going to accept it, I don't know; but in that tremendous storm we had over the Bank Holiday week-end his shop was apparently struck by lightning and was certainly burnt to ashes. He wasn't fully covered and it broke him. At any rate, he cleared out of Lodstone. The whole thing could be a coincidence, but it didn't feel like one.'

'This farmer he had his row with – he was a local man?'

'Yes. He farms in the village.'

'A Belling, a Stallard, a Valance or a Marston?'

'Oh grandmother. Yes, a Valance.'

'This storm when the shop was burnt – when was it exactly?'

'It was on the Saturday night. The Bank Holiday was on the second. The Saturday would have been the 31st of July.'

'It would indeed. Now – there was some incident on May Day, Were the two connected?'

'We haven't found a logical connection. But they had elements – and people – in common.'

'The time you stayed at the vicarage, you said Mrs Besson couldn't have you. Why was that?'

'I told you – I didn't warn her and she was booked up.'

'You think she really was?'

'Not now, no. I think she had been warned off having me. This was after the May Day business, of course. She was afraid of something. I tried to reassure her, but not very successfully.'

'And her cottage wasn't burnt.'

'Oh no. Do you think it would have been?'

'This May Day incident. Can you tell me more about that? You were not directly involved yourself?'

'No. By a very unlikely chance I came on – evidence that what looked like a crime had been committed. But then the evidence vanished and I found myself in a conspiracy of silence.'

'This suspected crime would have occurred the night before? You found evidence of it on May Morning?'

'That's right.'

'Yes,' said Mrs Canting, 'yes. Now – what do you want me to say?'

'I want you to tell me for a start why the farmer who had the row with Jack Simmons would have been a member of one of those four families.'

'Because it was never safe to quarrel with any of them, and apparently still isn't.'

'Do you mean they are organised in some way to circumvent the law and keep things in their own hands?'

'You must understand, Margaret, that I have no complete or proven knowledge of anything. I heard things, scraps of things, over the course of years in Lodstone. But they were mostly on topics which, in my day, a girl could not show curiosity about or even, in some cases, admit she understood. I have my own beliefs on the general nature of the underlying explanation. I have nothing definite and no solid evidence. Yes, I should say there was an organisation in which members of these families, among others, were involved. It would not be primarily a criminal one. That is to say, it would not be a sort of gang whose sole purpose was to defeat the law. But it would consider itself outside the law. It would claim the right to settle things its own way, and would certainly not hesitate to ignore the requirements of law in doing so. But secrecy would be of its essence. Any open clash would be avoided at all costs.'

'This would be the vicar's source of evil?'

'Yes, undoubtedly. I don't know what knowledge he would have of it. But he has clearly apprehended its presence. I don't know Mr Claydon, of course.'

'Who else would be associated with it, apart from the four families?'

'Many of the village people, I think, would be aware of it. Some would be actively associated with it. A great many more would be subject to its influence in varying degrees – Mrs Besson, for instance. I think there would be a central figure, probably not one of the four families I mentioned. One of the bogeys of my childhood was a farm-bailiff, an enormous black-browed man, who lived in a cottage on the Ebury road.'

'Was his name Robin?'

'No. No, it wasn't, but I find the suggestion a very interesting one. Is there a Robin in the present scheme of things?'

'There is an enormous red-faced man called Robin, who is, of all things, the village constable. He does seem to lie at the heart of our mystery.'

'The constable? That has something admirable in it.'

Margaret said, 'You seem amused rather than distressed. I get the impression that this organisation, whatever it is, is not wholly repugnant to you.'

Mrs Canting spread her hands towards the tea-time fire and looked long between them. 'I think – I'm afraid I cannot deny a great deal of what Sir James Utley and his like would no doubt call ambivalence over this. I offer no defence for this thing. But I cannot consciously wish it out of existence. It is like fox-hunting or the English winter: I avoid it as far as possible, but I would not subscribe to its destruction, unless this was forced on me. But what in fact amused me was the thought of Charlie Mayne, working away busily on the surface of events at Lodstone, and even aware of something below the surface, but unaware of his own local constable as the opposite pole of influence.'

'To do Charlie Mayne justice, I don't think he was wholly unaware. He prided himself to some extent, you know, on not going too deep. But he saw Constable Robin's hand in a good many things he did not choose to enquire into – or at least, that was the impression I got.'

'That is possible, certainly. Charlie is extremely shrewd, and his shrewdness would extend to a knowledge of his own limitations.'

'I'm sure it does. I know I was very much impressed by the fact that a great deal of what you told me about his limitations as a source of information was virtually repeated to me by Charlie himself. No, I think he knew Constable Robin was something a bit unusual, but decided to let alone as far as possible. And of course it was for Robin to see that it remained possible for him to let alone. Can you tell me anything more?'

'I could tell you a good many stories like your story of the television shop, which I must say brings the whole thing very nicely up to date. But it would not be much more than to multiply instances. One common factor I have already given you – the involvement of members of those four farming families.'

'Is this purely a Lodstone affair?'

'I should say that this – this particular manifestation centres on Lodstone though it probably spreads to some extent outside it. The thing itself is not, I suppose, peculiar to Lodstone.'

'You spoke of the four families as being one factor common to a number of incidents. Would there be others?'

'You would find, if you could establish the facts (which of course you cannot now do), a recurrence of certain dates – at any rate, some recurring dates.'

'May Day, for one?'

'Yes. You would not know, of course, but I was told that in my grandfather's day, and even in my father's, the Lodstone May Days were notorious. Those were the days of course, of maypoles and all the other celebrations. Half the children in the parish, whether undisguisedly illegitimate or at least ostensibly legitimate, used to be born around the beginning of February. In my day, of course, a sterner public opinion had prevailed and things had quietened down. But, sheltered as I was and ignorant as I was supposed to be, I remember catching hints that the old licence was not wholly dead. I remember an expression I still don't know the real meaning of, but it stuck in my head in the way these mysterious excitements do. When a village girl had got into trouble, they used to shake their heads and say she had gone the round. I always associated it with the maypole dances, but I don't know why or with what justification.

'There was another expression, too, or a set of expressions, which I'm even less clear about, but they all involved a way – some special way. Phrases like "going the way" or "walking the way" clearly had some special significance, not merely what a little modern chit would mean by "going the whole way." To have gone the way was something irredeemably shocking, for a man or a girl. I remember thinking it was vaguely biblical, the broad way as opposed to the straight and narrow, the primrose path; but in fact I think it was something more definite than this. It was a thing that once done couldn't be undone, not a continuing course of action. But I still don't know what it was.'

'And this was all part of the same thing, was it – this and the private vengeance organisation?'

'I associated them certainly. In my day we were all respectable and God-fearing, but there was always a suggestion of the ungodly in our midst, who were unspeakable in every way, but whom it was safer to ignore than to oppose. Even when I was a girl, you know, a village like Lodstone could seem very remote and isolated, especially in winter. You have no idea, now – you don't even remember the black-out, which revived the memory for many people – how dark the country was in the long winter months. The daylight was so short and grudging and the darkness so absolute and so impenetrable. I think a sense of evil came much more naturally to one in those circumstances than it ever can now. The hosts of darkness did not need much of a build-up. You could feel them, as in the hymn, prowling and prowling around.'

She shivered suddenly and leant closer to the fire. 'You still haven't told me the whole story of your case,' she said, 'and I suppose you still don't want to. But if the thing itself – this crime you say you found evidence of – if that's fairly serious, and these people are involved, I think you ought to be very careful, particularly when you are at Lodstone – that's if you do go there again. I'd much rather you didn't.'

'I think very likely I shan't. But there's one thing I've promised to tell you, which may reassure you a bit. Charlie Mayne made me promise that I would never go to Lodstone without letting him know in advance that I was going. And he made me promise to tell you that I had made this promise.'

'Thank you. Dear Charlie. Yes, I must say I am glad of that assurance. Tell me, if you can, one thing that puzzles me very much. Where in the world does Sir James Utley come into all this? The last time you mentioned him you said you had come to the conclusion that he was directly involved. I find it very difficult to reconcile that with the sort of thing we have been discussing. Now I come to think of it, I suppose there is a great deal in Lodstone to interest Sir James, if he

151

could ever get at it, but I can't see how he could get personally involved at all. You're certain he was?'

'Yes. More than ever now. In fact, we are inclined to see him as the star turn. Our difficulty is to know where, or why, the Valance lot come into it at all.'

'Then I give it up. I remember saying in the summer that anything he was involved in must be respectable. I seem to have been wrong.'

'Not on the man's character. I'm sure his instinct is, as you say, for respectability – or perhaps more for public respect, even if a slightly phoney respect. But his hand may have been forced here. Do you remember another thing you said – that he could be ruthless, especially in defending the position he had built up? We rather fancy you spoke wiser than you were ware of.'

'Oh dear. I like the sound of this less and less. But I can understand the fascination it has had for you, and I hope one day you will be able to tell me the whole story. For the moment, anyhow, you are leaving it alone?'

'That's what we have agreed. I've got my hands full, and Jacob is very busy at the beginning of the year. And as I say, the thing has reached one stage, and we can wait for the next.'

'Very well. Can I take it that you won't be going to Lodstone, at any rate, during the remainder of this month?'

'Oh yes, I think it very unlikely.'

'Well please keep to that. No Lodstone until this month is well out.'

'All right, but—'

'I had much rather leave it like that, Margaret. I find myself unwilling at the moment to be more explicit. I have told you I have no real evidence, and it would be far better for you, if you have, to find the explanation for yourself. But of course I'd much rather you put the whole thing out of your head and got on with your work.'

'I intend to. Now I must be getting back. It is nearly dark now, and I don't want to have to do too much in darkness. And I'll miss the worst of the traffic if I go now.'

But it was not until she was clear of High Wycombe that she had time to think coherently about what her grandmother had had to say; and then she found her mind gnawing at the last and at the time least interesting thing she had said.

'No Lodstone till the month is well out.' She wondered why there was this odd insistence on the month. She had said something earlier, too, about dates – dates that recurred; and she had asked the exact date of the fire.

Margaret did some counting, idly at first and then with sharply focused attention. The first of May to the first of August was three months, and another three months brought you to the first of November. If the Lodstone incidents tended to occur at three-monthly intervals, then clearly another might be due at the end of the present month. Hence presumably her grandmother's insistence on keeping clear of Lodstone till October was out. It was, of course, the last day of the old month that was important, or rather the night before the first of the new month. If they were right, Johnnie had died on the night before May Day; and the storm and the fire had certainly been on the night before the first of August. There was a name for that, unconnected with Bank Holiday associations, and she groped about for it in her mind.

The Wheatley bottle-neck took all her attention, and it was only when the traffic flowed out into the double road and cast off its slower elements that she said, 'Lammas' aloud. Lammas, that was it. Jack Simmons had lost his shop on Lammas Eve and Johnnie Utley his life on the Eve of May. And the danger ahead—

Suddenly she had it. It was grotesque and monstrous, but it must be right. She went over all the details she could remember, but found herself perpetually checked by her own ignorance of the subject. There was so much she had to know, but there must, she realised, be a literature. If there was anything a member of the University need never lack, it was the knowledge that is printed in books. She was for the Bodleian tomorrow as soon as it opened.

She garaged the car and almost ran to the nearest telephone box. But they were sorry, Mr Garrod was away. No, they were not quite certain, but they did not expect him back for another three days at least.

CHAPTER TWENTY

Margaret wrote, 'Thursday, October 17th, morning. Not meeting anyone (intentionally). Not staying. There is something I must see. M.C.' She addressed the postcard to Sir Charles Mayne at Ebury Manor and dropped it in the box as she came away from the library. Between the towered and gabled roof-lines the sky was motionless and a lowering red. The evening air was quite still, but struck home with the first real chill of winter.

She telephoned Garrod from college, but could get no further news of him. She set about cancelling her engagements for next day. Her mind worked restlessly in a world of fantastic speculation which repeatedly, as she explored it, offered unexpected footholds of fact. But the truth lay at Lodstone, and she had to go there and see for herself, with her mind retuned to a fresh receptiveness, what there was to be seen.

Thursday came dark but dry. The sky was hidden by an unbroken covering of low cloud, which the wind, chilly and intermittent from the east, seemed unlikely to shift. Today there was neither yellow sunlight, nor a misted warmth, nor even a ruffling west wind to take off the dead leaves. All the poets' autumns were out of commission. The year was dying without grace or comfort.

Lodstone stood on its mound under the threatening sky, and she came to it across empty country. Even in the village the positive evidence of life seemed lacking, and if anyone saw her drive through, they saw her through shut windows and from behind crimped curtains. She went past the vicarage, swung right-handed round the side of the hill and pulled up outside the northern gate of the churchyard. She switched off the engine and got out. Coldness and silence added themselves to the visible desolation. The breeze rustled intermittently in the tops of the churchyard trees, but nothing else moved. Propped on its earthworks, the green ring ran its perfect circle round the standing stones of the ancient dead.

Margaret turned up the collar of her mackintosh, shivering as the cold cloth touched the side of her neck. She wished she had brought a scarf. The turf of the ring was springy and close-set, like a sheepwalk on the downs. Once, twice, she went the round, hands deep in her pockets, head forward, eyes on the ground. Vicarage and church raised blank walls above her, and for the rest the trees, thick grown and still half in yellow leaf, shut her in.

She had often sunk herself in the atmosphere of ancient places, and knew how powerful, despite the most willing submission of a knowledgeable mind, were the sterilising effects of the empty years and the long lapse of human occupation. The surgeon-barber of Avebury, crushed in his unintelligible attempt to bury one of the great sarsens, always seemed to her more remote and more startlingly unfamiliar than the much popularised people who had set them up. Here it was not the barely imaginable founders who crowded in on her, the people who had set out the hill-top circle with stretched thongs and built up the earthworks with their blade-bone shovels, but the people of yesterday and the day before, Victorian Valances and Regency Stallards, who had come up here above the roofs of a recognisable Lodstone to perpetuate a mystery shown them by their fathers.

She went once more round the circle and then, on the south side, stopped and looked across at the Beacon. Colour-less but perfectly clear under the grey sky, the notched outline of the neolithic earthworks broke the line of the summit. On the nearest slope, straight across from her as she looked at it, a dark furrow ran clean up the side of the hill to the deepest central dip in the line of the earthwork. Here, at her feet, the grass path led out of the churchyard gate and dropped straight down to the village. There it merged into the road beyond the houses, a continuous line pointing straight across the width of the tree-filled valley to that dark answering line on the face of the hill. Once more, as in the car two evenings before, she suddenly knew. Without looking behind her she went down the path towards the village.

She joined the road just where it left the houses and went on down the hill. Her eyes were fixed on the dark curve in the sky ahead. She saw no one, and no one spoke to her as she went. She knew now where she was going. At the white gate the tarmac turned off half left, but she climbed the gate and walked on steadily on her undeviating line, along the line of the hedges, across the open field, straight for the crossing of the track and the farm road, where Johnnie Utley, nearly six months ago, had sat under the bank waiting for the Straightways tractor to take him home. Then over the twin gates and along the side of the field, past the dip in the bank where Garrod had thrown her into shelter and crowded in beside her while the same tractor snorted at the gate behind. At the far gate they had taken their compass bearing and turned off for the car park in the distant lane; but now her course was different.

She walked with her eyes on the Beacon, as she had walked unconsciously on May Morning, and today no small smiling man intervened to draw her away from her course. Always the track ran straight ahead, often following and forming the boundary of a field, sometimes cutting straight across one, but never at any point completely blocked. Every hedge or fence provided a stile, every bank a gate. Where the land was under plough she went steadily across for the gate or gap on the far side which stood perfectly aligned to let her through. On the old pasture the track itself was clearly marked, never rutted, but trodden into the turf by the long two-way traffic of persistent feet.

Lodstone was now well behind, and her apprehension, never far away in the silent and deserted village, eased steadily as the distance behind her grew and the exercise of walking unstrung her nerves. A stream, meandering through pollarded willows, crossed her way, but levelled its grass banks to a shallow ford at the point of intersection, and the track went straight on again to a stile in the far hedge.

Here a metalled road, coming in from the right, took up the alignment, and she walked for half a mile on the tarmac with the Beacon, much nearer now and showing steadily increasing detail, poised solidly between the lines of trees that grew along the sides of the road. Then the road turned off left, but for her the inevitable gate stood waiting, and beyond it the track led unhesitatingly across pasture to a dark belt of trees that stretched left and right as far as she could see.

A small stile gave access to the wood, and beyond the stile the track plunged straight in, deeply marked here in the leaf-littered mould and colonnaded on both sides by the boles of ancient trees. For all the thinning of the leaves it was dark under the trees. The breeze seemed to have dropped and the silence was absolute. The oppression of the silent trees rekindled her earlier disquiet, and she tiptoed with a touch of desperation over the fallen leaves, grey eyes staring and her mackintosh gathered tightly round her. She could see nothing but the trees all about her and the path driving straight through them ahead.

Then the ground fell away and she saw in front of her, framed exactly between two tree-trunks, the square tower of a church, which laid its top unerringly against the cloven ` skyline behind it. In another minute she was out of the trees and making steadily down a green slope to a village that sprawled at its foot. The church itself stood at the centre of a mounded churchyard. A cluster of old roofs clung round the church, and she could see the neat red-tiled ridges of council houses further out to the right. On the left a big house, set slightly up the far side of the valley, looked placidly across a long stretch of gardens; and it was then that she saw where she was. This was Ebury.

A wave of relief swept over her, followed almost at once by an apprehension of embarrassment. If there was one thing she did not want to do, it was to explain her present purposes to Charlie Mayne. But there seemed no reason why she should have to. The path she followed, as it had at Lodstone, cut clean through between the houses to the north of the church and brought her, across the village street, to the north gate of the churchyard.

She hesitated at the crossing, but there was no one about. She crossed the street, entered the churchyard by a lych-gate and walked quickly up the slope to the north door of the church. Here again she hesitated for a moment. Few churches, she knew, were left open at all times, and there was nothing to prevent her from making the circuit round the western side of the tower and picking up her line on the far side. But the urge to follow the line was very strong, and she put out her hand to try the door.

The stone eyes held hers suddenly, and she stopped with

one hand on the door-handle, staring into them. The face
was sheltered under the reveal of the arch and was little
weather-worn. The eyes that held hers were deeply socketed
and slanted slightly to the bridge of the broad, short nose.
The mouth was long and full-lipped, with the corners
drawn down in deep-cut lines. The whole face was alive
with an immense and sardonic intelligence. Above the broad,
low forehead two horns, hardly distinguishable among the
carved elf-locks of the hair, curved back to follow the line of
the head. The handle turned in her hand and she followed
the heavy door inwards. The eyes followed her as, headed
only for the Beacon, she stepped into the scented darkness
of the church.

The north door clanged shut, and for the first time since
she had left Lodstone panic took hold of her. She tiptoed,
almost running, over the flagstones to the south door. A
grey-green light filtered through the clerestory windows, but
the chancel was in almost complete darkness. On her right,
round the walls of the tower, the bell-ropes were looped
fantastically and the dusty curtains that hid the ringers
from the congregation run back along their rails. Up in the
tower the clock ticked steadily; but there was nothing to see.
The handle turned but the door would not move. She shook
it desperately, till the empty nave took up the echoes of her
desperation, and she stopped and, with her back to the door,
turned round to face the church. Nothing moved in the stony
silence but the hidden clock. She turned back to the door and,
stooping, found the heavy iron bolt that secured it. She pulled,
and it began to move. Then there was a rumbling over her
head and the clock struck, moaned and struck again. At the
twelfth stroke the door gave inwards suddenly, and she slipped
past it into the cold fresh air of the south porch. Facing her,
and very near now, the Beacon stood up over the white gate
that beckoned her from the far side of the churchyard. She
pulled the door shut behind her, turned the handle carefully
and hurried down the slope.

There were farm buildings over to her right but no buildings close to her line of going. From the foot of the churchyard
mound the ground rose steadily again, and her way led along
the edge of a broad stretch of plough which seemed to be
the last cultivation under the side of the down. Beyond it,

rough pasture, already broken and tagged in places with thorn, led to the foot of the towering chalk slope. Over the pasture the track was plain, a smooth and darker green in the rough grey grass. It made straight for the nearest footings of the hill, but was longer and much steeper than, by contrast with the great slope above it, it at first appeared. Suddenly and with some dismay Margaret realised that she was tired and, what was worse, very hungry. She had left Oxford early and since the moment of revelation at Lodstone had hurried, hard driven physically by her mental excitement, over miles of open country. Now it was past noon. She had a short but harassingly steep climb in front of her; and she could not turn back, least of all into Ebury. She must go on.

She trudged grimly up the last hundred yards of down, crossed a deeply-rutted chalk road that wound round the base of the hill and at once, without pausing or turning round, set herself at the green wall that now hung above her. It was, she saw at once, much steeper than she had suspected. Even with her weight well forward she felt constantly in danger of falling back, and had occasionally to clutch for handholds, so that for stretches she seemed to crawl like a fly on the great chalk face of the hill. In places the grass had been scoured off, and her feet found nothing but greasy slides of polished chalk, where they scrabbled and slipped back a foot for every six inches gained. Even the grass, dry, polished and hard laid with the slope, was treacherous.

After a few minutes of this she dropped forward on to her hands and knees, struggling for breath. Then she turned round and, sitting hard against the slope, looked back the way she had come. Already she had gained startlingly in height. Ebury church on its island mound was now well below her, and the whole tree-filled valley was beginning to open up beyond it. She could not yet trace in any physical appearance the unwavering line by which she had come, but something solid and dark among the trees might well be the top of Lodstone tower. The clouds hung so low now that they seemed to droop from the hill above her, and in front of her the unnatural darkness closed down on ranges of distant country that in clear weather would have been full of depth and detail. Even here the air was motionless, but the chill struck at her before she had sat many minutes, and she

159

clutched together at her throat the mackintosh she had been glad enough to leave open as she struggled on the hillside.

It was no good getting cold. She turned and set herself at the hill again, abandoning herself now to a systematic scrabble with hands and feet at the unrelenting surface of harsh grass and chalk. Time seemed to stand still, and she saw with alarm that the original skyline above her had disappeared behind the new, rounder skyline of what must be a convex slope. She was really tired now and conscious of that loosening of mental grip that always threatened when she was short of food. The excitement had died out of her, and her exploration was a purely physical one. It must be completed, of course, and her observations made and recorded; but work on them must be suspended till she was rested and fed. Let her only get to the top and complete her reconnaissance. What it all meant she would think later.

The angle of the slope eased momentarily, and she saw with relief the pale ridge of the earthworks above her and the V-shaped gap she had seen all the way from Lodstone straight ahead. She was over the shoulder of the slope. A dwarf thorn bush caught her foot and brought her down, and she could not summon the resolution to go on at once. Instead she turned and again looked back. Tired as she was, the excitement in her mind flared up again at the strangeness of it. Ebury was now an aerial view, uncontoured in the shadowless grey light, but full of curiously projected detail. The churchyard mound had flattened itself, but was defined by the silver-grey curve of the metalled road round its base. Across the width of the valley the trees had opened up into lines and ridges, and she saw with excitement the straight dark streak across the belt of yellow woodland that showed the way she had come. Beyond, the tarmac road picked up the line, and away above it, like a spearhead somehow separated from its shaft, the conical hill of Lodstone stood straight up out of the merging drift of trees. Down the huge slope of the Beacon, over Ebury mound, sheer across the valley floor, unwavering, unimpeded, the way led back to the green round on top of Lodstone hill.

She got to her feet and found the going at once easier. The track was deeply marked here, and she saw another and similar track converging from the right on to the same gap, in the earthwork. On either side of her the ground dropped suddenly into a shallow ditch that ran below the mound, but the track itself approached the gap on a level causeway that broke the line of the ditch. Then the green shoulders of turf heaved up on either hand, and she was inside the ring wall.

All round her now the uneven ridge laid its top against the sky. Other gaps at intervals let in other tracks, each carried across the ditch on its straight causeway of uncut chalk. She went in through two more concentric rings of turf, and now nothing showed through the gaps behind her. The drifting canopy of cloud lay over the turf walls and the walls themselves cut her off from the world of trees and villages that stretched away at the foot of the hill. The silence was absolute.

She walked towards the centre of the innermost ring, where a group of turf mounds stood close together, and a man got up from behind one of them and walked to meet her. He was neat and bearded, and he looked at her with a bright and quizzical eye. He said, 'Miss Canting, I think? We haven't met. My name's Utley.'

CHAPTER TWENTY-ONE

She shook hands politely. There seemed nothing else to do. He led her ceremoniously to a central space between the tumuli. Some sort of ground-sheet was spread on the turf, and a sling-bag showed the tops of two flasks. He said, 'Can I offer you a cup of coffee? You must be tired after your walk.'

Reason offered no more than a token resistance. Her physical needs clamoured for the hot drink, and her instinct insisted that she was useless without it. He said, 'It's harmless, as a matter of fact.'

Margaret said 'Thank you' comprehensively, gathered her mackintosh round her and sat down on the turf slope. Sir James took two exaggeratedly handsome flasks out of his bag and unwrapped a china cup and saucer, a spoon and a glass sugar-pot with a screw-on silver lid, beautifully polished. He uncorked one flask and said, 'White with sugar?'

He watched her eagerly as she drank it, and she saw that he was anxious for her appreciation. She said, 'I admit I'm cold and hungry, but that really is beautiful coffee, Sir James. You made it yourself, I imagine?'

'I did, yes. I am always nervous about it. It is one of the diffidences I cannot lose.' He poured her out another cup, and said, 'I happened to be in these parts. We were told you were walking the way and I came to meet you. My car is down on the south road, of course. How did you come to do it?

'By chance, largely. By intuition, partly. My grandmother mentioned the way, but didn't know what it was. I found the round for myself, and when I was there I suddenly saw the way and followed it. I still don't know what it is.'

'What did your grandmother say about it?'

'She remembered, but did not understand, references to a way. She said that to walk the way was an irrevocable step, the ultimate fall from grace. That is, of course, from the viewpoint of the respectable Christian.'

162

'An irrevocable step? Yes. And you, Miss Canting, do you feel that you have taken an irrevocable step?'

'Certainly not. Mine was a pure act of exploration. I still do not know what the way is or what it signifies.'

'Historically, or prehistorically, it is a ceremonial or processional way of the greatest antiquity, linking the local holy places with the high place that is their regional centre. The fact that in this instance it lies very nearly north and south is fortuitous. I don't think Christian practice shows any real parallel. It is as though a system of radiating ways linked the cathedral with all the parish churches in the diocese. But as the cathedral is not the centre of community worship for the diocese, this would not happen, of course.'

'Are they common, these ways?'

'In use, no. This is in my experience unique. The alignments are there, of course, all over the place. An earnest amateur antiquarian noticed them some years ago and wrote a book about them. Unfortunately, he fell a victim to the danger that has dogged every amateur since Stukeley saw the serpent's tail at Avebury. He got carried away by his theory and buried his genuine observations under a load of rubbish. The professionals were outraged. They closed their ranks and, I am afraid, their minds. They appeared to conclude that because a wrong explanation had been given, there was nothing to explain. There was, of course. Five ancient parish churches standing in a perfect line must have some explanation.'

'Why churches?'

'Because the Christians, like many other intelligent conquerors, adapted as much as they could of the old organisation to their new purposes. Among other things they built their churches – not all of them, of course, but a great many – on the sites already long hallowed to the worship of other gods. But they threw down the high places, and the system was left without its centre. This way, the way you have walked, has remained in vestigial use because the tradition of a ceremonial centre here on the Beacon has survived and because one at least of the local centres has maintained an extraordinarily perfect tradition. I discovered the way, of course, only after I was admitted at Lodstone. As I said, in my experience it is unique.'

'I see.'

'What, exactly, do you see, Miss Canting?'

'I see, or I think I see, where the way fits in – what its present significance is. There is still a great deal I don't understand at all. I don't understand your position in this, Sir James.'

He took her empty cup, wrapped it carefully in clean tissue paper and stowed it away with the flasks in his sling-bag. He settled himself on the slope with his hands clasped round his knees and his bright eyes fixed on hers. 'Miss Canting,' he said, 'you have been making some enquiries about me at Stancote. I do not know what sort of a picture of me you have formed.'

'So Charlie remembered, did he?'

'Charlie phoned me at once. He would have been in trouble if he hadn't.'

'I see. Well – I know that you were born in Banstead and grew up there with your brother Johnnie until you both went to Oxford. I know that your father was Jack Utley, very much an Utley, and that your mother was a Somerset woman he married and brought home to the consternation of his family. I know that your mother died when you were boys and your father died soon after you went up to the university. I know your mother was never countenanced in Banstead and I think to some extent I understand why. I thought she was enchanting, even in an old photograph.'

Nothing moved but his eyes, which opened suddenly and for a moment glared into hers. 'Who showed you my mother's photograph?' He spoke as if he had been running.

'Auntie. Fred's Auntie, that keeps the shop, or his wife does. Auntie was your father's cousin, I think. Yes, that's right. Her name is now Sykes. It was an old wedding-group – you and Johnnie and your mother are all in it.'

'You have been very thorough. I did not know you had been to Banstead. You say you can to some extent understand why my mother was rejected by the Utleys. What reason would you assign?'

'She was different in every way, mentally and physically. To them she was a foreigner. Your father adored her: and to crown it all, both her sons looked completely unlike Utleys. This all helped. There was something else too, but I couldn't

quite put my finger on it at the time. Since then I have thought
I knew.'

'My mother was a witch, Miss Canting.'

'Yes. I thought that must be it.'

'She came of fairy stock. Much mixed, of course—the pure
blood does not survive anywhere. But she was brought up by
her mother in the old beliefs.'

'And she handed them on to you?'

'Yes. I am not, I am afraid, a very religious man. I grew up
with an interest in and a devotion to the old beliefs rather than
with a strong personal faith. I know many professed Christians
whose position is very similar.'

'And Johnnie?'

He looked at her long and thoughtfully. 'Johnnie wasn't
interested. He knew a certain amount. But it meant nothing
to him.'

There was another silence. Isolated on their hill-top, shut
in between the green turf basin and its canopy of pendant
cloud, the small dark man brooded over the pale fair girl who
sat at his feet. Then Margaret said, 'I still don't understand
what brought you to Lodstone.'

He seemed to sigh. 'No,' he said. He took his eyes from her
face and looked round at the shallow ring of turf. 'Well, you
see, I grew up with a devotion to this thing that had been my
mother's faith. You have said she was enchanting, Miss
Canting. You cannot possibly know how apt and how inadequate, the word is. She was, of course, an enchantress. But I
had a scholar's bent, and my devotion took the form of study
and reflection rather than of personal involvement. I chose the
most suitable academic line and devoted myself to what was,
for all my own shortcomings, my ancestral religion.

'Now it is in my experience, which is now very great,
unwise and unsatisfactory to start the study of any religion
except in its concrete, day-to-day manifestations. My first
concern was therefore to find this religion, as I knew it still
existed, in an active and organised form. And you will understand that in my position I was not likely to be interested in the
antics of any catchpenny urban diabolist pandering to the
sensations of a corrupt public. I wanted the unadulterated
tradition.

'I tried Somerset through my mother's connections,

though I knew she had never been one of an organised community. I found, as I had expected, that the thing is still alive, and indeed that communities do exist. But I was not impressed by the strength or clarity of the tradition, and saw no probability of adding anything to what I had already had from my mother. Eventually I found Lodstone. You need not, I think, be concerned with how these enquiries were pursued or the discovery at last made. It would not be possible for an outsider, obviously, to do anything of the sort, or even for a convert. For many reasons, some of which you can imagine, there is an emphasis on inherited faith here far more than with most established religions. At any rate, I found Lodstone and was in due course admitted to the community.

'I have said that Lodstone is unique in its tradition of the way. In many other respects I should say it was quite exceptionally perfect, at any rate for this country. There are twelve families which by tradition supply a member of the coven each. At the time of the Domesday survey twelve families held the twelve farms in the parish, and the twelve in the community believe (with what justification I cannot say) that they are their descendants. Four of them farm in the village. Four other families, or their active branches, still supply their members and in most cases live near enough to take an active part. Whatever there is in the Domesday claim, these families have undoubtedly a very long Lodstone connection.'

'The Valances, the Stallards, the Bellings and the Marstons. The coven is not the whole community, I take it?'

'No, no. The coven is the governing and executive body, a sort of parochial church council or council of elders. The community as a whole is drawn from Lodstone itself and the surrounding neighbourhood – or even, as in my case, from right outside.'

'Why have I always been allowed to think of a coven as a bunch of old women under the thumb of a male leader?'

'Miss Canting, suppose someone with no preconceived ideas at all – let us say our old and useful friend, the visitor from Mars – suppose he were sent to make a survey of Christianity as it exists and is practised in this country today – and suppose he began, as he should, by dropping in unannounced at the services of one of your country parish churches: what would his first report be? I will tell you. Unless his choice has been very atypical, he is going to report that although the priesthood of this religion is strictly confined to men, the worshippers are all women, most of them old, though the old man seems occasionally to be admitted. You must not judge a religion by the practices and appearances of its decadence, Miss Canting, or by the reports of its declared enemies. My religion has been decadent longer than yours, just as it has existed much longer, and it is your religion, by the persistence, violence and sheer duplicity of its attacks, that has mainly induced that decadence. Now it is your turn. But I do at least know that it would be inaccurate to judge Christianity by the current manifestations of its practice.'

'Yes, I see. I'm sorry. Are there in fact no women, or is there no rule?'

'There is at least one woman in every coven. She holds office as the Maid. She embodies certain principles of divinity in human form. She is called the Maid, but she is maid, wife and mother, the moon in all its phases. But she is an officer of the coven. She is not herself divine.'

'The Lodstone Maid – she meets the others regularly?'

'Yes, yes. She is not a Lodstone woman now, but, as with all the rest, her family were Lodstone once.'

'And there is a – some sort of head or leader of the community?'

'Yes.'

'And he also embodies divine attributes?'

'He is himself at the appropriate moment divine, divine man. The conception is not unknown to other religions, Miss Canting. For the rest, he is mere man, as the unsanctified bread and wine in the vestry are mere bread and wine, and in many cases poor specimens as such. But even as man his authority is very great. Time was when his human personality had to be hidden, but nowadays no difficulty is felt.'

'Is this office also hereditary?'

'Not in the sense that it goes with a family name, like membership of the coven. The master may nevertheless often be in physical fact the son or grandson of a previous master. Apart from his inherited beliefs, the qualities he has inherited may contribute to his becoming master. But though the relationship is implicitly recognised, it is the qualities that count.'

167

'And he is appointed for life?'

'He is master for seven years.'

'And then?'

'Another is found.'

'And the outgoing master?'

'It varies.'

' "Every seven years," ' Margaret quoted, ' "They pay a teind to hell." And it is expedient that one man should die for the people. The appointment is in fact for life after all?'

'One life may serve for another. You are a very intelligent girl, Miss Canting. But you are of the wrong stock.' He sighed again, and she found that he was looking at her face rather than her. 'The wrong stock,' he said again.

She shivered suddenly and realised that, despite the coffee, she was cold and oppressed. She said, 'It was you I spoke to when the shop was burning?'

'Oh yes. It was curious and unfortunate that you should have picked on me for your question. I hadn't seen you before, but I knew who you must be; and I saw that you might have recognised me. It upset me very considerably.'

'Why did you have to burn that poor young man's shop? He was within his rights, and he was going to let the matter go, anyhow.'

'The shop was struck by lightning, Miss Canting. I saw it happen. I cannot, of course, compel you to accept this. I merely give you my assurance, for what you think it is worth, that no one went near the shop that night with matches or paraffin or any of the paraphernalia of the fire-raiser.'

'But you – your community, anyhow – had it in for Jack Simmons; and he was warned by a lot of people in the village not to pursue his quarrel with Mr Valance.'

'That is perfectly correct. And his shop was burnt. It is for you to take the facts as you like. Your easiest course is to reject my assurance and to assume that one of the community simply set fire to the shop. If you are not inclined to do that, your choice is more difficult.'

'My choice is in fact between howling coincidence and a supernatural explanation.'

'Miss Canting, I suspect that you and I are both what I may call instinctive rationalists. You are a practising Christian. Suppose someone is very ill and a person you regard as holy prays for his recovery, and he then recovers against the medical prognosis: are you going to say unequivocally that the prayer was answered and that God bent the causal chain on the sick man's behalf; or are you going to fall back on a half-in-half explanation involving faith-healing or mental therapy; or are you just going to observe the correlation of prayer and healing and find it right and comforting, but leave it unexplained?

'You don't answer,' he went on, 'and that is a sign of honesty in you. But I think I can help you. You will in fact take the third course. You will find it easier and even feel it is right not to proceed to a specific explanation. Then you must allow me the same latitude. You must have experienced the storm yourself.'

'And the storm was invoked?'

'Oh yes, a storm was invoked. But there are often storms over the Bank Holiday week-end, aren't there? It is one of the things people joke about.'

Margaret shivered again. 'Sir James,' she said at last, 'the situation is so far beyond me that I am aware mainly of the fact that I am cold. I think you must now tell me why you met me here, why you have told me all you have and what, having done so, you propose to do next. We are really concerned, aren't we, not with Jack Simmons but with your brother Johnnie? I saw Johnnie's body on May Morning. You know that. I didn't know at the time whose body it was. The body disappeared and an attempt was made to induce me to forget the whole thing. Since then I have, to my own satisfaction, identified the body as Johnnie's and obtained a few more apparently relevant facts. I have made no attempt to report the matter to any authority – except, of course, once in circumstances you will be aware of. You have now told me a great deal more. But you have not told me the circumstances of Johnnie's death or the connection between it and your Lodstone community. And you know – it was Johnnie's death, ultimately, that brought me here. The rest I am not – or at any rate, was not – concerned with.'

'Very well. As you say, we are immediately concerned with Johnnie. I was once very fond of Johnnie, you know, Miss Canting. But he was no good. He was no good at all.'

169

CHAPTER TWENTY-TWO

'The trouble with Johnnie,' said Sir James, 'was that he always took the line of least resistance. We do not place the same emphasis on asceticism as you do, but resolution and some degree of effort are a necessary virtue anywhere. The belief that God owes you a living seems to us a peculiarly Christian attitude. We do not see providence in the fall of a sparrow. We think that the sparrow wasn't quick enough to dodge what has knocked him down. Johnnie seemed to want the best of both worlds. He got away with it at Banstead, but from the time he left it he was in trouble.'

Margaret said, 'I know Johnnie's record, or at any rate the official version of it. You helped him a lot at one time. You must have helped him long after you knew he was hopeless. That was kind of you.'

'It wasn't kindness, Miss Canting. It was love. Later he put himself beyond the pale. I stopped helping him, not because he no longer deserved it, or because I thought it was bad for him, or for any other good Christian reason. I stopped helping him because by then I hated his guts.'

'Somebody told me not long ago that my emotions were less derivative than most people's. They said I never felt anything because I was expected to or thought I ought to. I don't know how far that is true, but I certainly find something immediately intelligible and admirable in your statement. Johnnie was a blackmailer. I have even met one of his victims. There was someone who loved him, but in a desperate sort of way. Did you know about Martha and her children? But I don't think most people would have done much to save him from what was coming to him. I know I shouldn't. I assumed he had been blackmailing you, or was attempting to do so.'

'I see. You think he was blackmailing me, and I therefore got rid of him?'

'It seemed the obvious explanation.'

'Yes. It is not exactly true, but the practical difference is immaterial. Johnnie found his way to Stancote. He must have broken in and then got a key made. He used the cottage in my absence, passing himself off as me, in so far as he let himself be seen at all.'

'I knew he had been masquerading as you. He had a false beard and make-up.'

'It was Charlie who ultimately discovered him: and I took steps to make sure it shouldn't happen again. But Johnnie had got the idea that I was using Stancote as a blind, and he must have followed me from there. At any rate, he found out about Lodstone. He knew enough, you see, to understand what things meant.'

'And that was to be the subject of his blackmail?'

'Yes. That's it. He thought that a – a public figure like myself would pay handsomely for silence about his membership of the Lodstone community. That was typical of his outlook. It never occurred to him, you see, that it was the community he was threatening through me, and that the community might exact silence whether or not I paid for it. Ultimately his own folly did for him before the thing came to an issue at all. He came – up here, do you see, on the May Eve.'

'There is a gathering of some sort here at the quarterly festivals?'

'Yes. I told you the tradition of a regional centre had survived. Johnnie came with a camera. Of course he was found at once. We have been a secret community for more than a thousand years, Miss Canting. It would occur to most people that the secret must be well guarded. There is no persecution now by church or state, of course, but the habit of secrecy becomes ingrained; and in fact we fear the breath of the profane multitude more than ever we feared the witch-hunter. We must grow – we are growing – in secret.'

'So Johnnie died at the hands of the community?'

He smiled suddenly, looking over her at the top of the turf wall, and for the first time she was consciously afraid of him. 'Do you remember the ram caught in a thicket? Johnnie died better than he deserved. We took his body to Lodstone. It was the most outrageous chance that, during the short time when it could be seen, you should have seen it.'

'But I did see it.'

'You did. And although you did not make trouble, you did

171

not let it rest. You wanted the truth. Now you have got it, Miss Canting.' He looked long at her again. She had the feeling that he was not so much trying to make a decision as trying to postpone it. Presently he said, 'This man who has been working with you in this – you have not mentioned him at all, but of course it is known that you have been working together. How much does he know?'

'He knows, or thinks he knows, that the body was Johnnie's. He does not know the explanation of things at Lodstone. I have not seen him since the conversation with my grandmother which first led me to that explanation. He does not know I am here now. Nobody does.'

'You mean none of your friends. Others, of course, do. I am here because they do. I am deeply involved in your danger, Miss Canting. I would give almost anything for you not to have come.'

'But I mean no harm. I do not wish you harm, you or your community. I don't know how I can persuade you of this. I have not tried to analyse my motives, and I suppose the truth is that I would avoid even an attempt to analyse them. My grandmother, as you may know, grew up as a girl in Lodstone, and she knows pretty well where the truth lies. She was a member of a respectable Christian household and is still, in a matter-of-fact, eighteenth-century sort of way, on the side of the angels. But do you know what she said of your Lodstone community? She said it was like fox-hunting or the English winter – she would avoid it as far as possible, but would not do anything to end it.'

Sir James laughed suddenly and disconcertingly. 'Admirable,' he said, in what she recognised uncomfortably as his television voice, 'quite admirable. But you still have not told me your own position.'

'I don't know why, but I am in fact to be trusted absolutely. I would – I think I would go to the stake for your secret, Sir James.'

'The gallows,' he said, 'not the stake. They hanged us in England. They burnt only other Christians of the wrong brand. Of course, opinions differed at different times which brand was for the burning.' He simpered over his little joke, and then suddenly got up. Margaret rolled forward on to her knees and found him standing immediately over her. She knelt thus, her hands hanging loose at her sides, her pale head tilted back, staring up into the dark, narrowed eyes that bored down into hers. He said, 'Margaret is a witch name, did you know that? My mother was a Margaret. You are of the wrong stock but have much of the quality. You could join us, Margaret.'

Her whole body shook suddenly with the cold, but she smiled up at him out of her physical distress. 'Where is your scholarly interest and lack of personal involvement, Sir James? Is it the theologian's job to evangelise to the heathen? Scholarly interest my foot. You are a devotee to your manicured finger-tips, and I honour you for it. But I can't join you. You know that.'

He nodded. The moving cloud dipped suddenly, and the dark translucent world round them was flooded with opaque silver. Even while they looked at each other the ring walls and the further tumuli were blotted out, and they were alone in a drifting white world with only a few square feet of visible earth under them. He put his left hand on her shoulder, and she found that the square white fingers were unexpectedly strong. His right hand went to his pocket.

She said, 'I've told you your secret is safe with me. What more can I say?'

He shook his head. 'It's no good,' he said, 'it's no good.' His eyes were wide open now, still staring down into hers, and she saw that he was in the grip of an almost paralysing fear. She said, 'I will swear to it – any oath you give me. For both our sakes.' His right hand came out of his pocket and his left, though it still held her shoulder, half loosened its grip.

Away in the mist behind her a man's voice called, 'Margaret! Margaret Canting!' and another voice from the farther side of the invisible earthworks took it up, 'Miss Canting! Miss Canting!' so that the mist and the surrounding walls trapped the sound and blended the two voices into a ubiquitous clamour, 'Canting! Margaret Canting! Miss Margaret! Margaret!'

His mouth opened slightly and shut again. 'You said no one knew you were here,' he whispered, 'and I believed you. I believed you, do you see?' His right hand moved again.

'It's true,' said Margaret, 'it's true. No one—' She gasped as the broad blade went slowly up over the left side of her

173

neck. It stopped, and she twisted convulsively, over-balanced and rolled backwards down the slope. She heard the grate and thud as the knife went into the turf above her. She gathered her mackintosh round her and ran into the mist, dodging and twisting between the encumbering earthworks as they rose suddenly to meet her. Feet came padding after her. The voices still called, 'Margaret! Miss Canting! Margaret Canting!' on either side, and she heard other feet running criss-cross in the choking white cloud. A hollow opened at her feet and in a moment she was down in it full-length, her mouth open, gasping for breath, but listening for the feet behind her.

For a moment there was complete silence. Then she heard movements again, stealthy movements from more than one direction. She sat up and, crouching, put her head between her knees. She was finished. There was nothing more she could do.

Nobody called out for some time after that, but she heard a hint of men's voices, as though people muttered to themselves or perhaps spoke quietly to each other in the fog. Every now and then she heard feet in the grass, but nothing appeared within the tight circle of visibility around her.

As suddenly as it had come the cloud pulled its trailing fringes clear of the hill. The world went darker, and the green turf banks stood up all round her, laying their tops against the sombre sky. Margaret raised her head and saw Charlie Mayne standing with his back to her, not five yards away. She got up and said, 'Sir Charles Mayne,' and he whipped round.

'Where the devil have you been? We've been shouting all over the hill for you. Didn't you hear? Are you all right?' She nodded and he let out a yell for Karim, who appeared on the far side of the circle. There were the usual quick and unintelligible interchanges, and he turned to Margaret again.

'There was someone else up here. Do you know who it was?'

They walked towards the central tumuli, but nothing appeared. Ground sheet and sling bag had gone. The grass was flattened in faint patches, and half-way up a slope there was a clean new rift in the turf, as though a broad wedge had been driven into it. She said, 'Oh yes, it's all right. I met them up here. It would have been all right – I think. But I am very grateful to you for coming. How did you know I was here?'

174

'Saw your car at Lodstone church. Couldn't find you in the village.' Very faintly, as if in the back of her own mind, Margaret heard a car start somewhere down the southern side of the hill. She watched Charlie Mayne without a flicker. 'Finally,' he said, 'I asked. Couldn't get anything solid. Lodstone all over – nobody knew anything, or if they did they weren't saying much. Then Emma Besson called me in for a minute and told me to come to the Beacon as quick as possible and look for you here. Wouldn't say any more. But she's an honest woman and fond of you, so I tried it. Drove off as for Ebury and then made our way up here as fast as we could. Then just as we got here that damned low cloud came over and we couldn't see a thing. We shouted for you but got no reply. Then we heard people running and ran ourselves, but it was all blind man's buff – we never saw anyone for certain. Then the fog cleared and there you were, as cool as a cucumber, just behind me. I'm relieved, I must say, but more than half inclined to shake you till your teeth rattle. I suppose you've got nothing to say either?'

Margaret said, 'I'm not as cool as a cucumber. I'm frozen stiff and hungry and dead tired. I'm sorry I worried you, but really I couldn't help it.' She looked at him defiantly as two large tears trickled slowly down her face and dripped on to her mackintosh.

'Lor,' said Charlie Mayne, 'don't take on. It doesn't suit you. Take a pull of this and come on down to the car. The walk will do you good, but get the whisky into you first.' He held out a silver flask, much battered but of impressive capacity. The spirit went down as smooth as silk and exploded startlingly in her empty stomach. 'One more,' he said. She took one more and handed back the flask. 'I don't mind if I do,' said Charlie Mayne, and joined her. 'Karim doesn't drink – not in public, anyhow. Come on.'

For the moment she was conscious of nothing but mental relief and a steadily increasing physical warmth. The smooth but powerful whisky floated her down the chalk hillside and into the car waiting on the rutted road at its foot. At Ebury she was fed and rested; and then the undercurrent of disquiet which she had been only half conscious of came to the surface, and she was restless to be gone.

'It's no good,' she said to Charlie Mayne, 'I can't tell you –

now, when I know more, less than ever. But if it's any comfort to you, the thing's over. I'll go no more a-roving. I'm going back to Oxford to work like mad for my finals. It's my last year and my last chance. Oh – one thing. You won't tax Mrs Besson, will you? She did what she could to help, and I hope she won't suffer for it. But please keep right away from her for a bit. It's the only thing you can do to help her. I'm sure of that.

'Now will you please, if I promise never to worry you again, do one thing for me? Take me as far as Lodstone, drop me at the bottom of the hill and leave me. I'll go up and get my car and drive straight to Oxford. But it is essential that I go into Lodstone alone. It's the middle of the afternoon and daylight such as it is. If you like, you can watch the Oxford road and see that I do get away. But you mustn't come with me into Lodstone.'

He looked at her for a moment or two of inscrutable silence. Then he said, 'Karim shall drive you wherever you want to go and drop you when you get there. Then he will bring the car straight back here and stay here. There'll be no watching the Oxford road. I'll go no more a-roving either. I have come to the conclusion that I am wasting my time worrying about you. I don't think for a moment that you are capable of looking after yourself, but I don't think you're the sort of girl things happen to. Bring your husband to see me when you have one. I shall be interested to see him.'

Margaret watched him as the car moved off, walking with quick, short steps up the immaculate gravel towards the great house. Ten minutes later she walked up Lodstone hill for what was, she knew with complete certainty, the last time. She ignored the path running up direct to the churchyard and followed the tarmac of the village street on its right-hand curve round the shoulder of the hill. The light had already faded behind the cloud-rack. The day had never made a fight of it and was ready to throw its hand in. There were no lights yet in the village, but the darkness had an air of defiance.

She passed Mrs Besson's cottage without a glance. The high sash-windows of the vicarage were blank and impenetrable, though there was a second-hand suggestion of light from the kitchen at the back. The trees that had rustled and whispered in the morning were quite still. Her car stood where she had left it. She leant on the top of the gate and looked at the grass round. The south door of the church opened and Sir James Utley came up the steps into the churchyard.

He came straight up to her and stood facing her with the gate between them. He seemed at a loss for words, but breathless, as though his lack of action was imposed by an intolerable effort of the will. Margaret said, 'Sir James, I did not know, and could not possibly know, that anyone would come looking for me on the Beacon. You must see that their intervention was against my interest. If it is not too late, I am ready now, as I was then, to give you assurance of my secrecy in any form you can accept. Or is it too late?"

'I don't think it is too late. I don't know. I went round and came here from the north. It is a risk we must take. Come with me.' He turned and walked to the south side of the churchyard, where the grass path ran downhill and the Beacon stood up almost black now through its gap in the trees. Then he turned and stood waiting for her. She opened the gate and walked after him. He said, 'You have a lot of courage, but we are both in great danger. Now say this.'

She took the appalling words from him and felt his fear close over her like a cold cloud. 'Go back to your car,' he said, 'quickly. Get in and start the engine.' She sat there with the cold engine turning uneasily, waiting for him to come to the gate. Twice she was on the point of getting out, but his urgency held her and she was afraid to move. Then suddenly the gate clicked and he was standing by the car. There was no disguise or control now. He breathed as if he had been running for his life and she saw that in the cold light his face was streaky with sweat. He clutched the side of the car, and she thought he was going to fall.

She said, 'Are you all right?'

He nodded, steadying himself. 'You will never come back here,' he said, 'and we shan't meet again.' He looked over his shoulder at the darkening churchyard. 'I don't think you need be told, Miss Canting, that my life may be in your hands. And much more than my life.' He shivered suddenly and violently. 'Much more than my life. Now go please.'

She backed the car and ran it quietly round the curve of

the hill under the trees. There were some lights now, but the village crouched in the cold dusk as she had once seen it crouch under the stifling heat. She set her course for Oxford, driving fast.

Chapter Twenty-Three

Majestic in academicals, the man Garrod doffed his cap ceremonially from the outer edge of the pavement. 'I didn't know you had come back,' said Margaret. 'I've been trying to get hold of you.'

'I hadn't until today. I kept trying to, but couldn't manage it.'

'Can we meet and talk some time?'

He looked at her sharply. 'I know that voice. I thought you said you were going to leave it alone and get on with your work.'

'I have now. That's what I want to tell you about, so far as I can. It's finished, Jacob. Not with a bang but with a whimper, I rather think. But anyhow, finished, certainly. When can we talk?'

'Seven at the Mitre, where we talked the first time?'

'Yes, all right. Seven, then.'

'Now,' he said later, 'what did Sir James have to say?'

'Sir James?'

'Sir James, girl, yes. Don't look at me with that exasperating air of startled innocence. If you have really settled the thing to your own satisfaction and made up your mind to have done with it, you must have seen Sir James. Look at the facts. We had concluded that Johnnie had tried to blackmail Sir James and had been bumped off for his pains and buried under the Straightways concrete. We didn't know what Johnnie had been trying to blackmail his brother about. We assumed it was something to do with the Lodstone business, but we didn't know what the Lodstone business was, or where Valance and Robin and the rest came in. Now you are going to tell me that you know all that and that the whole thing is explained. Sir James is your only remotely likely source of information. Therefore I conclude that you have met him and talked with him.'

'You are very swift and categorical. I should dearly love to be able to tell you that you are wrong.'

'But you can't?'

'No, I can't.'

'Then why the prevarication?'

'Because I can't tell you the whole story, and I wanted to make it as easy as possible for me to maintain this refusal and for you to accept it.'

'All right. I see. Tell me what you can, anyway.'

'A few days ago a new line of investigation opened up suddenly. What I really mean is that somebody gave me a clue to an explanation and I had to follow it – I really could not help myself. I tried to get hold of you – I tried twice – but you were away and they didn't know when you'd be back. So I followed the clue by myself. There really was no alternative.'

'And you found Sir James at the end of it?'

'Yes – or to be more accurate he found me. At any rate, we met in circumstances which more or less forced his hand. He gave me his explanation, but only on condition that I did not pass it on to anyone at all. I accepted that condition. I am satisfied with his explanation. I do not want to do anything more about it at all.'

There was a long and slightly threatening silence. Garrod rolled the stem of his glass rapidly between finger and thumb and seemed to be trying to stare through the table top. At last he said, 'If the circumstances in which you met forced him to explain things, why did you have to accept his condition of secrecy?'

'I had discovered too much, don't you see? It couldn't be left as it was.'

'All right. Now we're getting at it. You knew too much. So what did Sir James do? Make you a present of the rest and beg your discretion? It doesn't add up, Margaret, does it? I think you are trying to spare my feelings, or save yourself from looking silly, or probably both. But I won't press you. I am – I am glad you were still here when I got back. Was it a demmed close-run thing?'

'A neck,' said Margaret. 'No more than a neck.'

He nodded solemnly. 'But it really is the end this time? You are satisfied and will go no further?'

'Oh yes.'

'One of your two pre-conditions to marriage is fulfilled?'
'Yes.'
'Well, for God's sake get on and fulfil the other. In the meantime, mightn't we celebrate my safe return – and yours? Let's eat out of Oxford. Have you got time for the Ram? We'll be there a bit late, but at least we shan't have to wait for a meal.'

'I've got time, yes. But I'm worried about the head waiter and the marsh warbler.'

'Oh that? Good gracious, it's probably a different head waiter, and even if it's not, he won't remember. And even if he does, what the hell? This time we're out after owls. Our flash-light equipment is in the car. Come on.'

'Tell me one thing,' he said, as the orange lights fell away behind and the white headlights picked up the open road, 'did you on the whole retain the impression we had formed of Sir James? We were predisposed in his favour, if you remember. We did not think the secret he was defending from his nasty little brother would be likely to upset us much. Is it permissible to ask whether you still feel like this?'

'Yes. Oh yes, I can't help liking Sir James. He is a much darker horse than I had supposed, but when I finally did meet him, I warmed to him despite – well, difficult circumstances. And I think he to me, in an odd sort of way. We are steeped in mutual admiration. But don't worry. I shan't continue the friendship so exotically conceived.'

'I will keep my apprehension within bounds. But you found him, on the whole, as we expected – the Wiltshire lad culturalised and tarted up, but still the country boy at heart?'

'Yes. I did. And hardly a line to throw in private, though the television manner breaks through occasionally when he gets rattled. It was Johnnie that had sold his birthright. Jimmie is still Jimmie. I hope he's all right.'

'It's the same man,' she said, as they went in through the double glass doors, 'he's looking at your suit.'

'Two, sir?' said the head waiter. 'Yes, sir. I think the last time we had the pleasure of seeing you there had been some sort of accident. I trust madam was none the worse. This way, sir.'

'Thank you,' said Margaret, 'none the worse. I am a glutton for punishment.'

'That's right,' said Garrod, 'back on the old pitch, you see. Owls, this time. What can you recommend for us tonight? I'm afraid we're a bit late.'

They ate under an imponderable cloud of restraint, but presently Garrod said, 'This is a semi-anniversary, had you realised? It will be six months tomorrow since we met.'

'Six months?'

'Six months since May Day. The night is Halloween, Margaret, the morn is Hallowday.'

'Ah. Then win me, win me, if ye will, for weel I wat ye may. How very curious that you should quote that. I quoted it myself only the other day.'

'At any rate, I take note of your assurance. Should we be – I forget – bobbing for apples, or something?'

'No, indeed, no. But there will be a moon up presently, and I have a fancy for a breath of air before we go back.'

They drank their coffee and moved off through a deserted lounge, where the tables held only used cups and littered ash-trays, and a circle of empty chairs stood round the television set in the corner.

'The early Church,' said the exquisite, familiar voice, 'never lost an opportunity of absorbing the practices, perhaps even the places, of pre-Christian worship into its own organisation. The Christian festival of All Saints or All Hallows is of course a well-known example of this.'

Margaret whipped round and dropped into a chair facing the set. There he was, eyebrows raised, eyelids drooping, with always, as she now saw it, more than a hint of mockery in the small mouth above the sleek black beard. She knew what he was going to say, and let the rounded phrases flow over her without any very detailed examination. The great thing was that he was there, sleek, assured, quizzical and charming as ever.

Garrod, standing behind her, said, 'He is a charmer, the old sod. Johnnie should have known better than to try and upset that success story. You're well out of it, Margaret.'

The voice stopped and the face faded until it seemed to be only the screen that looked quizzically at her. Then the sad young announcer was suddenly with them. Sir James Utley, he said, had been telling them something of the popular associations of Halloween. Sir James had been unable to be present in the studio tonight and his talk had therefore been recorded.

A cold wave of apprehension touched her, so that she almost shivered in the close heat of the hotel. She saw him suddenly as she had last seen him, jaw dropped, fighting for breath, his face streaky with sweat. She said, 'Let's go. It worries me, seeing him like that.'

The moon was up now and the night clear and cold. Garrod looked at his watch. 'You've got a couple of hours,' he said. 'Which way home? Not Lodstone, I think.'

'Not Lodstone, no. Could you go somewhere in the Ebury direction?'

'I could try. It's not far.'

They drove in silence through ten miles of moonlit country and checked at a cross-roads. Garrod said, 'Right, here, I think.' He looked at the signpost. 'Yes, right. I'm sorry I can't help, Margaret. You have to carry this burden, I suppose?'

'Yes, but not indefinitely. Give me a day or two, and the whole thing should be over.'

He nodded, and swung the car downhill between trees, with lights showing faintly ahead. 'That should be Ebury, I think.'

'Stop the car, will you? Let's walk a little.'

They got out and tiptoed down the tarmac in the tremendous silence. The side-lights of the car glowed yellow behind them, but the world was black and silver. The road bent sharply through trees, and when they came out on the far side, the whole valley opened up before them in the moonlight.

Ebury was at the foot of the slope, its church tower a chunk of shadow with drowsy yellow lights clustered round its foot. On the left the trees came down almost to the road, and above and beyond them silver trees blended into silver trees as far as the sight went. On the right, bare and immense, the Beacon flung up its long curve to the still climbing moon.

They walked hand-in-hand into the valley, keeping to the grass verge rather than break the silence. Just above the village Margaret stopped. He put his arm round her and she leant against him but did not speak, watching the great chalk slope above them.

The edge of a shadow fell suddenly on its far side and

closed slowly along it. The cloud moved sluggishly across the moon and the darkness flooded in everywhere, though at the end of the valley they could see already the silver streak of returning moonlight. The top of the Beacon was invisible now, but its presence above them was almost palpable. Then on the unseen skyline a light flickered for a moment, vanished and then momentarily flared up again. She watched, straining her eyes, but saw nothing more.

'I'm tired,' she said. 'Take me home.'

'The moon will be out again in a moment.'

'I know, but I'm tired, Jacob. Let's go back.'

'Come on then.'

They moved on to the tarmac and then, sheltered under the immense shadow, walked briskly back towards the car.

>>> If you've enjoyed this book and would like to discover more great vintage crime and thriller titles, as well as the most exciting crime and thriller authors writing today, visit: **>>>**

The Murder Room
Where Criminal Minds Meet

themurderroom.com